JET CAPER

ERIC SMALL

Middletown Publishing Group

St. Augustine, Florida

Middletown Publishing Group
St. Augustine, FL

Jet Caper - Eric Small -- 1st ed. 2024

Dedication

For All the Female Pilots and Mechanics.

Acknowledgments:

I can't imagine writing and completing this book without my wife Denele's love, support and encouragement, not to mention her stellar editorial and proofreading assistance.

I owe much of my affinity for writing to the love and support of my late mother and father Sally and Richard, who both shared their love of reading with me at a very young age.

My eternal gratitude to my brother Steve, and my sister Nancy for their ongoing love and support.

I am grateful to Bob Eames for generously sharing some of the vast knowledge he amassed during decades of piloting large commercial aircraft. I no doubt failed in some respects to accurately portray many aspects of aviation and aeronautical mechanics, but that is emphatically not Bob's fault. Let's just chalk it up to literary license.

Author image used by permission from Lifetouch Portrait Studios, Inc. Stork Photography
Cover image: Photo **308829159**; Toni Morales; | Dreamstime.com

1

In the early summer, at a small local airport in Florida, a group of tourists gathered for an air show. They watched with interest as a small airplane executed various stunts for their entertainment. Their enjoyment quickly turned to dread as the small jet turned and headed straight downward, plummeting directly at their little group.

"That plane is crashing," frightened voices cried in unison.

There was no time to do anything but pray. They froze like a display of ice statues, as the gleaming silver Cessna rocketed toward them. It hurtled in an almost vertical trajectory as it exuded a thundering noise and the noxious stench of gasoline. Still, the crowd remained immobile, anticipating their impending demise, while the acrid taste of petrol filled their gaping mouths. But at the last moment, the jet abruptly curved upward, and away, with plenty of room to spare. As the crowd exhaled with a relieved murmur, the jet made a series of loops, and barrel rolls, before one final loop, ending in a picture-perfect landing on the runway. The jet taxied to a stop in a marked space on the tarmac, and a diminutive woman sporting long blond hair, blue eyes and a grinning countenance, popped out of the pilot's seat.

A twenty-something man stepped out of the small

office.

"Show's over, folks. That was the one and only Daisy Wilson, stunt pilot extraordinaire. Lessons available inside."

***

Meanwhile, on a makeshift stage in a converted warehouse on A1A, a small group of actors rehearsed Shakespeare's Twelfth Night. The place had no air conditioning, just a large fan on each side of the stage. Their loud hum did more to annoy the actors than it did to provide relief from the oppressive heat.

As the newest community theater in the county, and the only one on the island, it did not attract the most accomplished actors. Instead, it was a haven for the aspiring, the untalented, and the rejected. But there were a few gems who had both talent and modest prior success. One such pearl in the otherwise drab-looking oyster was me, Tripper Steele. I'm a tall, leading man type, with dark brown, close-cropped hair, brown eyes and a slender physique. I briefly starred in an off, off Broadway production of Squeaky Partridge, which was a well-known avant-garde production in New York.

When both the show and the theater closed, I fled the cold and headed to Florida. But I had no better luck finding an acting job in the Sunshine State, having struck out in Jacksonville. Local community theater groups likewise were oddly unimpressed with my earlier claim to stardom, and I gave up and took a job as a server at a small family restaurant. Shortly thereafter, I discovered the startup theater in which I stood at the moment.

"What the hell was that? One of the greatest lines in the history of theater, and you deliver it like you're ordering lunch in a diner. Some feeling, please. Now do it again, like you have a passing knowledge of Shakespeare."

"No need to get nasty about it, Carleton. It's not like I've never acted before." I cleared my throat and belted out an impressive rendering of my line:

"Some are born great, some achieve greatness, and some have greatness thrust upon them."

"Cut, cut, cut. That's just awful. Obviously, Tripper, greatness was neither born nor thrust upon you. Let's call it a day. Maybe tomorrow you'll find your Muse, or your inner Olivier, or something. Or God help us, this play is screwed."

I shrugged and headed backstage with the rest of the actors. As I walked off the stage, I noticed a man and woman standing in the back of the auditorium. They'd attended all the open rehearsals, but their identity and purpose were a mystery to me. But I gave it no further thought, and hurried to drop my stage stuff and head to the parking lot. I had to get to the restaurant where I worked. Given the paucity of professional acting jobs, I needed something to pay the bills. But I love acting, and if the only opportunity for it was in a community theater with an antagonistic and obdurate director who thought he was channeling Stanislavski, so be it. I know I'm a talented actor, even if my strong suit is emphatically not Shakespeare.

I parked my vintage, um, old, broken down, 1987 Plymouth Duster in the restaurant parking lot, and entered through the back, directly into the kitchen.

My best friend, Derek "Hippo" Thurston, looked up from his workstation. He was an assistant cook at the restaurant, and his workstation was a long table, on which he was currently slicing raw vegetables.

Derek's physique mimicked his moniker. Large, heavy, and strong. He had a shock of brown hair, parted on the side, a round, unshaven, rough-hewn face, and a goatee. The goatee looked menacing, which stood in stark contrast to his toothy smile.

At present, he wore a white apron over his customary T-shirt and jeans and sneakers.

"Hey Hip," I greeted him.

"Hey Trip, how's my favorite thespian?"

"Good, good, very good."

"That bad, huh? Tough rehearsal?"

"Carleton is an asshole."

"No shit. I met the guy. I know of what you speak. Anyway, better punch in." He pointed at the time clock, where they had cards to time stamp an employee's arrival. I did so and was officially back to work as a server at the ritzy establishment known as "Bert's Eats."

Bert's was not a diner, exactly. It was more of a small, family-owned restaurant, which served basic American food. Think steaks and burgers, roast chicken, stuff like that. Not gourmet, or even close, but the food was good, the vegetables fresh and locally sourced, and the atmosphere was much better than one would think from the restaurant name. I once asked the owner, Bertram Wolfe, why he didn't change the name of the place to something that more resembled the actual ambiance of the place, like maybe Bertram's Fine Food, and he just pointed to a dollar bill taped to the wall.

"That's the first dollar I ever earned in the restaurant business. A customer paid for a burger and fries at my glorified hamburger stand, which had a cardboard sign with 'Bert's Eats' scrawled on the front. The name was good enough then, and it's good enough today. Now get back to work. A couple just sat down at Table 3."

I grabbed my order pad and a pen, gave a little wave to Derek, and headed out to the dining room, where I surveyed the situation. There were a few couples sitting at checkerboard tablecloth covered tables, with white cloth napkins. Several other similarly set tables were vacant. A pretty server attended to the occupied tables. She'd pulled her long, blond hair back in a ponytail.

Daisy Wilson, also known as "Daze," flashed a smile when she spotted me, and I returned it while hustling to a newly occupied table.

Daisy was an accomplished pilot. She gave flying lessons at the local airport. Waiting on tables was a necessary sideline for her. Like me, she needed something to pay the bills other than doing what she loved. Daisy, at one time, piloted commercial aircraft for a major airline. She no longe had any job opportunity as a pilot. The entire industry blackballed her from any other commercial airline for reasons that had nothing to do with her aviation acumen. Daisy was a superb pilot. She could fly anything, from giant jets to helicopters. If it had wings, she could fly it.

As for me, I could act. And maybe fly a little, because I was a licensed pilot, and a student of hers at the flying school.

Part of Daisy's meager compensation at the airport included periodic access to a two seat Cessna 152. It had a single Lycoming engine capable of producing 110 horsepower, and could cruise at 100 miles per hour with a range of about 350 miles.

I often manned the co-pilot's seat on her periodic jaunts with the aircraft, and could say for a fact that she could never make the full 350 mile range of the Cessna, because she spent so much time doing barrel rolls, loops and other aerial stunts. The first time she pulled one of those when I accompanied her, I almost soiled myself. I knew I was very close to throwing up. But that unpleasantness never happened, and now I enjoy it. You can get used to anything.

Anyway, the restaurant stayed busy for a couple of hours, then it was completely dead. I was ambivalent about the customer hiatuses. I love the breaks, and they give me time to talk to Hippo and Daze, but waiting tables is very much a tip-based occupation. No customers, no money.

But this one fell into the grateful category. The three of

us huddled in the kitchen.

"Are you guys flying today?" Hippo asked.

I looked at Daze. "Are we?"

"Nah, let's take a day off. You're learning so much, I hardly have anything left to teach you." A snicker followed this absurd statement.

Hippo and I both smiled. I could take a thousand lessons and never come close to learning all she knew.

"You have something else in mind?" I inquired.

She looked at Hippo. "Is Willy performing tonight?"

"She is. You guys want to come?"

Daze looked over at me, and I nodded. "Yeah. If she's not too tired after work, we can grab a bite somewhere."

"Anywhere but here," Hippo said. "And preferably outside."

Hippo's longtime girlfriend was Wilhemina Danvers, the only well-paid member of our foursome. Derek agreed to pick up Daisy and me in the early evening, and, noticing a few customers filing in, we all went back to work.

2

After work, Daze and I walked to my Duster. We are good friends, sometime lovers, and currently the latter. We headed back to the apartment we shared to shower and get ready for our evening in Jacksonville, where Willy performed.

At the appointed time, Hippo picked us up in his SUV, and we drove to the Orpheum, parked, and went inside to take the ringside seats Willy had arranged for us.

Shortly after we sat down, an announcement blared.

"Ladies and gentlemen, hold on to your seats. The most thrill-packed, death defying example of human carnage is about to begin. Let me introduce the first contestant. Raised by wolves, taught her skills by living among vicious grizzly bears, she has the teeth of a piranha. Let's give the appropriate thunderous boo to the half-human, half animal, Deathtrap! Loud boos filled the arena. I looked over at Hippo to see if he joined in, and saw him waving his arms and shouting with everyone else, as his very own costume-bedecked Willemina Danvers, aka Deathtrap, took her corner.

"And now, for the goddess of good, the tough as nails but soft as silk, sweetheart of the ring, Angelheart!"

Loud cheers followed the announcement, and Daisy, Hippo and I joined in. The match, or fight, if one wants to call it that, was predictable. Right from the outset, Deathtrap pressed her height and weight advantage, kicking, biting, punching and strangling the poor Angelheart, who looked defeated before they even started. But somewhere along the way, the tide turned, and good triumphed over evil. It was a good show, and the two "fighters" were very skilled. They had to be, if they didn't want to kill each other by accident, and kill the golden goose that produced enormous crowds every night.

After the match, Hippo led Daze and me backstage to Willy's dressing room. They exchanged greetings while Willy stood behind a screen changing out of her costume. When she emerged, the difference in her appearance was startling. Un-costumed, she looked nothing like her alter ego. A tall, long-legged brunette with flowing, thick hair and a pretty face, Willy looked more like a well-muscled fashion model than a wrestler. You could see that she was strong, but the resemblance to a fighter ended there.

Fully dressed in street clothes, she emerged from behind the screen, kissed Hippo, and hugged Daze and me. She didn't hesitate when asked if she was too tired to go out to dinner.

"I'm not tired at all. Just another day at work. Flossie and I are pretty good at missing each other. We work hard, but try not to wear each other out too much, without affecting the show, of course."

"Of course," I said. "What a fabulous performance."

"Terrific," Daze chimed in, while Hippo just beamed with pride.

As we exited the arena, I noticed a man and woman standing outside. I was certain it was the same two who attended my theater rehearsals. The two stuck out like sore thumbs. Who wore a dark suit to a wrestling match? The woman looked a little better, but my glance picked up a string of pearls around her neck. Too formal for the setting.

I asked the others whether they'd noticed the man and woman, but they demurred. They likely only caught my attention because I'd seen them before. I just shrugged and resolved to keep an eye out for them. If they were following me, I wanted to know why.

We all boarded Hippo's SUV, with Willy sitting in front, or "shotgun" as she called it, with Daze and me in the back. We all dined outside at a restaurant halfway between Jacksonville and St. Augustine, and then headed home. Hippo dropped me and Daze at our apartment and headed over to Willy's home, a few blocks from the beach.

***

"He spotted us, you know."

"Yeah, he did. I picked up on that, too."

"It's your fault. You insist on wearing that suit. You look like an idiot, wearing a suit in ninety-degree weather."

"It's only about eighty right now," the man said.

"With about 100 percent humidity. And this is the evening. You wore that suit to the rehearsals, too. And that warehouse is a blast furnace."

"We're not really trying to hide, anyway," the man said. "Why do we care if he sees us?"

"We're not ready to approach them."

"I don't know about you, but I'm ready right now. They could make a great team."

"True. They have all the required elements, and they all need money."

"Except maybe the wrestler lady," the man mused.

"I'll bet she'd help out of loyalty."

"Probably," the man agreed. "But we only need Wilson

and Steele."

The woman nodded.

***

Derek "Hippo" Thurston was a college football star at the University of Florida. His hometown Jacksonville Jaguars drafted him in the second round. He never played a down in the NFL. Prior to a single snap, his required physical exam disclosed a neck condition known as diffuse cervical stenosis. One cervical fusion surgery later, Hippo could live a normal life, but his football career was over. So instead of having a lucrative NFL career, Hippo was working as a cook and just making ends meet.

He and Willy met at the University of Florida. She was a drama major, and he graduated with honors with a degree in business administration, and a fully punched ticket to the National Football League. Hippo planned a ten-year football career, followed by a long broadcasting career. Big plans for a big guy. And a smart one, too. Hippo was his nickname, but his teammates at UF referred to him as "Einstein."

But the big plans temporarily dissolved with the big neck issue. He had a much better chance of being hired by a network as a former NFL player than he did as one of many college graduates with a business degree. So, he was a cook who unsuccessfully submitted many applications for broadcasting jobs, internships, or anything at all. So far, no luck. But Hippo kept trying. He was persistent, as a big-time college player who always finished his tackles; as a college kid asking Willy for a date time after time until she accepted; as a loyal friend; and even as a cook. His friends knew he'd get a chance at his dream at some point. Just not now.

***

The next day, Daisy and I headed to the airport for another flying lesson. We parked in the employee parking lot and walked the short distance to the office managing private planes and flying lessons. The assistant manager, Dennis

Weber, was a pimply faced, twenty-three-year-old kid who was head over heels in love with Daze.

"Hi Daisy," he said brightly when we walked in. He gave me a brief, wordless nod, then turned back to Daisy. "Looking great today," he said, then quickly added "For flying. It'll be clear sailing. South wind, only about two knots." He kept staring at Daze.

"Thanks Denny," Daze said, reaching over to pat his arm.

I watched the interchange with amusement. Daze was just being her usual nice self, but the kid acted as if she'd given him a lap dance when she touched him.

I waited while Daisy did her usual preflight on the Cessna, then we buckled up and took off. Dennis was right. It was beautiful flying weather. Blue skies, sunny, but not so bright that the glare blinded you. And very few adjustments due to wind speed.

"Where to?" Daze asked me, while still manning the controls.

"What am I learning today?" I asked.

"How to fly," was the cynical answer. "You're not ready for any acrobatics." She executed a barrel roll, then continued. "But I am."

"Didn't you file a flight plan?"

"Yeah. As an instructor, I have a little leeway. But the FAA frowns on 'flying around aimlessly,' so I wrote Daytona."

"We're not strafing the speedway again, are we?"

Daze grinned. "Maybe."

I didn't think any races ran that day, and considered myself fortunate. Daze had a well-developed crazy streak, and wouldn't mind playing disrupter to the rabid NASCAR community, even if the storied Daytona 500 was running. It wasn't so much that she relished creating havoc as it was that she rarely gave a ton of thought before doing something. She is the most impetuous person I ever knew, and I absolutely love that part of her.

Our hookup, if anyone wanted to call it that, was not serious. We are good friends, and both of us have had multiple prior relationships, both with each other and with others. But at present, we are an adorable couple, flying together like a pair of old geese.

3

At present, the old geese headed towards Daytona, about fifty miles south of our origin airport. We reached it fast, and, without a racetrack to torment, we discussed alternatives.

"How about a baseball field?" I offered.

"Okay. Is there one in Daytona?"

"There must be at least a high school one. Circle around a bit while I check."

"Sure. In circles. I can do that." She immediately executed a barrel roll, followed by another and a third.

Used to this kind of behavior, and no longer prone to stomach upheaval, I calmly waited for the acrobatics to end and gave my answer.

"Yup. The Daytona Tortugas. Single A minor league club. And we're in luck. There's a game going on right this minute."

"What's a Tortuga?"

"An island in the Caribbean. Also, a tortoise."

"Who names a sports team after a slow-moving reptile?"

"Another team in the league is the Fire Frogs."

"At least they're fast, and can jump like hell. A tortoise either slowly plods, or hides in its shell. It's a terrible name."

I just listened. When Daze was done, I assumed the role of navigator to the field, where, sure enough, a baseball game was in progress.

"I'll do a few tricks for the fans, and then you can unfurl the banner."

"Okay, go to it."

Daze performed a few stunts. I pulled out my binoculars and watched the crowd all crane their necks and point at us.

"Okay, let 'er rip."

I unfurled the banner, tied it securely, and let it fly, treating the crowd to a long banner reading "Caution: Student Pilot."

Daze circled around the park twice, then I pulled in the banner, and we headed back home. She turned the controls over to me, giving instructions the entire time, leading me to complain about "back seat pilots."

"Your flying is okay," she said. "But you have some bad habits."

"Like what?"

"Complaining about your instructor, for one."

"Fair enough. But name another."

"Leaving the toilet seat up."

"That has nothing to do with flying," I protested.

"I said you had some bad habits. I didn't say they had anything to do with flying. Your flying is fine. You can co-pilot me anytime."

"I learned from the best," I said.

"True enough. Now land this old jalopy, and stick the landing like I showed you."

"Aye, Aye Captain."

I landed the plane and taxied off the runway.

"Stop here," Daze said. "This spot is out of view of the tower."

"So…ooh!"

Daze had stripped off her blouse and unhooked her bra, letting two beautiful breasts pop out. Framed by that long, blond hair, she looked more like Lady Godiva than a pilot.

"Flying makes me horny," she said.

"Looking at you does the same for me. But do we have room?"

"Get those shorts off, and I'll show you how to maximize a small space." She unbuttoned her own shorts as she spoke.

I needed no further encouragement, and the two of us executed a maneuver requiring great skill.

As we struggled to reposition ourselves to put our clothes back on, the radio squawked.

"Everything okay, Daisy? Any engine-trouble?"

Daze flashed a grin at me before responding.

"Everything is in perfect working order."

With what I'm sure was a mischievous smile, I leaned in and said, "She performed beautifully, Dennis," drawing a light punch from Daze, who added, "See you in a couple of minutes."

"Roger," Dennis said.

Before we taxied the rest of the way, I looked over at Daze, and said, "Oh crap, we better stop."

"What's up?"

"Your blouse is on backwards."

She laughed. "I better fix it. I don't want to fuel Dennis' imagination." She took off her blouse, turned it around, and put it back on.

"How do I look?"

"Maybe a little flushed, but otherwise, perfectly respectable. How about me?"

"The picture of rectitude."

"Works for me. Let's go."

If Dennis noticed anything amiss, he said nothing, and we headed home in the Duster.

I knew the ban precluded Daisy from flying to or from Jacksonville International Airport, and getting jobs ordinarily readily available for a pilot with her outstanding skill set, but I was hazy on the details, and on the way home, I asked her.

Daisy recounted her blackballing for "borrowing" some well-connected billionaire's Gulfstream for an impromptu trip to Maui with some friends before she met me.

"Hey, I cleaned and pre-flighted it when I brought it back. Even put gas in it. And he wasn't even using it that weekend. But the bastard was furious. And he contacted some friend at the FAA, who contacted all the major airlines. But they let me keep my license as long as I agreed never to visit that airport again. He still hates me," she said. "Probably spends every waking hour figuring out ways to get even."

We arrived back at our apartment, took showers, and headed to Bert's Eats. Hippo was already at work and waved us over. "How was today's flying lesson?"

"His performance was exemplary," Daze said with a snicker.

"She's an outstanding teacher," I said with a nod.

"Then why did your compliment sound facetious?"

"We kind of mixed business with pleasure," I said.

"Ah. A double entendre."

"Your perceptive abilities are well-honed, my good sir."

Upon entering the dining room, I encountered an unexpected sight—none other than the couple I'd seen following us. I played it cool. Let them say something first. I approached the table, handed them menus, and asked whether they wanted something to drink.

The man looked up at me. "Gin and tonic. Easy on the tonic."

"A glass of white wine, please. Any type is fine."

"Gin with a hint of tonic and one glass of house white wine coming up." I walked away, caught Daze's eye and signaled for her to go into the kitchen with me.

"Did you see those two in Table 2?"

Daze nodded. "I wonder what they want?"

"They didn't say, at least not yet. They just placed drink orders."

"Are you going to confront them?"

"I hoped they'd say something first. They're following us for a reason."

Daze grimaced. "Not a bad one, I hope."

"Agreed. But somehow, I don't think so."

"Just ask them. Being in the restaurant is an open invitation."

"Yeah, I guess it is. Okay, here goes."

I retrieved the couple's drinks from the restaurant bar and delivered them to the table. Placing the glasses before each of them, I said, "Are you ready to order? And are you ready to tell me why you're following us?"

"Strip steak, medium rare, baked potato, and house salad with ranch dressing," the man said.

"Grilled salmon, extra lemon, mashed potatoes, green beans, and this is not a good place to talk. Please meet us at this location." She handed me a piece of paper with a written address, date and time on it. "And please invite your pilot friend to join us. I think what we have to tell you is very much in your interest. And it will cost nothing to hear us out."

"One strip, medium rare, baked potato, house salad with ranch, salmon, extra lemon, mashed and green beans coming up. And one appointment under consideration."

I caught Daze's eye again, and once again we conferred in the kitchen, where I told Daze and Hippo what they'd said.

"It sounds crooked," Hippo said.

"It does," Daze offered.

"Should we just ignore it?"

The other two took a moment to think about it, then Hippo said "Maybe not. The location is an office on A1A in the morning. Not a dark alley at night. Seems like low risk to listen."

"I am curious what they want with both of us," Daze said.

"Yeah, me too. So, we agree to listen with great skepticism?"

They both nodded.

"Do you want me to come along? I can be very intimidating."

I chuckled. "Yes, you can. But as you pointed out, it's a public place in the morning. Low risk. We can always scare them to death later."

When the food was ready, I delivered it to their table and acted like a waiter until they finished their meal, paid the check and left without further discussion.

I picked up the $48.00 cash paid check folio, with a crisp $100 bill included and a note with a brief scrawl on it reading "Outstanding service. See you tomorrow morning."

I showed it to my friends before depositing it into the shared tip box.

"Nice tip," one of the college student busboys told me, seeing the bill drop into the coffer he shared with the servers. "What did you do to earn that? Are you selling drugs? If you are…I have, um, a friend…who…"

I held up a hand, palm facing the kid. "Stop. Before you say something you'll regret. I did not and do not sell drugs.

Occasionally you get an extra generous customer. That's all."

"Sure, sure, Trip. Nice addition to the tip box. Thanks."

4

"**I**'ve given it some thought," Carleton said.

"That's a first," I mumbled.

Carleton looked sharply at me. "That's what I get when I'm about to do you a big favor?"

I sighed. "Sorry about that. But giving me favors, or even thoughtful help, has not exactly been part of your directorial relationship with me."

Carleton ignored my response. "I think I've miscast you."

"How so?"

"You're much more suited to the role of Feste."

"The court jester? Hey, that's the lead. But what about Gary? It's his role."

"Gary left without so much as a phone call."

"Where'd he go?"

"It doesn't matter. What matters is that you have new lines to learn."

"I know them already," I said. "How's this? 'Foolery, sir, does walk about the orb like the sun, it shines everywhere.'"

Carleton looked upward, as if beseeching an unseen deity to rescue him from catastrophe. But he cut his eyes back to me.

"That's good, Trip, especially off the cuff. We'll work on it, okay?"

His response blew me away. Carleton hadn't said two friendly words to me in all the time I'd known him. I guessed his need for someone to play Feste trumped his overt dislike of me.

"Okay," I said. "I welcome your help and guidance."

Carleton didn't hear me, because he had already turned away to bark orders at the rest of the cast.

I returned to our apartment after rehearsal at about eleven p.m. to find a fully awake Daisy pacing nervously in the living room. Daisy was not prone to anxiety. She had to have nerves of steel to perform her aerial acrobatics.

"What's up?" I asked upon entering.

"You're back. Good. I don't like this at all. Something's wrong. I can just feel it. Oh, um, how was rehearsal?"

"It went well. Carleton gave me the lead. I'll tell you all about it, but you first. What's bothering you?"

"The meeting with those two strange people. I have a bad feeling about it."

"So, we'll skip it. We don't have to do anything. We just won't show up." I wrapped my arms around her and discovered a very uncustomary shivering. "Does that make you feel better?"

She nodded into my shoulder and stopped shaking.

We disengaged and stood face to face. She spoke first. "But I'm overwhelmed with curiosity."

"Yeah, me too. But our lives are fine without hearing them out, and they'll continue to be fine. Some things aren't worth it, especially if you have a foreboding of doom."

"It's more like a premonition, but you get the idea."

Having decided on a course of action, or lack of action, we went to bed.

As we lay there, her head nestled in the crook of my arm, she said, "You got the lead. That's great." And we both fell asleep.

***

As we sat at the kitchen table in the morning, I drank my coffee, and Daze sipped her herbal tea. She avoided all caffeine. We ate a simple breakfast of whole grain toast and apple slices.

"No work until the afternoon," I said. "Shall we fly somewhere?"

Daze seemed not to hear me, so I tapped her gently on the arm, and she popped out of her meditative state.

"Oh, sorry. I was just thinking."

I waited for her to elaborate.

"Maybe we should find out what those two people want with us?"

"I thought we decided your premonition overrode our curiosity."

"We did," she acknowledged. "But, as Hip pointed out yesterday, it's in full daylight right on A1A. What could possibly happen by listening to their story?"

"Your premonition, not mine. I'm okay with going if you are. I'm even okay with canceling the meeting on the way there, and heading to the airport instead."

"I love your flexibility," she said.

"And I love yours," I said with what I thought was a lascivious leer.

Daze just giggled. "We both showed remarkable flexibility yesterday on the plane, wouldn't you say?"

It was my turn to giggle. "I didn't know the human body could bend that way."

We headed to our big appointment via the beach road to start, and Daze gazed longingly toward the ocean. A meeting in a stuffy office building did not fit her personality. At all. She was at home in the air, or in the fresh air on the beach, with the vast ocean giving her space.

"Maybe we should just turn right up here, skip the meeting, and spend the morning at the beach," I said, slowing down.

I heard a deep sigh of…relief?

But it wasn't relief. It was resignation. Daze was determined to see this through, or so she said.

We pulled up in front of a nondescript two-story building, with no signage in front. I parked and checked the address against the note.

"This is it," I said. "Should we just turn around and go

do some paddle-boarding?"

She shook her head. "No… I don't think so. This doesn't feel right, but it doesn't seem dangerous, either, so we might as well hear what they have to say."

I had some trepidation of my own, and frankly would have been fine with ditching the whole thing and going to the beach. Where Daisy was impetuous, I was cautious. We complemented each other beautifully. She made me less cautious, and I…well, became more spontaneous. And I'd never want to dampen her wonderful spirit. But at present, her crazy streak had run up against one of her premonitions. And for the moment, we were both appropriately skeptical.

"Okay," I said. "Let's do it."

We went into the building and found various doors with numbers on them. We found 4A, and knocked.

The door opened a moment later, and the woman we'd seen the previous evening greeted us and ushered us into the office.

She extended her hand and introduced herself as Abigail Adams.

"Like the…"

"Second First Lady, yes. I'm told she was a distant relative. And this is Jeffrey Bailey," she said as her partner appeared at an inner doorway. He extended his hand and Daisy and I shook their hands. We could hear sounds one would associate with an office, but saw no one else.

Abby and Jeff, as they told us to call them, ushered us to a conference room, and we all sat down.

Abby spoke first. "I'm sure you're wondering what this is all about, and why the cloak and dagger stuff. But some extremely powerful people might not like what we do."

I interrupted her. "What do you do? And why would we ever want to get involved in anything that powerful people hate?"

Daze moved her chair closer to me. She didn't like this any more than I did.

Jeff spoke up. "Look, we get it. We've shown you nothing. We're the good guys, I promise you that. Let us explain and check us out before deciding anything. Your only task right now is to listen, and you don't even have to do that. But we'll give you another hundred dollars each to just sit here and hear us out. Is that fair?"

I looked at Daze, and she slowly nodded. We could use $200 for not doing anything.

"Good," Jeff said. "I don't think you'll regret it. Your respective skill sets could benefit our business and make you a ton of money."

It sounded great, but easy money was usually too good to be true, and often illegal. I was getting impatient. Daze was fidgeting next to me, but she said nothing.

"Out with it," I said, with not a little exasperation. "What do you do? And why do you need us?"

Abby answered. "We don't need you. We want you. You're perfect for what we have in mind. And what we do is property reclamation."

"Property reclamation? You restore things…oh, no. You're a repo company."

"A name associated with some organizations that are not always…ethical. We're not that."

"Look," I said. "I think I can speak for Daisy when I say this, but she will speak for herself. We won't seize a poor family's furniture, or cars from people down on their luck who can't keep up with their payments. We're leaving."

"We'd never do that," Daze said. "That's a hard no."

5

Daisy and I stood up, and Abby said quietly, "We don't do that, either. We have a very particular kind of business. Please sit down, and let me tell you what I should have told you upfront. Jeff and I abhor the kinds of things you describe. We don't do them, and dislike other companies that do. We reclaim, okay repossess, very large ticket items, like airplanes nominally owned by billionaires." She cut her eyes to Daisy. "Like Mikhail Bachenko."

We sat down. Bachenko was Daisy's nemesis, if you could call him that. She'd borrowed his Gulfstream, returned it in perfect condition, but he'd held a grudge against her ever since. And he was in danger of losing his plane?

Daisy said, "How is that possible? He's a billionaire. Doesn't he own that plane?"

"Ah, I've piqued your interest. We have it on good authority that he continues to do anything he can to cause you harm."

"How do you know that?" I demanded.

"Our business puts us in contact with many people in the aviation industry, and that rarefied group of wealthy people. But I digress. Let me answer your question, Ms. Wilson."

"Cash purchases of aircraft of that type are extremely rare. Large corporations and very wealthy individuals more commonly lease the jets. They have the cache of a 'private jet,' without actually paying the enormous purchase price. Bachenko possesses an exclusive lease of that Gulfstream. Exclusivity requires a much bigger monthly payment."

"No way that guy is behind in his payments," Daze said emphatically.

"True enough. He is rich and is not behind in his payments. But he violated certain other conditions of the lease."

"Like what?"

"Let's just say taking his plane back wouldn't alter your moral compass."

"If it's legal, and doesn't hurt ordinary people, it probably won't."

"It's legal, and it hurts a vindictive billionaire. So, here's some more detail," Abby continued.

"Jeff and I are software engineers by training and experience. Together, we developed a specialized database program with unique advanced features that are wildly popular with businesses. I won't explain the technicalities of the program right now," she said, and stopped. "Would you like to hear more about the software? It can get a little technical, but I can explain it now, or maybe later?"

"I think you can tell us that later," I said, but how does this explain your involvement in a reclamation business?"

"Alone, it doesn't," Abby acknowledged. "But as you'll see, our, um, electronic eavesdropping talent dovetails perfectly with a particular reclamation. And yours do, too, as I'll explain."

"To continue, Jeff and I are not business people. We

know nothing about finance, or the fundamentals of forming a business, but we somehow, with help from friends, pulled it off and founded AbbJeff. The purpose of the business was to market and sell our proprietary software, and to develop new software."

She paused, then continued, "We're good at developing software and bad at business, as I just said. But we knew enough to know we needed funding to market our products effectively. We needed a sales staff, a marketing manager, a bookkeeper, lawyers, accountants, way more than that, but you get the idea. When you start off, you need little, but our software is very popular. We needed a structure to sell our product both nationally and internationally. And you wouldn't believe the regulatory nightmare to sell software overseas, but I'm seriously digressing." She glanced at Jeff, who picked up from there.

"We needed money," he said. "And we tried the conventional bank route, but for a variety of reasons, we had little success. It seems that conventional banks were very skeptical of software startups like ours. So, we had to turn elsewhere, and ultimately settled upon a smooth- talking internationalist, Mikhail Bachenko. He had loads of money to lend, an interest in the software business, and many, many political connections both here and abroad."

"Does he develop software himself?" Daze asked.

"He's no software engineer," Abby almost spat the words.

"But he employs people who are," Jeff said. "Abby and I no longer work at AbbJeff, the company we founded, and headed up as president and CEO, respectively."

"There's a story there," I said. "And you're about to tell us about Bachenko's role in that sad state of affairs."

"Yes," Jeff said. "Abby and I will cast aside any concern about how you will use the information we give you. We're going to tell you everything, and let the chips fall where they may. Some individuals have burned us in the past and maybe that makes us over-cautious."

"Abby and I thought we were being smart," Jeff said. "We only knew about the usual banks. We knew nothing about so-called hard money lenders, and we tried to steer clear of them, because they seemed like loan sharks to us. I guess some of them are not, but we didn't know what we were doing, and just wanted to save and expand our business. We raised some money by getting some tiny investments from people we thought we could trust — friends of friends, people like that. We didn't really know them, but they seemed trustworthy. Three investors with a five percent ownership of the company, with the two of us keeping 85 percent. It brought in some money, and the demand for our software grew exponentially."

Abby spoke up. "We had a tremendous expansion of our business, and a tiny business structure. We needed more resources, both physical and human, to handle the vast increase in business, and frankly, to expand into international markets."

"We needed more money," Jeff said. "Plain and simple. Our little start-up was not so small anymore. But there were no more friends or friends of friends to invest."

"So, when Mikhail Bachenko approached us with a proposal, we almost jumped at it. He offered a significant investment for forty percent of the company."

I could see where this was going, and I was pretty sure Daze could as well. But we let the two of them tell their story.

"The money was like a shot in the arm," Jeff said. "Our revenue exploded. We took on enormous expenses, but we had the revenue to support them. Or at least that's what our accounting staff advised us."

"They were telling the truth," Abby said. "Our company was very profitable. Still is. But that's getting ahead of the story."

"Abby and I are superb software engineers, but the

demands of the business side of things overwhelmed us. We trusted professionals more and more, and the advice was not always great."

"The lawyers who signed off on transferring our personally owned intellectual property patents is the most blatant example."

"We were unbelievably dumb," Abby said. "That lawyer must have been in Bachenko's pocket. I'm sure of it, but I can't prove a thing. Bachenko told us to have our own attorneys look over the transaction. He said he needed the company to have assets in order to invest. And the only real asset was the intellectual property."

"So, we chose our own intellectual property attorneys, or so we thought. And they advised us it was okay to transfer our patents to AbbJeff, Inc. Because he flatly stated, 'you two are very much in control of the company. You presently own eighty-five percent of the company, and you have friendly investors holding the other fifteen percent. The new investor, Bachenko, is only receiving forty percent of the stock. You still have control. And it's not unreasonable for a big investor to want value in something he's buying.'"

"What the lawyer told us seemed reasonable, and we very much wanted the investment. The three minority investors, who never interfered a bit in the past, and had expressed vigorous support for our leadership, supported the investment by Bachenko."

"We signed the agreement, transferred the patents and the trademark AbbJeff, the logo, everything we owned personally, to AbbJeff."

"Bachenko was as good as his word, invested millions into the business, which skyrocketed. An independent valuation of the company today conducted by a major accounting firm is almost two billion dollars."

"Whoa," I said, and Abby and Jeff nodded.

"I think you can figure out the rest. Our three friendly investors were bought out, bribed, threatened, who knows what, but they sold their shares to Bachenko, who exercised his fifty-five percent controlling interest to oust the two of us from our positions, and from the board of directors, and ultimately fired us."

"But we still own forty percent of a very valuable company. But it's not publicly held. It's not like we can just sell our shares and get forty percent of the value. The shares have value, but only to Bachenko, who'd love to get rid of us entirely."

"We're also developing new software products that AbbJeff won't own. But some creative successes occur once in a lifetime, and our database program is a thing of beauty."

"I get it," Daze said. "You hate Bachenko for good reason. He effectively stole your proverbial baby from you. What does that have to do with repossessing a plane? Or Trip and me?"

Abby exuded an enormous sigh. "Our situation…and yours, has very little to do with repossessing Bachenko's Gulfstream."

"Then what…?"

Jeff interjected. "After Bachenko fired us, we were recruited by Imperial Reclamation to repossess his jet. And that's precisely what we intend to do. That's where you two come into play. Your skill sets are perfectly suited to that task. Alistair Brooke, the company's chief, believed we'd be motivated and informed enough about Bachenko's practices to develop a plan for repossessing the Gulfstream. We know that Bachenko is a very dangerous, extremely well-connected man, not to be trifled with."

"But you're going to poke the bear with a sharp stick, and you want us to help you do it," Daze said.

"In a word, yes. Look, you stand to benefit as much as

we do. Bachenko has screwed you over for doing nothing more than taking a joy ride. Don't you think his idea of retribution for your impulsive action was completely out of proportion to what you did?"

"I hate to admit it, but in hindsight, I understand his anger," she said. "But the extreme nature of his response was bafflingly vindictive."

"Let's get back to some more information for your consideration," Jeff said.

"First, what Mikhail Bachenko did to us was totally legal. Sharp business practice is not a crime. There may have been illegality involved in how he went about it, such as the manner in which he turned our friendly investors against us, but we can't prove a thing. They're not talking, maybe from embarrassment that they were so easily bought off, or maybe from fear of retribution. We just don't know. Abby and I suspect he had our attorney in his pocket, but we have no proof of it. Similarly, what he did to you, by all appearances, was completely legal. And he has an army of attorneys that will say that everything Bachenko does is legal. We didn't even try to fight his hostile takeover in the courts. It would have been a fool's errand. But we have some suspicions, lots of them, about a variety of things. And a lot revolves around that plane. Let me explain."

"But first, a little more background. We told you we developed proprietary database software, and that it's very popular with business. Well, it's very popular with governments, too. Both the United States and abroad. And it's cloud based." Jeff looked at both of us to make sure we knew what he meant. We did.

"Backups of all data in each database are stored in the cloud. The U.S. Government makes certain to store sensitive information in its secure local servers, outside of our database. But it stores a ton of information outside of its locked-down server. And the U.S. Government is much better at securing its top-secret files than many other nations. Just a piece of information to file away while I continue giving you the background. It becomes important in a moment."

"So, we have a very wealthy international industrialist who is very interested in a particular start-up company. Interested enough to invest millions of dollars, and more or less steal the company away from its founders. We have a cloud-based database program that is used by business and government. And we have a plane that the rich guy is fanatic about. Fanatic enough to freak out when a 'crazy bimbo pilot'—his words, not mine—borrowed his jet for a trip to Maui."

We stared at him. "You know the details of that?" Daze asked.

Abby and Jeff both smiled. "Surprised you, didn't I," Jeff said. "Yes, we know all about it because Mike—the name he often uses in this country—told us about it while we were still on good terms with him. The incident completely unhinged him. I had to stifle a smile, because he was so incensed. I have a question about it, though."

"What?"

"Bachenko treats that plane as his personal office. He never allows it out of the sight of his trusted pilot and crew. Never."

It was Daze's turn to smile. "I was only there because he needed a skilled pilot on call at a moment's notice. I took the job because the commuter flights bored me, and thought I'd get to do something interesting and exciting flying such a long-range aircraft. But he went nowhere. He just left supervision of the jet's maintenance to me. He explicitly forbade me from actually boarding the plane."

"So how…?"

"Did I borrow it? After about a week, I grew tired of waiting around doing nothing other than befriending the equally idle crew, and ignored his prohibition, first by having a small shindig in the plane itself, and then…well you know the rest. I was itching to fly, and the so-called trusted crew members were, too, especially when the flight was to Maui for a non-stop weekend party. They agreed to come along, including a fellow who had pilot training who served as my co-pilot. We had a great blow-out party in Hawaii and returned. I paid to gas it up, which is not cheap, and put the plane in tip-top condition. I figured he'd fire me, but I was going to quit, anyway. After the way he responded to me, I shudder to think what happened to the crew."

"We don't know. He told us he was going to make you very sorry you crossed him, and that he would get you banned from any commercial flight. Abby and I had the unmistakable impression that he believed he could get that done. He didn't tell us how, but we know he's very connected politically, and in the business world, which is why Imperial created a special unit to deal with people like him."

"Imperial recruited us for one subject—Mikhail Bachenko. Getting it done could be very profitable for us, and for you. We don't care about any payout from Imperial, even though it will be substantial if we're successful. We have money. No, we want the same thing you do—our old lives back. Hopefully, there is evidence in that plane that could help both of us. And every single dollar paid out by Imperial will go directly to the two of you, to divide any way you see fit. And if there is no money from Imperial, we'll pay you ourselves."

"How could information in that plane help me return to flying anywhere I want?" Daze asked.

Abby and Jeff looked at each other and made a silent agreement.

Abby spoke up. "We honestly don't know it for sure. And we're not sure any evidence exists. There might be nothing, in which case Jeff and I pay you a large sum of money. We'll do more than that if we find what we're looking for. With those caveats, let me answer your question with a hypothetical. Say, for example, that a hard drive exists which contains evidence of Bachenko's felonies, maybe bribery, or blackmail, or fraud?"

"It would seriously discredit him and maybe send him to jail. And you might return to the helm of AbbJeff. And my restrictions might end. Appealing thoughts, but a lot of maybes," Daze said.

"As we said, we're not sure evidence exists, or that it is on the plane. But we have more than guessing to support our beliefs."

Daze and I waited for elaboration, and Jeff offered it.

"We created a back door to our software. We can access the data in the databases."

At our expressions, he hastened to add, "Every single cloud-based storage company discloses that up front, and so do we. No one routinely accesses the data. In fact, we never did. But a back door is necessary to provide any kind of technical support. No one reads the documents in the databases. And there are serious controls over any access. All cloud-based services, including ours, prohibit reading, downloading or in any way reviewing the actual data. That remains private and secure. We monitor any access, both with keystroke programs on the workstations, and by video surveillance. The security staff would catch any unauthorized access in a matter of seconds. It was flat out impossible to read any data in our databases. Our clients, which as we said, include governments, require, and routinely review, our security procedures."

"You used the past tense when you told us it was impossible," I said.

Jeff sighed. "I did. I don't know if it's impossible any more. Oh, the security procedures will be intact, for sure. The clientele would continue to insist upon it. But a new security staff installed by the new CEO…might not take their jobs as seriously as they should."

"Meaning he could bribe them," Daze said.

"Let's just say I think the man is capable of anything."

"He's aware of the back door?" I asked, although I knew the answer.

"No question. The more I think about it, the more I believe that's the reason he targeted our company. Access to business and government data could be very enticing, and very profitable if used improperly."

I had no trouble imagining what a criminal could do with sensitive information from businesses and countries.

"This is way bigger than a simple repo," Daze said the obvious. "How can a pilot and," she smiled slyly, "a Shakespearean actor be of any help? It sounds like you need a full, professional team, not us."

Before I could sputter a denial of my affinity for performing the Bard's plays, Jeff interjected.

"You're not just an ordinary pilot. You're a superstar stuck in the junior circuit. And he is a first-rate actor stuck in a third-rate theater. Oh, I'm sure he will perform Feste admirably, but he belongs in that converted warehouse performing Shakespeare about as much as Michael Jordan, giving up basketball to play the flute. And his improvisation skills are an asset in any tough situation."

"What is Imperial's basis for repossessing the plane, anyway?" I asked.

"It's not nonpayment. But there are other conditions he ignores, whether from arrogance or design. I couldn't tell you. For example, he's apparently never filed a single maintenance report; not a single flight log; has never provided information regarding the number of miles the plane has traveled; or other information detailing the condition of the 'collateral,' as Alistair phrases it. He's a very secretive guy, so Imperial is clueless regarding the physical condition of the aircraft. Those are only a few of the dozen breaches of the terms of the sales contract. Alistair wants the plane back to sell or lease to someone who is more accountable."

"It sounds like a tough job," Daze said. "Do you have a plan to get past all that security? It was one thing to do it when I was on the inside, almost in physical possession of the plane. It will be a lot tougher now."

"Does that mean you're interested?" A hopeful sounding Abby asked the question.

Daze looked at me. "We have to discuss it first. It was more of an observation."

"A good one, too. But yes, we have a plan, but we cannot assure its success by any means. You'll get paid even if it's unsuccessful. But you'll get paid much more if it's successful. Because Imperial and Jeff and I will both pay you. But we know you'll want to verify our story."

"We'll give you an answer as soon as we do."

"That's fair," Abby said, and Jeff nodded.

"Check us out, but please don't take too long. We need to put things in motion pretty soon. Here is a paper with our company name and contact information at Imperial, including that of Alistair Brooke. I'm sure you can understand why we want to keep the specific details of our plan to ourselves until you're in or out."

I looked at Daze, and she nodded. Time to verify their information, and give it careful consideration. That was precisely what we needed.

We rose, and Abby said, "Don't forget this." She handed a $100 bill to each of us. "Thanks for listening."

We left the place and got into the car.

"We don't have to get to work until one o'clock. How about we go home, change into our swimsuits, and go to the beach for an hour?"

Daze seemed distracted.

"Hey, are you okay?"

She trained her pale blue eyes on me. "What do you think of their pitch?"

"They told a very interesting story. Tough to make up that kind of detail. But we still need to check them out."

"We do. I agree it was a well-crafted request for our help, backed up by a tale of woe that would engender sympathy. And they dangled a lot of money as an incentive. I also bet they were sure I'd jump at the chance to take down Bachenko."

"That was a big part of their package, for sure. You know, something about that whole jet caper of yours with Bachenko's Gulfstream I wondered about."

"What?"

"He did all these vindictive things to you, but never sought to have you arrested or prosecuted?"

"No, he didn't. I guess what I did wasn't illegal. He left the plane in my care. It's not like I stole it. And I returned it in pristine condition."

"I think that tells us something."

"What?"

"Bachenko doesn't like the police."

***

"We're back home," I said, as we pulled into the apartment parking lot. "A trip to the beach?"

"Sure," she said.

We put on our swimsuits, donned our surfer shirts, and headed to the beach. We had a fun time, and I thought little of the job offer. Daze seemed at peace, as well. She loved the beach and especially gazing out at the ocean.

We arrived at work a little early. We wanted to tell Hippo about the meeting, so we huddled together in the kitchen. He was the only one working there at the moment, as one chef was running late. So, it was a perfect opportunity to debrief Hippo.

"That's some story," he said, and we both nodded.

"What do you think about it?"

"We should do what they said. Check them out as best we can," I said.

"We thought you might help with that," Daze said to him. "You're good at that kind of stuff."

"Ah, calling upon my computer wizardry, are you?"

"We are," I said. "Neither of us is good with computers or social media."

"I wasn't either," Hippo admitted. "But I need to be if I want to blow this lousy joint and become a network star."

"You'd be great at it, for sure," I said. And I meant it.

Daze smiled at Hippo. "I'd hire you in a second."

"I'll see what I can find out."

"I still have that premonition," Daze said quietly.

We both looked at her. "Should we just shut this down right now?" I asked.

"No… I guess not. It could be life-changing money, and worth spending a little time deciding."

"We have good lives, now," I said.

"We do," Daze said. "And I doubt we'll do this. But I'm willing to figure it out a little longer."

"If you want my opinion," Hippo said, and we turned back to him. "Get the facts before deciding. But I don't think this pie in the sky is real."

"I don't either," Daze and I said at the same time.

Work was uneventful. A few customers and meager tips.

"If it keeps up like this, I won't be able to pay my share of the bills," I grumbled to Daze, and we headed home.

"I know," she said. "Sometimes it's pretty good. Lately, not so much. I get a little extra money from flying lessons, but not a lot."

"You won't start charging me, will you?"

"Perish the thought. That's fun. Teaching bloated old retired guys who played with computer game simulators and think they're already pilots, and keep trying to get in my pants—I should not only get paid, I should get combat pay."

We arrived back at our apartment and changed out of our work clothes.

"Heading for rehearsal?" she asked.

"Yeah. The show must go on, and I'm the lead now. Gary quit. He wasn't half-bad as an actor. Probably left screaming in dismay at such a third-rate production."

"Why do you stay?"

I sighed. "It's all I have. I couldn't get into any other place around. Gary couldn't either, but he must have found a place to take over for someone who got sick."

"If we had a lot of money…" Daze began.

"I could spend more time finding a good role, or maybe even have the cash to produce a play myself. Yeah. And you wouldn't have to babysit obnoxious, handsy old guys."

"No. But we both know neither thing is likely. Even if we agree to their proposal, there's no guarantee they'll actually pay us a lot of money."

"I know. But fun to dream, isn't it?"

"It is."

"It could happen someday without us selling our souls," I said.

"I'd love that," Daze agreed. "But we're not getting to the promised land working at Bert's."

"Are you leaning towards taking the job?"

"No. But let's see what Hippo finds out for us."

"Yeah. If he finds they're awful, the decision is easy."

I left for rehearsal, and Daisy sat for a while, then called Willy.

"I have a quart of mint chocolate chip. Come on over and share it with me."

The two women sat at the kitchen table and began devouring the ice cream. Daisy filled her in on the offer, and she nodded. Hippo had already given her a short version.

"Derek's instinct is that it's all bogus," Willy said.

"We have our doubts, as well…"

"And?"

"And I have a premonition."

"Oh, honey. Pay attention to a premonition."

"I know."

"If both of you have reservations, and you have a premonition, why consider it at all?"

Daisy looked at her. "Money. Neither of us have much of it."

"There are a lot of ways to earn extra money. You're a stunt pilot. Trip is…well…a great guy. And a hard worker."

"Bachenko made sure most of my job opportunities have dried up. He's out to get me."

"That guy had an incredible overreaction to your little joyride."

"It sure seems like it to me. Almost a vendetta. But I have my flying instructor job at the airport, and free use of the Cessna. I need little more than that. But Trip…he loves acting, and he's stuck in that hot, stuffy warehouse doing Shakespeare, for crying out loud. He hates Shakespeare. He's a fine actor, but he was born to do improv, not a classical soliloquy."

"He's the Court Jester," Willy said. "Feste. That's the lead. Derek told me."

"He hates the play, hates the director, and detests the oppressively hot atmosphere, and the amateurish production values. But he loves acting as much as I love flying, and that's a lot. So, if there's something I can do to help him with that, I'll do it. The job involves flying. I'd do that for free. So how bad could it be?"

"You love him," Willy said.

"Of course I do. He loves me, too. We're friends and lovers, and great together. We're not the run off and get married types—neither one of us. But our affection for each other is real and intense."

6

We headed to the airport the next morning for another flying lesson. On the way, Daze told me how she and Willy devoured a quart of mint chocolate chip ice cream, and asked me how rehearsal went.

"Okay, I guess. As the lead actor, I get a personal dressing room and trailer. A converted motorhome. Very snazzy."

"You didn't get any of those things. But was it different in your new role?"

"Yeah, I guess so. A little. Carleton was slightly less mean to me. I think he's afraid I'll leave him in the lurch just like Gary did."

"Well, that helps a bit, right?"

"I don't know. It's Shakespeare. All that funny talking and classical stage work. I know many people love it, but I'd rather think expansively and act according to instinct."

"Like in your own production," Daze said.

"Yeah, like that. Pick my play, cast my own actors, make all the financial decisions and risk my money…oh my

God. I want to act, not run a business."

Daze laughed. "If you made a small investment, you could probably influence some of those things."

"I could," I agreed. "They offered you a chance to get back at Bachenko."

"Yes, they did," Daze said pensively. "But maybe they misfired on that."

"What do you mean?"

"Am I a get even sort of person?"

"God no. You're the definition of easygoing. Live and let live."

"I just want that creep to stop interfering in my life. Flying for big airlines did not suit my temperament, but he seems to have kept me from every job that might interest me. I can't even fly to Jacksonville International Airport anymore."

"You can't even visit the airport?" I was curious how far the prohibition went.

"I can visit all I want. Taking a flight from there is fine. I can't fly a plane there or from there. That's the deal. I thought it would last only a short time, and Bachenko would forgive me. It's my home airport and I can't use it."

"They hired you here," I said.

"Yes, and it's a good thing I have access to the Cessna. I'd go nuts without it."

"So, having the money to lease or even own a plane would be nice," I said.

"I guess so. But it wouldn't be necessary if Bachenko went away."

"You told me he hit on you right after hiring you, and you turned him down. Do you think he's holding a grudge because you rejected his advances?"

"I doubt it. He's a ladies' man. Has a lot of money, and women flock to him. And honestly, I just turned him down because I thought the business relationship shouldn't start that way. I might even have given him a romp in the hay after a flight. But we never went on one." She gave me a suggestive look. "You know how I get after I fly."

I smiled. "I do. What do you do when you babysit the old guys after their flying lessons?"

"I rush home and find you," she said sweetly.

"You should fly as much as possible," I said.

"I couldn't agree more."

We parked in our usual spot at the airport and headed into the office. Dennis had the day off, so the general manager, Scott Eastman, and I engaged in small talk while Daze did her usual check in and preflight.

"Nice day for a lesson, sir," Scott said.

"Ms. Wilson is a fine teacher," I replied.

"That's what all her students say. She's all business. Flying is a serious matter. Be careful every second."

"Ms. Wilson emphasizes safety all the time," I assured Scott.

"Good head on her shoulders," he said.

Daze signaled me, and I bid Scott goodbye and headed out to the tarmac.

"You have a good head on your shoulders," I told Daze.

"Scott's a dear. Stickler for safety."

"Probably wouldn't approve of sex in an airplane," I said.

She smiled. "No, Mother Superior would certainly oppose that."

"Where to?" I asked.

"I thought we'd go to Orlando. It's within range, and if we do too much stunt flying, we can always refuel there."

"Works for me," I said.

"I hope so. You're the pilot. I'm your co-pilot. Let's see your takeoff technique."

I waited for clearance from the tower, taxied into position, and started rolling down the runway, gathering speed until I pulled back on the stick and experienced the magical feel of lifting into the air. I ended the ascent, leveled off into the requisite altitude, and glanced over at Daze, who gave a silent clap of her hands.

"Well done, Captain," she said. "Very good. As you know, I like to give positive feedback." She lifted her blouse, unhooked her bra, and flashed those beautiful breasts at me, leaving the undergarment on the floor. She then lowered her blouse back over her uncovered chest.

"That's outstanding positive feedback," I murmured, eyes fixed straight ahead, but seeing her through the corner of my eye. "Do you give the same positive reinforcement to your other customers?"

"I don't give it to customers. You pay nothing. That's a special benefit for non-paying clients."

"I promise never to pay you," I said.

She flashed me again. "Good. Now keep your eyes on

the controls and do regular visual inspections. It's a clear day, but it won't always be this way. You're never flying blind. You always have sophisticated equipment, providing you with the rough equivalent of sight. But it's clear sailing today."

"Hard to keep my eye on the controls, and the visual field in front of me with you doing—that." She flashed me again.

"Part of your training," she said. "Flying with distractions."

"Okay, keep it up."

"Yes, Captain." She removed her blouse entirely, as I kept all six eyes trained on everything I was supposed to watch.

After about a half hour of straight flying, Daze donned her blouse and took over the controls. She promptly took us into something she called a Bell Tailslide, a 1/4 vertical loop.

She looked over at me. "You want to actually go to Orlando?"

"No, let's head back in the other direction. I'd like to take back the controls. But I won't try that…this myself."

Daze had taken us into what she described as an Immelmann—an ascending half loop followed by a half roll, heading us in the opposite direction. At a higher altitude, I noticed.

"Good catch," she said. "Our flight plan called for this altitude on the way back."

"Interesting way to turn around," I observed.

"Oh, there are many others. Okay, take over."

I did so, and flew us back to our own airport, where I executed an almost perfect landing.

"Well done," Daze told me. "I think I'll defer the positive feedback until we get home," she said, picking up her bra and stuffing it into her pocket.

"Won't Scott notice you're braless?"

"Nope. He has a one-track mind. FAA regulations. The only reason he'd notice me with no top on at all is because it violates the rules. He'd notice that, but not this," she said, pointing at her chest.

And she was right. Scott examined her flight log, gave me a nod, and expressed thanks as he went back to his ledgers and rulebooks.

And we returned home and barely made it into the apartment before shedding our clothes and heading for the bedroom.

***

After our enjoyable early afternoon romp, Daisy and I dressed for work.

"Same thing every day," I said.

"Other than work, I'd say it's a pleasant life. And you know me, if I get to fly every day, I'm happy."

"It is great fun," I agreed. "I wish rehearsal was as much fun as flying."

"That bad, huh?"

"Oh, I don't know. I get to act. But I can't help being jealous of Gary. He escaped the warehouse. I understand they gave him a part in the new production at the Creighton Theater."

"You auditioned for that," Daze said.

"Yeah, and I didn't get it. It's almost as if someone is

keeping me from getting into local productions. But I guess they think Gary is a better actor."

"No, he's not," Daisy said loyally.

"I appreciate that, and I agree with you, but the director at the Creighton obviously doesn't."

I looked at my watch. "Time to go to work."

"Maybe Hip has news for us," Daze said.

"Maybe. But don't we agree we don't want to do it?"

"Yes. But if the whole thing is legitimate… maybe it will get you out of the warehouse and into a real theater?"

"I don't believe it's legitimate."

Daze nodded. "Yeah, I guess it's a nutty idea. I'm okay with insanity, but even I have my limits."

"I love the unpredictable part of you," I said.

Daze just smiled.

We arrived at work and punched in. Hippo was already there, cutting vegetables.

"Do you live here?" I asked.

"It sure seems that way. I'm saving like a madman. Got to get a stake together to start my career, and blow this joint forever."

"I should save more. It might give me time to find a better class of theater production."

"Keep striking out?"

"I've whiffed so many times, I've almost given up trying to get a hit, much less a home run."

"Don't give up," Hippo said. "I've seen you act. You have the chops."

"Thanks." I glanced in Daze's direction. "I have two fans."

"We're not making it up," she said.

"I appreciate the support. Thanks."

"I have some information for you," he said, his eyes pointedly cut to his fellow sous chefs. "But maybe it's best we talk after work."

"Okay," I said. "But we have serious doubts about the whole thing."

Hippo nodded. "Understandable."

7

We worked our shift, and it was moderately busy. I made decent money, and I spotted Daisy scooping up some cash tips as well. I thought about Hippo's aggressive saving and sighed. It was all I could do to pay my share of the rent and utilities. I had little spending money. All Daze's extra money went to fuel for the Cessna.

Money, or lack of it, was an issue. Daisy made little money from flying lessons. But the perk of the job was essential. Personal use of a plane, which she mostly used for our flying "lessons."

We finished our shift and met up with Hippo and Willy at an outdoor cafe near the beach.

The two of them were already sipping margaritas when we arrived, and I signaled the server to bring two more.

"I was just telling Willy about your 'repo' people." Hippo used the universal hand signal for quotes.

"It's not a repo company?" Daze asked.

"Oh, the company they referred to is very real. It's a legitimate company, if it's fair to characterize such a sleazy business that way."

"So, what's the problem?" I asked.

"Abigail Adams and Jeffrey Bailey don't show up in their company directory," Hippo said, folding his arms in front of him with his elbows on the table.

"I suppose a separate unit might not appear in a company directory. I mean, why approach us with something so easily checked…by someone who knows how to check?"

"Good question," Hip said. "I searched the names, but it's surprising how many people have the names Abigail Adams and Jeffrey Bailey. I didn't meet them, and have no photos, or I could have searched their faces. The company could have recently hired them, or the directory is out of date. Or it's just a separate unit, as you said, or there's another reasonable explanation."

"What about AbbJeff?" I asked.

"It's pretty much what they told you. A software company headed up by Mikhail Bachenko. No listing of Abigail Adams or Jeffrey Bailey, or even any mention of them as the company's founders. As of now, you know what I do."

"One more thing. You might as well check out that Alistair guy. I can't reach out to him directly, but you two can. See if he's real, and if he verifies the story. It's information worth knowing."

We both nodded, and our foursome spent the rest of the evening talking about other things.

***

"Nice evening with Hip and Willy," I said the next morning.

"It was fun." She rubbed her temple. "I might have had one too many margaritas. Did I do anything outrageous?"

I smiled. "More than usual?"

She reached over and punched me in the arm.

"Ow," I said, then cracked up laughing. "No, you were fine. Of course, I had severely impaired judgment."

"I remember you standing up and singing show tunes," Daze giggled while she said it.

"I did, didn't I? Oh, what the hell. Musicals are more fun than Shakespeare."

"You have a wonderful voice," Daze said. "At least it sounded that way to a tipsy woman."

"Tipsy?"

"A lady never gets drunk. She gets tipsy."

"Works for me," I said.

At that moment, my phone chirped. I looked at the caller ID. Hippo.

I answered it and immediately started laughing. I tapped the speaker icon, and we were both treated to an unbelievably awful version of "Singing in the Rain."

"Make it stop," I said into the phone. "There's a shrill, grating, off key sound in my ear."

Hippo stopped and chuckled. "Music filled the air last night."

"Daze told me," I said. "How bad was it?"

"Actually, not bad. Willy and I especially enjoyed your duet with Daisy."

"My what?"

"You and Daisy sang a two-part harmony of Easy Street from Annie."

"I can't even think of the words to that," I said. I looked at Daze. "Can you?"

Daze smiled and belted out "Easy Street, Easy Street. That's all I know."

"Yeah, me too."

"Well, that's pretty much all you two sang. Repeatedly."

"Hmm. I wonder if that was a subliminal wish that those two charlatans were offering us a chance at becoming wealthy."

"That's what I figured," Hip said.

"So why the morning call? Just to mock two…um…" I looked at Daze. "Tipsy friends?"

"I know this one," Hip said. "We were both drunk. Willy and Daisy were tipsy."

"How did you know that?"

"Willy told me that this morning. A lady is never drunk."

"You were drunk, too. I can hardly remember."

"Wasted, my thespian friend. The singing performance was not at the restaurant. We all went down to the beach after, and you two were singing at the top of your lungs."

"A song that we didn't know the words to," I said.

"Right. Anyway, Willy and I are going windsurfing today. Want to tag along?" He paused. "After we all get over our hangovers?"

I looked at Daze, who said, "Sure. Give us an hour."

"Okay, I'll pick you up in an hour."

Even though the three of them were born and raised in Florida, and I grew up in New York, I'd spent a lot of time at the New Jersey shore every summer, and much of my time in Florida at the beach. I was comfortable surfing, windsurfing, and paddle boarding, and so were my friends.

So we spent the morning and early afternoon windsurfing until the three of us had to go to Bert's and Willy had to head to Jacksonville for a pre-performance rehearsal.

"We'll have to get up to see you again soon," I said, and Daze and Hippo chimed in with agreement.

"I'll leave tickets for you anytime you want. Just let me know."

We headed back to our apartment to change out of our wet swimsuits and into work clothes.

"When are we flying again?" I asked as we headed to work.

"Can't do it tomorrow, unfortunately. I have a client."

"Another retired old guy who thinks he knows everything already?"

Daze grimaced. "Probably." She looked at me. "It's no fun at all. I don't even get um…you know."

I smiled. "I do. Day after tomorrow, then?"

"It's a date."

"Great. I have rehearsal tonight."

"I figured. The show must go on."

***

"Many a good hanging prevents a bad marriage." My lungs almost hurt as I projected my line, and Carleton loved it.

"Yes, yes, more like that. Great work, Feste…I mean Trip. Just great. Okay, let's take a break. Trip, can I talk to you for a moment?"

Amazed as I was at Carleton's sudden transformation to a supportive director, I was even more surprised by the topic of discussion. It came out of the blue.

"That was great, Trip, especially for someone who is not a Shakespearean actor. I'm not a Shakespearean director. Not an improv fan, either. I'm more of a Gilbert and Sullivan, or musical comedy theater person. That's my training, and what I frankly was born to do."

I stared at him. "Then why are we doing Shakespeare? If Pirates of Penzance is your thing, let's do that. I'd even audition for the part of the Modern Major General."

Carleton sighed. "And if it was the part you wanted, I'd cast you in a second. You're an excellent actor, Trip. You don't belong here. Neither do I, but here I am." He looked at me. "And here you are."

His comments flummoxed me. "Why are we having this conversation, Carleton? I'm actually happy to hear it. But forgive me if I'm a bit confused."

He nodded. "Understandable. Look, I want you to be all in with our production. It's very important to both of us." He put his hand up, palm facing me, when he saw me interjecting. "Let me explain. We're doing Shakespeare, not because that's what I want to do. And you've loudly stressed that it's not what you want to do. Doing Shakespeare sets us apart. It's a new theater. We can't compete either for actors and actresses or for funding. That all goes to the other production companies in this area. And there are a lot of them. We could only open by promising a few wealthy Shakespeare lovers to bankroll a Shakespearean Theater. It is very popular. It's not like the man wasn't a giant in the theater. He obviously was the greatest playwright in history. And Twelfth Night, well, it's a terrific comedy."

"So, we do Shakespeare, even though it's not our preference?"

"For us, it's the only option. Until it isn't. Let's put on a great show. Impress them with the best production ever, and maybe do one or two more, establish ourselves, and maybe we can do a few other things as well."

"This was a pep talk," I said.

"I like to think of it as an explanation coupled with rallying the troops. But yes, it's a pep talk."

We left the side room in which we'd talked, but before we did, Carleton said, "I'm only hard on the best actors. I go kid gloves with everyone else."

I gave him a half-smile, and we returned to the rehearsal, during which he immediately berated me for insufficient emotion in my lines.

***

"How was your rehearsal?" Daisy asked me when I returned.

"Oh, it was very interesting," I said, and told her all about what Carleton said.

"It makes sense," she said. "Don't you think so?"

"Yes, I do. Shakespeare festivals and theaters have sprouted up all around the country, and are very popular. The competition for funding around here, or anywhere, is fierce. Our little production company was very astute to create an unfilled niche that had built-in funding."

"So..."

"I'll see this play through. And then...well, I can decide that later. Who knows, maybe this wild Bachenko thing will pan out for both of us."

"Time to check out Alistair Brooke."

8

"Let's first check out the website listed on the paper Abby gave us," I said Daze produced the paper, and we leaned our heads together to look at it.

"It has a logo on it. Looks like intertwined A, J and S."

"The A and J make sense. I wonder what the S stands for?"

"It's right here. Software. AbbJeffSoftware.com," I said.

"Time to check out the website. It piqued my interest."

"Yeah, mine, too." I opened my laptop, navigated to the website, and we gazed at a picture of…

"Mikhail Bachenko," Daze blurted out. "Just like they said."

I kept reading. "Mikhail Bachenko, Latvian-American financier and software engineer."

"Abby and Jeff were pretty emphatic that he was no such thing," Daze said. "I thought he was a hedge fund manager, or something like that."

"Abby and Jeff obviously named the company after themselves."

Daze clicked on a directory for the business. "No Abigail Adams, and no Jeffrey Bailey. Some other names."

"It's a software company. They make a sophisticated database software, among other products," she said. "That checks out with what they told us."

"We have a business named after two people, with a website showing their logo, but no mention of them at all. Again, consistent with their story."

"That's about the size of it," Daze agreed.

She fingered the piece of paper with the names and phone numbers of the executives at the repo company, Imperial Reclamation.

"Sounds British," I observed. "Like Her Majesty commands this repossession. Make it so."

Daze gave an impish smile. "Or Your lordship has not payeth, you must returneth."

"You're channeling Shakespeare," I said. "I'll bet Carleton will give you a part."

"No thanks. I'll stick to what I know. The stage is not for me."

"You never know," I said. "There might be a latent Lady Macbeth in you."

"I'm more Amelia Earhart than Lady Macbeth."

"Too bad it's a Shakespeare company," I said. "You'd be perfect in the lead role of Take Flight."

"There's a musical about Amelia Earhart?"

"Yes, there is. Okay, do you want to call one of those numbers, or should I?"

"Shouldn't we check to see if these people are really executives at Imperial Reclamation? And that these are their direct phone numbers?"

"How do we do that? We didn't look into the company, Hip did. And I'm guessing the internet rarely contains executives' private numbers."

Daze was already navigating to the website for Imperial Reclamation, or IR for short.

She pointed to a company directory. "Look at this."

"What am I looking at?"

"Phone numbers for the company's executives."

"So? Those are probably the public general numbers, leading the valued public into a myriad of menu driven choose 1 for this, choose 2 for that, choose 3 to be put on hold interminably, choose 4 for instant disconnection."

Daze listened to my rant patiently, and said, "Maybe so, but those numbers match the ones Abby and Jeff gave us. They're the correct phone numbers. Maybe not direct, but they did not lie about it, either."

"Okay, sure, but no one ever gets through to the company president or other executive by calling the general numbers."

"I wonder," Daze said. "Maybe if we can actually reach an operator, or any human at all, we just give our name and say they're expecting our call. Because if Abby told us the truth, they are expecting a call."

Daze looked at me. "Who should call, you or me?"

I thought about it for a moment. "You, I think."

"Okay, she said, picking up her phone. But you'll be right here, anyway."

I nodded as she looked at the paper, picked a number, and punched it in.

"Who did you pick?" I asked.

Daze looked back up at me when she finished tapping.

"Right to the top," she said. "Alistair Brooke. The president of Imperial Reclamation. That's who Abby and Jeff named. The others may not know all the details."

"More and more British sounding all the time," I observed, while Daze listened to the predictable menu system. I watched her tap a number, listen again, tap another number, then a third. I watched her wait a moment again before saying "representative."

She waited a few moments more, then listened, and responded to the apparent question. "Daisy Wilson. Mr. Brooke is expecting my call." She listened to the response and said, "Abigail Adams and Jeffrey Bailey."

I watched Daze give me a thumbs up and waited while they presumably connected her to the great man himself.

"Yes, this is Daisy Wilson. With me here is Tripper Steele. Okay, great." She waited a moment and said, "Mr. Brooke? Abby Adams told me to call you to verify that she and Jeffrey Bailey work for Imperial Reclamation."

I watched Daze listen a moment and saw her smile.

"Yes, he's right here. May I put you on speaker? It's only us alone here at home."

The next voice I heard was that of a man who introduced himself as Alistair Brooke.

"Mr. Steele and Ms. Wilson, I can absolutely confirm

that Abigail Adams and Jeffrey Bailey work for us. They are part of a special unit we created here at IR, as we call it, to deal with particularly difficult, ahem, politically sensitive issues. We recruited Abby and Jeff. They have an unusual combination of skills and mindsets that we found useful for a particular project involving a man very familiar to you, Ms. Wilson."

"Mikhail Bachenko," Daze said quietly.

"Yes. And I'm sure you have many questions, not the least of which would likely be how do the two of you fit into this project of ours? Or 'why you?'"

"We have more questions than that," I said, speaking for the first time.

"No doubt," Brooke said. "But I'm not the best person to answer them. Abby made it clear to me that there was no way she could recruit the two of you without confirmation that she and Jeff work for us. You have that confirmation. Abby and Jeff are best suited to answer the rest. Also, the section chief of that special unit, Clover Taylor."

Daze and I both tried to get more information from the guy, but it was clear he had completed his task, and was a busy man who had a lot on his plate. He didn't hang up on us, but it was clear he had ended all further discussion, and gave us a peremptory goodbye. Daze disconnected the call, and we took a moment to look at each other with the unspoken, huh? What just happened?

I spoke first. "Well, we got confirmation. That's pretty much what we were looking for. If we want more, we'll have to call Abby and set up…another appointment."

Daze nodded. "But do we even want to? This gets crazier and crazier. I just want to fly. You just want to act. Why do we need this agita?"

"We don't," I agreed. "And I don't just want to act. I want to fly with you, both literally and figuratively."

Daze smiled at that. "Time for another joint flight, um, flying lesson."

9

On our way to the airport, I turned to the five-foot three blond spitfire next to me and asked her how she started flying.

"You weren't in the military," I said. "So, where did you start?"

"We lived two miles from the airport," Daze said. "I grew up hearing planes overhead all the time. I think I was three years old when I decided I wanted to be a pilot."

I smiled. "It probably was hard to get a license at that age."

"So I was told," Daze said. "I just had a very early fascination with flying that you would think would have dissipated as I grew older, but the desire only became greater and greater. I actually thought about the Air Force Academy as early as age thirteen, but was immediately turned off by the height requirement of 5 foot 4. I was only four foot 10 and I guessed I'd be lucky to even get to five feet, because my Mom and Dad were so short themselves."

"You had a growth spurt," I observed

"A veritable beanpole now," she quipped. "Like you," she added.

"I am not," I said.

Daze laughed. "Maybe it just seems that way when we stand next to each other."

"I think we look nice together," I said.

"Yeah, me too. Anyway, I got a part-time job at the airport. Reservations, baggage check-in, women's work."

Daze didn't sound bitter about it, just factual.

"That's the way it was back then," she said. "Still is."

"How did you get out of the terminal and onto the tarmac?"

"I went out there every single day. During lunch break, after school, after work. Every day. At some point, I became a fixture there, and one day, a kind old pilot, Kinkaid McCord—I will never forget his name as long as I live, took me under his wing. Taught me the value of the pre-flight process, the necessity for a pilot to understand the workings of an aircraft, to even be almost an aircraft mechanic. And one day, Mac, as they called him, gave me a flying lesson. We went on a flight, and he showed me everything he did. And many, many lessons later, I got my license. Since that time, I've flown thousands of hours. I learned the stunt stuff much later."

"Do you regret not going to the Air Force Academy?"

Daze laughed at that. "You know me, right?"

I nodded.

"What part of your knowledge of me includes an ability to follow rules, obey orders, and do conventional things directed by someone else?"

"Um, none."

"Exactly. Not a fit for the military. That was just a way

to learn how to fly. Mac solved that problem for me. I'm still in awe of the guy—he died a couple of years ago, and I cried like a baby. But what possessed this well-respected, old school guy to teach a girl, because that's what I was when I met him, how to become a pilot? He endured, almost laughed at, the other old-timers who mocked him for teaching a girl—a short one at that, to become a pilot. I'll always wonder if he fancied himself Henry Higgins, and I was his Eliza Doolittle. Take on the impossible. He never told me, and I didn't want to know. I loved flying and wanted to do it as much as possible."

"Do they still have the 5-foot 4 height requirement?"

"I think so, but I'm not sure anyone honors it anymore. The seats are all adjustable. The height requirement is a little stupid. Someone probably put it in place to keep as many women away as possible. I think there's a two-star general who stands four foot eleven. I doubt anyone ever tells—I don't know who the guy is—old blood and guts or something like that, that he was too short to fly. Pull in over there, great."

I parked where Daze told me, and we walked together into the office.

Dennis gave his usual exuberant greeting to Daze. She checked in, filed a flight plan, and did her usual preflight.

"Don't the mechanics and flight personnel here do that stuff?" I asked, while watching her usual procedures.

"I hope so. But Mac taught me to never rely exclusively on anyone else to check out a plane. I'm the pilot, and I'm responsible. Also, it's my life and my passengers who are at risk."

"Mac was an excellent teacher."

"The best. To this day I don't have a clue why he helped me as much as he did. I was a pimply faced teenager who just wanted to fly. I guess I showed him just how much I wanted to learn, and someday to pilot a plane myself."

"He never made you feel…um, uncomfortable?" I said.

Daze grimaced. "Oh God, no. Like I said, I was a pimply faced kid. He was like my grandpa. Maybe I reminded him of his own grandchildren. Who knows?"

We boarded the Cessna, strapped ourselves in, and Daze did a few more pre-flight checks. Then we taxied toward the runway, got clearance from the tower, and took off. Daze watched me closely as I executed my many lessons well, and we climbed to the requisite altitude.

"Nice takeoff," Daze said. "Okay, what do you do to get us in the direction I put in the flight plan?"

As she'd taught me, I had bent my head over the chart along with her, and we drew a line between home and Ft. Myers. I checked the navigation panel, made a few adjustments, and Daze smiled in approval.

"You've learned your lessons well," she said. "Knowing how to get where you want to go is almost as important as taking off and landing."

"You need to know a lot more than those three things to fly a plane," I observed, while continuing to keep one eye on the panel, one eye ahead of me and a third eye on Daze. Or so it seemed.

"We'll have to refuel in Fort Myers," I said.

"We're not going there," she responded. "What would we do there? It's true that we know of some nice beaches to visit, but we'd have to rent a car, or take a taxi or something. And we have to go to work. No, we're heading in that direction, but turning around at some point short of Fort Myers."

"Too bad," I said. "I like Fort Myers. But you're right. We have no time today."

"And refueling is a nuisance," she said. "I'm really fed

up with the 350-mile range of this thing," she muttered. "And operating out of a little regional airport."

I looked over at her. "Maybe we should give Abby and Jeff a call."

"Do you think so?"

"That guy at Imperial sounded legitimate, I guess. He had a British accent." I paused. "But that's stupid, right? He sounds legitimate because of where he lives."

Daze smiled. "I don't think his accent matters, but he confirmed what Abby and Jeff told us."

"He did. The whole thing seems unrealistic, but you were born to fly. This is fun, for sure, but maybe we can help take down Bachenko, and get rid of these silly restrictions on you doing what you love."

Daze gave me a grateful look.

"Let's turn around in about twenty kilometers. Do you want to take over now?"

"I'm on it," I said.

"Let's see what you've got, cowboy."

I executed the maneuver, and we headed home.

"That was good," she said, and told me how to make it better.

"But it was good, right?"

"We didn't crash. I didn't have to take over, and we're headed in the correct direction. That's a home run in my book."

"Isn't a home run the best thing you can do?"

"A grand slam is better," she said sweetly. "Seriously,

Trip, it was good. I want you to be great."

"Like you?"

"Don't try to be me. I've logged thousands of hours of flight time. You have, well, a few hundred now. You can certainly fly a plane on your own."

"I don't want to fly a plane alone."

I landed, and we taxied to the designated spot. There is no gate at the airport. You just park. I did so, and we disembarked and walked to the office and checked out.

We boarded my Duster and headed home. En-route, I asked Daze whether she was sure she wanted to call Abby.

She set her chin. "Certain. I wasn't before. I thought I was comfortable with things the way they are—flying regularly. And I love flying with you. But mostly I fly with people who don't love it like I do. Like we do," she added. "Mostly, its unappreciative jerks who want to tell friends they're pilots. That's short bursts of flying, and a ton of babysitting and fending off amorous advances."

"That bad, huh?"

"That's only the half of it. You're smart enough to always pay attention to the complex processes involved in flying a plane." She paused and flashed a grin. "No matter how much I try to distract you."

"It's difficult," I said. "I'm a big fan of the distractions."

"Yeah, me too. I'm feeling very distracted right now."

I smiled. "We're almost home."

She unbuttoned her shorts. "I'm not sure I want to wait that long."

I pulled into the apartment parking lot and looked around. I saw no one, and unbuttoned my own shorts, while Daze slid hers and her underwear off. The Duster has a long bench front seat, so no need to go to the back of the car.

After we pulled our shorts on, we headed into the apartment.

"When's the last time you had sex in a car?" I asked. "High School?"

She looked at me. "I had no boyfriends in high school. Awkward and shy does not lead to boyfriends, and I guess something of a tomboy. I wasn't particularly attractive, and unlike the other girls, I spent no time trying to look good for boys, and used all my free time going to the airport."

"A unique path, but it worked out well," I said. "You realized your dream of becoming a pilot and a pretty woman who attracts boys like me."

"Guys like you would have blown me off in high school," Daze said.

"Oh, I doubt it. I was pretty awkward and shy myself. But look at us now. Fumbling around in a car just like teenagers."

Daze smiled. "I guess I'm a little impulsive."

"Flying makes you horny," I said.

"Flying is exciting. You make me horny."

We sat at the kitchen table and decided on a course of action.

"Are you okay with maybe getting involved with that repo company?" Daze asked, a bit anxiously.

"Sure. I needed you to tell me that the status quo oppresses you. If you had nothing to gain by the whole thing, I would have just put it out of my mind. I might get enough money to advance my acting career, and have more money than Bert's Eats can provide. But I don't have a long list of things I want to get with more money."

"Neither do I," Daze said. "Eliminating these artificial limits on my flying is paramount on my list. I'm an experienced pilot, and can fly anything with wings. I'd be much in demand. But I'm limited right now to a two-seater Cessna, and making extra money by waitressing and teaching a bunch of dolts. Present company excluded, of course."

"Thanks. I am not a dolt. Good to know."

Daze punched me in the arm. "You know what I mean. You're a more than decent pilot. I teach glorified video game players who think mastering a computer flight simulator makes them pilots."

"So, let's find out just how we can change that. Alistair Brooke seems to want Bachenko stopped. As do Abby and Jeff. And it could be fun to repossess his plane, right?"

"If it reverses my restrictions, I don't care if it's fun or not. Nor do I care what happens to him."

"I might care," I said. "What he did to you is unconscionable."

Daze smiled at me and picked up her phone.

"Here goes," she said.

Abby answered immediately. "Ms. Wilson. I'm so glad you called. Alistair Brooke advised us you'd contacted him."

"Can I put you on speaker?" Daze said in response. "Trip's here with me at home. No one else is around."

"Of course," Abby said.

"We did. Mr. Brooke assured us he employs you and

Jeffrey Bailey; that you two are part of a special unit; and that Mikhail Bachenko violated some term of the lease agreement on an airplane. We also looked at the two websites, which seem consistent with what you and Jeff told us. While we admit to some reservations, we're prepared to give you conditional agreement, subject to hearing your more detailed plans for us."

"Fair enough," Abby said.

"We had the day off today, and have plans for dinner. We're both busy tomorrow and the next morning. How about we meet at three o'clock the day after tomorrow?"

"That's great, just great. You won't regret it."

"I hope not," Daze said, and she disconnected.

"We have plans tonight?" I asked.

"Willy is cooking. We're having dinner at her place."

I slapped my forehead. "With all the, um, excitement, I completely forgot."

"She's making her famous roast chicken."

"Ooh, I love that."

We spent a pleasant evening with our friends, enjoying great food, a couple of glasses of wine, and our usual comfortable conversation.

Hippo told us about an interview he had scheduled with a major sports network, and we quizzed him on it.

"Entry level," he said. "Any hopes I had to rise right to the top on the strength of my NFL career went poof." He rubbed his neck.

"My neck mostly feels fine. Playing professional football, however, might have killed me."

Willy put her arm around him. "I'm glad you aren't playing football."

Daze and I nodded our agreement.

"You'll rise to the top on smarts and hard work," Daze said.

"I know you," I said. "It won't take you that long. You'll pay your dues, and work harder and smarter than anyone else. They'll see your qualities."

"I hope so. Getting a foot in the door would help the journey a lot."

"When's the interview?" Daze asked.

"Next week. Thursday."

"You'll wow them," Willy said.

We told them about the latest news on the repo front, and they peppered us with questions.

"What made you change your mind? What exactly did that Alistair guy say? Are you getting more details? You guys know to be careful, right? They may still scam you. Even if everyone seems sincere, they'll likely hide something."

"We'll stay vigilant," Daze said.

"Neither of us is harboring any illusions. We're going to listen, and walk out if they don't lay their cards on the table. And we know their full disclosure will omit something. There's nothing stopping us from turning them down, and nothing stopping us from quitting in the middle of whatever they have in mind."

"I just want to fly," Daze said. "It's my lifelong dream. If this can help me end the restrictions, it will take a lot to have me want to pull out."

I pointed at Daze. "I will do almost anything to help her."

"We don't know what's involved," Hippo said. "But we're on your side. If you need help, we're here for both of you."

We did a sort of one for all and all for one football hug and cheer, and moved on to other topics. A nice evening with friends.

10

The next day, we headed to Bert's. We both had the lunch shift, and we were already running late. But we pulled it together and made it to the restaurant just barely in time to punch in.

We spoke very little about Abby and Jeff. I know I needed time to process everything, and I'm sure Daze did as well. I frankly harbored no illusions that any plan to repossess Bachenko's plane would not have serious hazards. I figured it would be both incredibly difficult, and outright dangerous. And the offer of substantial payment had no actual figure attached to it. So, they'd offered us a tough job, wrapped in a rank guess that something would be on the plane, for a speculative payment. These were my initial thoughts, but I left them mostly unspoken. For once, I did not know what Daze was thinking. I knew getting the ability to fly more than a Cessna in a limited area mattered to her. A lot. And I also knew that if there was any truth at all to the story we were told, she might get that. So, I didn't even mentally rule the whole thing out. I kept my reservations to myself. At least for the present. I was certain we'd discuss the matter fully at some point. Just not in the car, and not at work. And I had a rehearsal at night. So we'd discuss the whole thing either after work or tomorrow.

Hippo wanted an update and had something he wanted to tell us. He pointed to the listening ears all around us. We made an after work but before rehearsal appointment with him.

***

We were sitting outside at a parkette. It wasn't quite a park, hence the diminutive suffix. It a small, outside seating area, surrounded by a couple of palm trees, and set back a few feet from the sidewalk. The town scattered them all around the area, and we chose this one because it only had room for the four of us, where we could talk in private. Also, because I had a rehearsal in the evening, and couldn't afford to get even the slightest bit inebriated. Willy had joined us, but she had a night performance, so she didn't want any distraction from that delicately balanced simulated violence at which she shined.

"I don't want accidentally to kill Flossie," she explained. "Or make a wrong move and have her kill me. Everything depends upon pinpoint movement control."

We knew this, and none of us felt like drinking that night, anyway. We had lots to report, and a lot to think about.

"We want to hear all about your scheduled meeting," Willy said. "But first, Derek, tell them about your interview."

"They know I have an interview next week," Hippo said, and we both nodded. He'd already shared the exciting news.

"Tell them where it is," she said.

"London, England," Hippo said. "I thought it was New York, but I guess I'm interviewing for an international job."

"Wow, that's exciting," Daze said.

"They play NFL games there every year, don't they?"

"They do, and the NFL is trying to expand all over the world. But they have an established presence in London."

"Would you have to move there?" Daze asked.

"I don't have the job yet. I'm sure I'll get more details

at the interview."

"How are you getting there?" I asked, "And where are you staying?"

Hippo smiled. "They gave me two first-class tickets, and are putting us up at the Savoy."

"Hippo hits the big time," I said. "I'm going to really enjoy that trip."

The three of them just looked at me. "Oh," I said. "You're not taking me, are you?"

"I'm taking Willy, you imbecile," Hippo said with a smile.

"You get to fly first class in a private plane all the time," Willy said. "It's my turn."

"They have a fantastic theater district there," I said. "Someday, maybe I'll get to go there on business. Anyway, what an opportunity! Congratulations. Not everyone gets an interview, much less the royal treatment. It's very encouraging."

"A step closer to the dream," Daze said. "I'm sure you'll wow them."

"I don't want to get ahead of myself," Hippo said. "But I can't help hoping. I just want a foot in the door. After that, I'll work hard, and hope for the next big break. But enough of that. Tell us about the meeting."

"Nothing much to say. We're scheduled to hear their plans tomorrow. If they make sense, we told them we're on board. But we can still get out."

"Do you believe their story?" Hippo asked.

I looked at Daze, and she nodded. "I kind of do. They probably left out some things, but the gist of what they told us was believable. If they were acting, I didn't spot it. But if they were, they're damn talented actors."

"I agree with Trip," Daze said. "It was well told, with understandable pauses, additional information filled in later. Not a canned statement anyway. But I think we can respect Trip's view of their performance."

"He'd recognize acting, for sure," Hippo said.

"There's a lot of potential gain." I said. "We don't yet know what the risks and costs are, but we can guess crossing a guy like Bachenko will not be easy or risk-free."

Daze nodded. "I know that for a fact. And doing this to him is not the same thing as turning his plane into a party-mobile."

"It will tick him off, for sure. Probably make him dangerous," Hippo said. "Is risking that worth it?"

"That's the precise issue we need to decide before fully accepting the challenge Abby and Jeff have presented to us."

"We wanted to keep you informed, and have no time this evening." I looked at my watch. "Oh crap. I'm late. Carleton will have a cow."

"I have to leave now, too," Willy said, and we all rose and went our separate ways.

***

"Better a witty fool than a foolish wit." I said and waited for Carleton to yell at me. But he didn't. I saw an almost imperceptible nod from him. The rehearsal continued on with few interruptions from our director. I wondered why, and took the time afterwards to inquire.

He gave an enormous sigh when I asked. "It wasn't horrible," he finally said.

"That's borderline high praise from you," I replied.

"I think I'm being too hard on the actors here," he said.

"I can take it. I want good direction. It makes me a better actor and makes for a better production. You've whipped this motley group into something close to an ensemble. Why stop now?"

"Because it's a group of well-meaning, trying their best, spare-time hobbyists. You can take it for sure, because you're a professional actor. But the rest of the troupe are not, and never will be. And if I want a successful production, I can't have half the actors leave because of a tyrannical director."

"But you stopped being hard on me, too."

"They see you being yelled at, and they feel bad themselves."

"Oh, I doubt it. I haven't heard that anyone else is leaving. One or two may at some point, but we have understudies for every role."

"You have heard no one complain about me?" His tone was incredulous.

"Are you kidding? I hear it all the time, even from myself. I have even referred to you as an asshole."

"Then why…."

"People need to complain. But they also value learning and feedback, both positive and negative. If I had to give you a star rating as a director, I'd give you four stars."

"Why four stars?"

"You're a talented director," I said. "But you're an asshole."

Carleton just broke out laughing at that, and we shook

hands.

"I promise to live up to that characterization at the next rehearsal."

"I look forward to it," I replied, and we walked out to the parking lot together. As we walked, Carleton offered a constructive suggestion, and I thanked him before we both drove away.

***

When I returned home, I expected to find Daisy already in bed. Instead, when I walked in, she practically ran to greet me.

I kissed her and took an obviously distraught Daisy into my arms as she sobbed into my ear about how she'd been pacing almost the whole time I was at rehearsal.

"What's going on, Daisy? Why the extreme anxiety?"

She let go of me. "You never call me Daisy."

"I do when I'm concerned about you. Some other times, too. It's your name. And I like your name."

"I do, too," she said. "I like Daze, too. Anyway, I'm upset because of my premonition."

"Back again?" I asked, and she nodded vigorously.

"About Bachenko? And AbbJeff?"

"Yes. I keep thinking something horrible will happen."

"So, we won't do it. Problem solved."

"That's the thing. I want us to do it. Subject to knowing more details, of course."

"Sure. More details. But if you have a premonition,

shouldn't we avoid something horrible from happening?"

"Of course. That's the problem."

"It is. Caught between a rock and a hard place."

Daze looked at me. "Um, yeah, I guess so. Funny expression, and maybe a tinge off, but I guess it covers this situation well enough."

I thought about it. "Let's sit down at the kitchen table and figure it out. We're still standing here by the door."

"Oh, sure. Let's sit down."

We sat at the table, and I said "Why don't we start with the premonition. What exactly is it telling you?"

Daze thought about it, and said, "It's very clear it deals with Bachenko. And Abby and Jeff. Other than that, it's a little hazy."

"And it says danger, right?"

"Well, yes, I guess so. More like something bad is going to happen."

"Something bad will happen if we take the job?"

"Well, no. I don't think that's exactly it."

"Okay, is something bad going to happen to you, me, or someone else?"

"Us," she said. "Both of us."

"Okay, close your eyes."

She complied.

"Okay, how do you feel if we don't take the job? Better, worse, or no change?"

Daze opened her eyes. "Worse," she said.

"Let's try the other way around. Scientific method," I added with a smile.

Daze closed her eyes again, and I asked the opposite question.

"How do you feel if we take the job? Better, worse, or no change.

Daze opened her eyes again. "No change. What do you think it means? Scientifically speaking, of course." She added a smile, and I was happy that she had her sense of humor back.

"I don't know," I admitted. "But maybe the decision on whether to take the job is not the question. You have a premonition of danger to us, which we will not ignore. But maybe it relates not to taking or not taking the job, but to how we conduct ourselves in the job if we take it. Does that make sense?"

Daze thought about it and nodded. "I think so. Maybe the premonition is a warning to be careful, that this is a very dangerous job, and we have to treat it seriously."

"No more hijinks until the job is done?"

"Oh, there is plenty of room for hijinks. Just not during the job itself."

"Let's get some sleep," I said. "We'll decide tomorrow."

I held Daze in the crook of my arm, and we fell asleep right away.

11

We headed to the airport the next morning for my next flying lesson. On the way, I asked Daze if she had any paying clients lined up.

"I have nothing. Dennis would have called me if I did. And while I don't much like teaching people who really don't want to learn, or think they know it all already, when business is good, I can pay the bills a lot better than waitressing."

"Why do you think it's slow?"

Daze shrugged. "Your guess is as good as mine. It goes in spurts. I'll have several in a week and as now, nothing."

"You don't think Bachenko is keeping people away?"

"Oh, I wouldn't put anything past that guy. But this is so small time, I doubt he'd take a moment of his time trying to screw this up. No, it's probably just a seasonal, or haphazard thing. And the good news is that I get to fly with you, anywhere we want."

"Except Jacksonville International Airport," I said dryly.

Daze seemed undaunted by my comment. "Except that," she said cheerfully.

"You seem awfully chipper," I observed.

"I get to fly today."

"Ah, of course."

When we arrived at the airport, Dennis pointed to the waiting room. "You have a last-minute client," he said. He eyed me with obvious jealous disdain. "A paying one," he added.

I looked at Daze. "Duty calls. Paying client. I'll do the grocery shopping, drop them off at the apartment, and come back and pick you up in, say…an hour."

"The client paid for an hour lesson," an eavesdropping Dennis pointed out.

I smiled at him. "An hour and ten minutes, then. Have a good lesson, and I'll see you a little later."

I kissed Daze and walked out to the parking lot to retrieve my Duster.

As I was checking out at the grocery store, I heard a voice behind me. Willy. We exchanged greetings, and she asked me if I had a few minutes to chat. I looked at my watch and said "I have plenty of time before I go back to the airport to pick up Daisy. What's up?"

"I thought you were today's lesson," Willy said.

"A last-minute paying client. I'm a freeloader."

Willy smiled at that. "Listen Trip, I just wanted to ask you something. Something I should just come out and ask Derek, but I don't want to burst his bubble. He's so excited about his interview."

"Justifiably so," I said. "It's his dream. But what do you mean by bursting his bubble? Do you know something you're not telling him?"

"No, and I feel foolish asking you. But when I saw you in the grocery store, I…well… thought Derek might have told you something."

I looked at a distraught Willy, and asked as kindly as I could "What's this all about, Willy? Please, just come out with it."

Willy sighed. "Does Derek want to move to London?"

"Oh," I said. "I understand. You don't."

Willy almost sobbed the answer. "I have a life here in Florida. I could even make New York City work. But another country?"

"Look, Willy, Hip has not told me he wants to move to London. He probably hasn't given it much thought. He's just trying to get his foot in the door somewhere, anywhere. If his first big break is in London, well, I doubt that's his first choice. Mainly because he knows it would disrupt your life. But no way he wants to move to London if it's not with you. No way at all. You come first. He'd skip this interview if he thought it might cause him to lose you."

"I know. That's what I'm worried about. I don't want to be an obstacle to his dream."

"You'll work something out if he gets a job offer. Right now, you two have an all-expenses paid luxury vacation in one of the great cities in the world. Enjoy it. And Willy… talk to Hippo. You're both smart people. You can figure this out. But you have to talk."

"I know," she said. "Thanks, Trip. Are you going to fly when you pick Daisy up?"

"I don't know. Dennis might not want a double flight this morning."

"Daisy's always happiest when she flies with you," Willy said.

"Me, too. Take it easy, Willy, and good luck."

"Thanks."

I delivered the groceries to the apartment and headed back to the airport. From the waiting room, I saw Daze and a fifty-something guy with graying hair walking towards the office. They weren't speaking, and Daze was letting the man get ahead of her. Their interaction didn't look friendly, and I wondered what it was all about.

The man entered the office, and after a few words with Dennis, he walked out to the parking lot. Daze entered after he'd left, and I walked into the office in time to hear her tell Dennis in a furious tone that "I will never teach that guy again."

Dennis asked her what had happened, and she said after takeoff on their training flight, she was demonstrating a technique, and he'd reached over and felt her breast, then tried to slip his hand up her shirt.

"I almost lost control of the plane trying to stop him. And I think the near crash scared him enough to stop. We hadn't gone far, so I returned and landed immediately."

I headed for the door, thinking I could catch him and kick his ass, but Daze told me to stop.

"It's too late," she said. "He's gone. I've listened to a lot of crass language, and dealt with groping here, but always on the ground. What was he thinking? He was clearly not experienced enough to take over flying. We spent a long time in the cockpit before even taking off, and he made only a passing remark about how great it was to have such a pretty teacher. But that was it."

"He could have killed you both," Dennis said. "I'm putting his name in the system. He won't do that again."

"Not if I find him," I muttered.

Exhausted and aggravated, Daze had no desire to fly. I suggested we go to the beach for a while before leaving for work.

"We can find a quiet spot, and sit and talk," I said.

Daze nodded. "I need to calm down. I'm so angry, I could scream."

"That guy's behavior was despicable. And dangerous," I said.

She looked at me while I drove. "Over and over again, I've dealt with crap like that. The other pilots called me sweetheart and asked me to get them a cup of coffee, or…much worse. I was too small to be a pilot. I was a woman in a man's world. I made it anyway."

"You're a strong person," I agreed. "Becoming the skilled pilot you are today against all odds requires inner strength."

"And yet, I'm stuck in a Podunk airport flying a two-seater Cessna, and prohibited from flying to my own international airport. And putting up with cretins like the guy today just to make a few bucks. The dope could have killed both of us. I guess he figured I couldn't stop him if I needed to control the plane. He sure as hell couldn't fly for shit to take over while I was trying to stop him."

"How did you stop him?" I asked.

Daze smiled. "I think I broke one of his fingers. And popped him one on his nose when he pulled his hand away in pain."

I laughed. "Good for you."

Neither of her actions surprised me. The name Daisy evokes images of a delicate flower. She was certainly pretty, but also strong as hell. A lifetime working on airplanes had given her very defined arm muscles and incredibly strong fingers.

"Do all your students treat you that way?" I asked.

Daze sighed. "Most. But usually just crass comments. This was the first airborne assault. Most people have the good sense not to interfere with the person flying the plane." She paused. "You were different," she said. "You thanked me for the lesson, said you knew you had a lot to learn, but that you intended to work hard, and that you believed you had an outstanding teacher."

"I did, didn't I?"

"I was even disappointed you didn't hit on me," Daze said playfully.

"I waited until after the third lesson," I recalled. "Then I asked you to join me for coffee."

"You were so cute," she said. "Very proper and respectful. I wasn't used to that."

I laughed. "Oh, I wanted to get into your pants the moment I met you. It was all part of a carefully orchestrated strategy."

Daze gave me one of those dazzling smiles. "It was all I could do to keep my hands off of you."

"And look at us now," I said.

Daze slid over on the bench seat and leaned against me. Our arms and thighs pressed close together as I drove to the beach. Once there, we found a quiet spot, spread out the blanket I keep in the car, and sat down.

"Today's events pushed me in a big way towards accepting the AbbJeff proposal," she said. "I'm in this situation because of Bachenko."

"I agree. He needs to be stopped. If Abby and Jeff have

a way of doing it, I'm all in. My situation is okay, but yours is bullshit."

"One more visit to a nondescript office in about an hour, and we'll know for sure what we're doing." Daze said.

"Funny," I said.

"What?"

"I'd hate to disappoint Carleton by leaving in the middle of the production."

"Maybe you won't have to," Daze suggested. "We'll ask Abby and Jeff when we go back. Maybe you can do both. But I'm curious. Are the two of you actually getting along?"

I laughed. "We agree that he's an asshole. But an excellent director in an awful situation. He needs this production to work, and frankly, so do I. I don't have any other acting jobs lined up. Shakespeare is legitimate theater. Not my preference, but an actual role."

"Are you just agreeing to do this just for me? You know I don't want that."

I assured her I had several reasons to take part in…we didn't quite know what yet. "What Bachenko did to you was despicable, and I would do it just to take the bastard down. And you know I'd do anything to help you get your ability to fly back. So those are the primary reasons. But we're also getting paid. By both Imperial and AbbJeff. We don't know the amount, but it could be more than sufficient for us to get out from under this hand to mouth financial situation we're in. And maybe put me in a position to fund a production, or you to lease a big plane anytime you want. And even if I lose this role, it's a volunteer acting gig. It's not that hard to find those."

"The money would be good to get," Daze said. She leaned over and kissed me. "And thank you for wanting to help me."

We enjoyed the sun and the ocean for a long time, and I briefed her on what Willy had told me.

"Hip has said nothing to you?" she asked.

"Not a word. I think he's so excited about maybe getting out of the kitchen at Bert's and into the job of his dreams that he hasn't spent a lot of time figuring out the details. I know Hip. He won't move without Willy. So, I hope they can work something out. Maybe the job isn't even in London. He doesn't know where they'd station him. I told her to talk to him."

"Good advice."

12

Abby and Jeff greeted us at the door and ushered us into the conference room. I heard sounds again emanating from another room, and when we sat down, I asked how many other people were in the office.

"Two," she said. "But we have access to more if needed. And depending upon how this goes, we might. I'll explain."

"Please do," I said. "We know almost nothing other than Imperial wants Bachenko's plane repossessed, and you want to look inside. And we all agree that we dislike the guy."

They both nodded. "Fair enough, Mr. Steele," Jeff said. We have an idea how to accomplish that, and we know we need your respective skill sets. An accomplished actor who has learned how to fly a plane, and a skilled pilot who trained him. The two of us have specialized knowledge both of the software Bachenko is exploiting, and a certain cleverness, if you want to call it that, in breaking into secure databases, whether in the cloud or on a hard drive."

"You two are hackers?" Daze asked rhetorically.

"Let's just say software engineers, with some additional skill sets."

"You want to break into Bachenko's databases," I said.

"You know that already. But we don't think he'll keep sensitive information there. But if he has a hard drive on that plane, we need the ability to access it. And we think we can."

"So what other people do we need? And what do you have in mind for an actor and a pilot?"

"I'll answer the second question first. Bachenko heavily guards his plane. We hope to get around that without violence, but those guards of his are trained mercenaries that are big and burly and carry automatic weapons. We hope to use finesse, but we may need some muscle."

"And the two people we haven't met…" Daze said.

"Lars and Liam. Big, tough Swedish men with finely honed mean streaks."

"Will we meet them?" I asked.

"Sure, right now."

Jeff left the conference room and returned with two giants. He introduced us and the two huge guys with Popeye type muscles nodded, but said nothing.

Jeff thanked them, and they left the room.

"Okay, they're big," Daze said. "And they're on our side?"

Jeff smiled and answered in the affirmative. "They are."

"Good guys to have on your team," I observed.

"Yes, they're smart, too, but not talkative."

"So, what's the plan?" I asked. "And is it possible for me to take part in it without walking out on the play I'm in?"

Abby and Jeff looked at each other. "I don't think that will be a problem. Your rehearsals are at night. You might have to miss one or two, that's all."

"Okay, good. Understand me. It's my preference to continue with the play. It's not required. If I'm needed, I'll let it go."

"Appreciated, but likely unnecessary. This is why." Abby paused. "There is no way we can just waltz up to that plane, board and search it, and fly it away. In our present roles, we likely can't even approach it. We need someone on the inside."

Daze and I just stared at them. "No way Bachenko hires any of us," Daze said. "He has a close-knit staff of loyalists. Especially after, um, our incident. And he knows me on sight. No way he hires me as a pilot again. I guess he doesn't know Trip, but again, he won't hire Trip, either."

"We know that," Jeff offered. "We don't expect Bachenko to hire anyone right now. Maybe for AbbJeff, but not for anything having to do with the Gulfstream. No, we meant the airport."

"Why would the airport hire us?" I asked.

They both smiled. "Because the two of you are shining stars in your respective fields. Mr. Steele here is an expert in aeronautical oversight and inspection. You, Ms. Wilson, are not a pilot, but are a first-rate airline mechanic, certified in both airframe and power plant, valued skills at any airport in the world. While the first role is fiction, of course, yours is not. You are an A&P certified mechanic, and can fill that role easily."

"I have many questions," I said. "And we can get to mine in a moment. I can play that role for a short time, with a lot of study. But she's banned from that airport."

"No, she's not. She agreed to cease flying a plane to or from there. She can go to the airport any time she wants, just not as a pilot. And she won't be going there as Daisy Wilson. Both of you will have cover names."

I looked at Daze. "Don't they know you there?"

She thought about it for a moment. "Not the mechanics. I received that training back in Illinois. I'm still A&P certified by the FAA, but I've never worked as a mechanic in Jacksonville. The pilots, flight attendants and all the other support staff would probably know me, but not in the hangars."

"That's what we thought," Abby said. She looked at Daze. "Cutting and dyeing that hair would probably help…" she saw our joint dismay, and quickly added, "but unnecessary, especially since no one knows you in the area you'll be working. You can put your hair in a bun and hide it under a cap."

"How am I going to convince anyone to hire me in a field I have no background or skills in?"

"You're an actor. A good one. You can learn any role." She eyed Daze. "And you have a built-in teacher. I bet she taught you plenty already."

I nodded. "Yes, and she has a lot more to share. But I guess I was asking a different question. How do we even get jobs at the airport?"

"Leave that to us," Jeff said. "And Alistair Brooke. You'll get hired, all right. But you should study before you get to the interview. It will be a foregone conclusion, of course, but appearances need to be maintained."

"So, airport management will be in on the plan?"

"Not exactly. One or two will know Imperial's goal. No one but us will know the secondary plan."

"So we'll get jobs because Alistair Brooke will make it happen."

"Yes."

"Couldn't someone find out we're not who we say?"

"Yes. Someone could. But if all goes well, you'll both hold those jobs for a brief period."

"The plan is still unclear," I said.

"It is, and we welcome any suggestions, but the idea is to get into Bachenko's plane and fly it out of Jacksonville. Easier said than done, but much easier if the two of you both have official reasons to be there."

Daze and I peppered them with questions, and had still more by the time we left for work. We agreed to meet again after taking some time to study our respective roles. Or more to the point, me taking a crash course in aeronautical oversight for the part I would play in the biggest production of my life so far in Florida.

***

"That was… something," I said as we drove to work.

"Something that we still know little about," Daze said. "I have a million questions."

"I do, too. But right now, I guess my job is to learn my lines. How many times have I done that?"

"As long as I've known you, you've walked around the apartment reciting lines for some play or other."

"Some actors dread learning their lines. Me, I revel in it."

"You do,' Daze said, "I learn most of your lines just by hearing them over and over. And over." She was smiling when she said it.

"A little boring for you, huh?"

"Not really. I kind of enjoy it. It's like the drone of the television you're not watching, but it gives off a kind of comfortable background noise."

"Droning is not a wonderful sound for an actor," I said huffily. "I do not drone. I project."

"You project droning," Daze said, and burst out laughing.

"Hey, I take my acting seriously. It's not…okay it's hilarious." I broke out laughing, too.

"Anyway," Daze said with a giggle, "The language of aeronautical mechanics must be easier to learn than Shakespeare."

"'Truly, sir, the better for my foes and the worse for my friends,' nah, Shakespeare is easy."

"You just got that role a couple of days ago. You know the lines already?"

"Yeah, I do. Spooky, huh?"

"You're a savant. Teaching you mechanic speak will be a piece of cake."

"You've spent a lifetime learning how to be a mechanic. How am I supposed to learn in such a short time?"

"You don't need to learn to be a mechanic. A good thing, too, because it's difficult to learn, and I had an outstanding teacher in Mac. He made sure I knew all the mechanics before he even let me in the cockpit with him to fly. But you don't need that to be a fake inspector. You need to know the language and what it means, and I can teach you that. Just treat it like learning your lines for a play. And treat spotting issues as knowing when to speak your lines. A loose lug nut is another actor saying his line. Like, I'm loose, I'm loose, nay, I'm broken, fix me, forsooth there is no one I trust more than you."

I looked at Daze with amazement and then cracked up.

"Using nay was great, but correct use of forsooth was inspired. And by the way, a great method to teach an actor the language of something he knows nothing about."

Daze grinned. "I listen," she said. "And by the way, you already know a ton about being an airline mechanic, because I've shared it with you. I'm teaching you almost the same way Mac taught me, except I spent years doing it. But the principles are the same. Learn how a plane works before you try to fly it."

I knew what she meant. Daze was a wonderful teacher, and we never even entered the Cessna before completing what amounted to classroom work. She couldn't do that with her other clients, because they wanted to at least take a training flight with Daze at the controls for their $300, but she'd insisted on doing it right for me.

As we pulled into the parking lot of Bert's Eats, I turned to Daze and said, "We might have forgotten something. I am worried about walking out on the play, but rehearsal is at night. What about our jobs here? If we don't figure something out, we'll lose our jobs if we are spending our days at the airport."

Daze nodded. "I didn't think about it, either. We don't yet know how long we'll be at the airport. And how long can it be?"

"It could be too long for Bert," I said. "But I guess we'll have to figure it out. A brief vacation is one thing, but anything longer than say, a week, might be a problem."

"Another thing to figure out, I guess," Daze said. "Let's clock in, work our shift, and decide on an approach later."

13

As we punched in, I noticed Hippo was not at his station.

Carlos, Hip's fellow sous-chef, saw me look, and offered the information that Hip had called and said he'd be late. Some personal business to take care of.

I shrugged, donned my server gear, and headed into the dining room.

***

Hippo was late because he and Willy were having an extended conversation.

"Did Trip tell you I ran into him at the grocery store?" Willy asked.

Hippo didn't have to get to work for at least an hour, so he and Willy were sitting in the living room of Willy's condo.

"No, I haven't spoken to him in a while. Did he fill you in on what he and Daze plan to do?"

"No. I don't think they've decided yet. We grabbed a cup of coffee and sat down and chatted.

"Anything new going on?"

"Well, not exactly. Derek, honey, I want to talk to you about London."

"What to wear? The clothing to bring? What to do while I'm in my interview?"

"Oh, maybe all those things at some point, but I mean if you get the job."

"Wouldn't that be great? I don't even want to hope yet," he said. "There are probably a bunch of people being interviewed."

"With an all-expenses paid deluxe trip to London? I doubt it. They want you, honey."

"I wonder why? I never made it to the NFL."

"You were the defensive captain of a top ten football team, and a shoo-in to be drafted. You know college sports, and you're smart and good-looking. Lots of reasons."

"Well, thank you. I think I'd be better off having you decide whether I get the job."

Willy smiled. "I'd hire you in a second. But I want to talk about that."

"Sure. What's up?"

Willy bit her lip. She didn't want to puncture his dream. But she knew she had to raise her concerns sooner rather than later.

"Um, if you get the job, will you be moving to London?"

Hippo stared at her. "They could station me anywhere, but if it's London, we're both going. No way I'm moving away from you. I'd never do that. I love you."

Willy sighed. "I know. I love you, too. But honey, I have a life here. Is there even female wrestling in London?"

Hippo smiled broadly. "I'm taking you seriously, Willy. Don't worry, we'll talk about it as long as you want. And we'll figure something out. But I know the answer to your question. I was planning to surprise you in London, but there is absolutely female wrestling in London." He reached for his laptop, keyed in a website, and pushed it over to Willy. "Check out EVE, Riot Girls of Wrestling."

Willy looked at it and smiled. "A lot different from what we do here, but looks entertaining, for sure. I don't know if it answers my concerns, but knowing it's there helps."

"Whatever we do," Hippo said. "We'll do it together. This job seems to be internationally based, but as you pointed out, my knowledge of players and coaches are here in the U.S. So before we panic, let's see what the offer is, if there is one at all."

Willy leaned in close to Hippo. "Okay. Right now, we'll just plan our exciting trip to London."

***

I looked at the long list of terms and definitions Daze put in front of me and sighed loudly.

Daze smiled at me. "Don't worry. You know a few items on that list already. Those will be easy wins for you."

"Wins? And why are you putting a sweater and necklace on? Are you going out? And if so, it's like eighty degrees out there. You won't need a sweater tonight."

She pointed at the pages in front of me. "Knowing full well how unbelievably dry and technical that stuff is, and having a full awareness that the usual lines you learn are actually interesting to someone other than a flight mechanic, I've devised a little game to…shall we say…incentivize you."

"How is putting a sweater and necklace, and, um, toe ring on going to…ah, I think I know."

Daze affected her best British accent, which wasn't half-bad. "I think he's got it."

"How will this work?" I asked.

"You see that list? Take an hour to memorize as much as you can. Then we play the game."

"There's like a hundred technical terms and explanations here," I said. "I'll need more than an hour."

"Too bad," she said sweetly. "There's a price to be paid for wrong answers during the quiz portion of the game."

I wondered what she had in mind, but started studying the list. I have an excellent memory. You need one if you act. Memorizing lines came naturally to me, but this wasn't for a play. And there would be no cue cards or teleprompters during this performance. I had to show a working knowledge of what was on the list to both recognize mechanical issues on planes and use the correct terminology that looked halfway like I knew what I was talking about. Daze knew it, too, and I was fortunate to have someone as knowledgeable as her teaching me right at home. Home, I thought. The rent wasn't high, but we had paltry income. Maybe this thing with Bachenko would pay off in multiple ways, including financially. So, I put my mind to work and studied the terms and explanations until Daze returned to the room and announced, "Study period is over. Quiz time."

I looked up and saw she'd put on shoes and socks, a scarf, and a floppy hat.

"That's some getup," I said. "More items to remove?"

Daze just smiled. "Give me the papers," she commanded, and I handed them to her.

"Okay, ground rules. You get five questions right, I take

off a piece of clothing. You get two questions in a row wrong, and I put a piece of clothing back on." She pointed to a pile on the chair. "And I have unlimited clothes to put on."

"What happens if I don't get two wrong answers in a row, and keep getting five in a row correct?"

"You win the game," she said.

"Is there a prize?"

"Other than seeing me naked? And successfully learning this stuff?"

"Exactly in that order," I said with a smile.

"I certainly hope so," she said. "And I have a good idea of a bonus prize for exemplary work."

"I kind of wish I knew the rules when I was studying," I said. "I would have worked my ass off learning all about airplane mechanics. My knowledge might exceed yours."

"Not likely. I spent years learning it, and I'm A&P certified."

"And Mac didn't even incentivize you like you're doing for me," I said.

"He did it a different way. Letting me actually fly a plane."

I nodded. "Both are good ways to encourage learning. Okay, quiz away."

Daze read off terms, and I was supposed to give the definitions and brief explanations. Or she read it the other way, giving the definition and asking for the term. I answered the first five questions correctly, and she removed one shoe. I had a wrong answer, and sweated over the next question, desperately not wanting to have two in a row wrong, and thankfully got it right, followed by five correct answers and Daze's removal of the other shoe.

"Pretty good so far," Daze said. "Ten out of eleven."

"A lot of terms left," I said.

"More opportunities for clothing removal," she said with a grin.

We continued the game in the same fashion. Daze returned to questions I got wrong, and asked them again. I rarely got the answer wrong twice, and only a few times made two mistakes in a row. I was making steady progress. After about an hour, Daze had both shoes and both socks off, and her floppy hat sat on the chair with the other clothes. She had bare feet, but still wore all her regular clothes, plus the added necklace and sweater, and the tiny toe ring.

"You're doing pretty well," Daze observed. "Getting a lot of those terms down."

"You're still wearing most of your clothes, though," I said.

"And I'm a little tired of wearing this sweater, so please get the next five questions right."

And I did. And the next ten after that. I was on a roll. The sweater, necklace, and toe rings were gone.

We continued the game, and I had a wrong answer, followed by five correct ones and, at long last, removal of her shirt. She sat in front of me, wearing only a bra, shorts, and probably panties. I say probably, because you never knew with Daze. But I found out soon, because I had five correct answers, and her shorts came off, revealing bikini type underwear. And a very distracting underwear clad beauty in front of me.

"Very few terms left," Daze said. "And getting chilly in here."

She read off the next five terms and I answered them all

in a row. I wondered what article of clothing was coming off next, and she rewarded me by springing free two beautiful breasts.

"Hard to concentrate," I said, when she started reading questions again.

Daze looked up from the papers. "Not the only hard thing," she observed.

Daze read the next five questions, and to my utter joy, I answered them all correctly, and watched as Daze removed her panties.

"Bonus time," she said. "Congratulations. You've learned your lines."

14

We headed back to the unmarked office building on A1A, and sat down again with Abby and Jeff in the conference room.

We briefed them on my recent near mastery of technical aeronautical terms, and they expressed amazement at the short time it took.

"I'm used to studying lines," I said. "For plays, of course, but this wasn't much different. And I had a brilliant teacher," I added, with a look at Daze. "Also, a great deal of incentive to learn it." I let them think it was the money.

"Great, let's hear some of it," Jeff said.

I complied by talking like I'd been a certified airline mechanic for twenty years. It was a role. I was good at that.

"Perfect," Jeff said. "I knew you were a great actor, but seeing you in the role we conceived is fantastic."

I gave an exaggerated bow, which drew smiles from them.

"We have something to show you, courtesy of Alistair Brooke," Jeff said, handing each of us identification cards and single sheets of paper.

I looked at my ID, and read it out loud, "Terence Rogers, Aeronautical Inspector, Jacksonville International Airport, Private Aircraft Section. Lofty sounding title. Is it real?"

"Yes. All but your name. We didn't think using your real names was a good idea."

Daze looked at hers. "Tracy Bell, A&P Certified Mechanic, Jacksonville International Airport, Private Planes Section. We're in the same section," she said with a smile.

Abby looked to see if she was kidding, and obviously decided she was, although she said the obvious, anyway. "This will put you both where you need to be to get the job done. Both IDs are real, and only the airport director knows any other information. He's cooperating with Alistair at Imperial. And supposedly dislikes Bachenko for his own reasons." At my look, Abby added, "We don't know the reason. Alistair didn't tell us. But he's an ally, although one we should never reach out to."

"As far as anyone knows, this is a repossession operation. An owner is in default, and his plane is being reclaimed by Imperial. No one other than the people in this room knows otherwise."

"This is all legal?" Daze asked.

Jeff produced an official-looking document and pushed it across the table to us. We leaned our heads together to scan its contents. The document identified the lender, the borrower, the make and model, serial number and tag numbers for the Gulfstream, the nature of the defaults, which were primarily failure to report and provide requested and required information, and set forth the grounds for and authority for repossessing the aircraft. It was signed and certified in London, England, and bore the name of a British solicitor.

I did not know what an official repo authorization looked like, and I was sure Daze didn't either, but the thing looked official and proper, and we both murmured approval.

Abby handed Daze a package. She looked inside and gave a wry half-smile. I looked at the contents and put a hand on her arm.

"Don't worry. That's makeup hair dye. Washes out with shampoo, and leaves no residue. We use it all the time. Both men and women. It's theatrical hair coloring. Pick a color, any color, from alabaster to yellow." I looked at the package more closely. "Or in this case, stunning brunette."

Daze examined the package, and looked at Abby, who quickly said, "It's for your safety more than a need for a disguise. Bachenko knows you as a long-haired blonde. We can change your height a little with shoe inserts and push your hair into a bun under a baseball cap. And it will be brunette only for as long as you need it, after which you simply wash it out, and let your hair down. Back to being the pretty blonde ace pilot."

"I guess that's okay," Daze said. "I don't want to even run into Bachenko, but if I do, I'd rather he didn't recognize me."

'That's the idea. We want the job done, but we want you both to be as safe as possible."

I doubted that Abby and Jeff cared much about our safety, but their precautions, which likely ensured as well as possible the success of the dual operation, helped enhance our safety. So, I had no problem with what they had in mind.

"When do Tracy and I start?" I asked.

Abby smiled. "In character already, Terry? Great. Why don't we say the day after tomorrow? You'll need time to get yourselves prepared. Is that too soon?"

I looked at Daze, who gave me an unspoken agreement, and I gave an affirmative answer to the start date.

***

"We need to tell Bert about our expected leave of

absence," I said to Daze as I parked in the restaurant parking lot.

"What should we say? Vacation? Family crisis?"

"Family crisis would be a tough sell to apply to both of us," I said. "Either we're related and don't know it, or we're pretending to have two separate family crises at the same time."

Daze looked at me in mock horror. "I sincerely hope we're not related."

"Yeah, me, too. The vacation thing might work. Where should we pretend to go?"

"Ooh, that's a tough one. Somewhere we don't have to show pictures of, like the two of us on the beach in Aruba."

"We could pull some picture off the internet, and show those if anyone asks."

"The only one we'd need to really convince is Bert. He's very old school. He might not even know there is an internet."

"He knows, but fake pictures might convince him, if we can put ourselves in the pictures. And I don't know how to do that."

"I don't either," Daze said. "Hippo might."

"Maybe, but why don't we think of something else? We'll be spending a lot of time in Jacksonville. Why don't we have a fake vacation there?"

"Pretty crappy vacation. Our beaches are much better than theirs. And we'll be working, anyway."

"Maybe we should say we're doing something else."

"Like what?"

"Taking a staycation."

"Not bad. We need a vacation, but have no funds to go on one. Perfect."

We headed into the restaurant and both went to Bert's office.

"Hey Bert," I said. "Can Daze and I have the next week off? We have a lot to do around the apartment, and I'd like to take a few pilot lessons in a row, so I can learn a difficult maneuver without killing us both."

Bert looked at the two of us. "Why don't you take a real vacation, like the Cayman Islands, or something like that?"

"We have no money," I said. "And you don't have a problem with us missing a week of work?"

"You've seen how slow it is right now. No money for either of us. I was considering closing down for a week, to remodel, or whatever sign I'd put on the door. I was worried about putting you out of work. Now we can both get what we want, and I don't have to pay you anything."

"Except our pre-tip substandard wages," I said.

"Yes, well, about that…oh, okay. I'll pay you. And go. But not today. We're still open, so get out there and get to work."

"Thank you, Bert," Daze said. "We know you're doing us a favor, and we appreciate it."

The corners of Bert's mouth turned up ever so slightly, and we left, with our leave of absence firmly in hand.

"He's not closing down, is he?" I asked Daze.

"Nope. He's letting us take a paid vacation."

"I wonder why?"

"He's right. It's been slow. Not close the restaurant slow, but not packing in the restaurant busy, either. And we better make some money from this Bachenko thing, or we're totally screwed financially. No work, no tips."

"And very few flying lesson customers, either. Just a few."

We punched in and headed out to the dining room. Before doing so, I glanced in the kitchen, but saw no Hippo. I didn't recall any reason for his absence, and thought of him always being there. I even teased him about living at Bert's saving time, commuting to the place when he worked double shifts, scrupulously saving money.

***

I told Carleton I might need to miss a rehearsal sometime next week, but I couldn't tell him which day, because I didn't know. That part of it was hard to explain, because appointments usually are on a specific day. But I thought my outright lie was pretty well executed.

"What did you tell him?" Daze asked when I returned home.

"It turns out I need to see a dermatologist."

"That's all?"

"Dermatologists are impossible to get appointments with, right?"

Daze nodded. "They are. I had something on my arm that looked odd, so I tried to get to a dermatologist to see if it might be skin cancer. We live in Florida. Lots of sun, not enough sunscreen."

"Did you see one?"

"No. I got it checked out with a regular doctor. And it was fine. Is that your pretend issue, too?"

"No. I thought of that, but decided it was too easy to check. So, I invented a growth on my ass."

Daze giggled. "Which cheek?"

"The left one, if you must know. A tiny pimple on my left buttock. But I need it checked out. You can't be too careful."

"If you actually get to see an imaginary dermatologist, I bet ass pimples will be right in his or her wheelhouse."

"No doubt. Anyway, Carleton bought it. Seems he's had a lot of trouble getting in to see a dermatologist, too, and respects my desire to fill any office cancellation."

"One issue," Daze said.

"Only one?"

"Yes, one. Your rehearsals are at night. I'm pretty sure there isn't a single dermatologist that works after, say, 3 p.m."

"I don't think it's that bad, but I get your meaning. Carleton didn't ask, probably because we have a few afternoon rehearsals coming up."

"How were you going to work at Bert's and go to rehearsals?"

"I was going to ask to do the breakfast shift, or tell him I had to work. And I might have needed to tell him that anyway, because of my inspector job. He knows rehearsals must fit into actors' private lives. But I don't need to anymore."

"That was fortuitous," she noted.

"Yeah, it had totally slipped my mind until today."

"Wasn't Carleton freaked out about his lead actor taking a rehearsal off?"

"Less than I expected," I said. "It's the new Carleton. Not exactly warm and fuzzy, but so desperate to have a successful production that he doesn't want to aggravate anyone. He's more afraid that I'll just walk out, than he is about missing a single rehearsal for a good reason."

15

Hippo took the day off from Bert's, doing some shopping to prepare for his interview in London. He brought Willy along, because she said he was "style challenged."

"Part of the problem," she told him, "is that you have no reason to dress up living near the beach in Florida. Shorts, T-shirts, sneakers without socks, or flip-flops covers most people's daily wardrobe." She eyed Hippo. "Including yours. That will not fly in London. It's a very sophisticated, big city. British formality and all that."

"You saw the website for EVE, the Riot Girls of Wrestling. It was very punk rock."

"And it looked fun as entertainment. But you're applying for a job that will be more like Savile Row."

"Yeah, I know. That's why I asked you to help me. I'll need a suit, for sure, and I don't currently own one."

"Didn't you have award dinners or other football events at the University of Florida?"

"Yes, but the suit I wore to those events was so worn out, I tossed it after I graduated. You don't need one to be a sous chef."

"No problem, so first stop is Rivers Brothers."

"Not a department store, or one of those gigantic men's clothing stores?"

"If you want to look your best, Rivers Brothers is the place to go."

"I don't even know how much a suit costs now," he said.

"It can range from a couple of hundred dollars to many thousands."

"Aren't we more likely to see the 'many thousands' type of suits at Rivers Brothers?"

"Maybe. But my understanding is that they have suits in all different price ranges. I don't know that for sure," she admitted. "But we can always leave."

They pulled up in front of the venerable store. It was a four-story building in Jacksonville. Upon entry, they viewed a bustling first floor arrayed with cashmere sweaters, dress shirts, even cufflinks and cummerbunds, but no suits.

Willy pointed to a directory, and they peered at it.

"It says that suits are on each of the top three floors. I wonder how they're divided? By color, size, maybe price?"

"I bet it's price," Hippo said. "We might as well start with one floor up. Lowest floor, maybe lowest price."

They proceeded to that floor and saw many racks of suits. All were gray, navy, or black.

"Maybe this is the dark suit floor," Hippo observed, walking over to a rack, then following the suits down the aisle, looking at sizes.

"I don't see my size," Hippo said.

"I don't see prices, either. And what is your size? Do you know?"

"If I remember correctly, I squeezed into a 52, with an 18.5 neck and 40 -inch sleeve length."

Willy gave Hippo a once-over. "I bet it was bursting at the seams."

"Yeah, it was. All the guys looked like that. Some agents looked like their suits fit better, but they were all, maybe half our sizes."

"Probably wore tailored suits, too."

"Yeah, I guess so. They fit them like gloves."

At that moment, a perfectly coiffed man hurried over to us, expressing a profuse apology for not immediately seeing the two enormous people gracing the area.

"No problem," Hippo said. "I'm looking to buy a suit, but I don't see my size. Or any prices."

They could almost hear the man exude a sniff from his upturned nose.

Uh oh, Hippo thought. We're on the wrong floor. If you need to know the price, you can't afford it.

But to his surprise, the man was kind. He pointed to the suits on the rack and said that someone of Hippo's athletic build was unlikely to find a suit on that rack that fit properly.

"There are some suits on the third floor that might come close to fitting you, sir, but we have nothing on this floor." He waved his hand toward the racks. These are primarily for customers to pick a color, cut and style they want, with the fabric choice. We then have a tailor on site who will do all the alterations to make it fit perfectly. He eyed Hippo. "If you wish, our tailor can fashion something for you. He is a creative genius."

Hippo thought employing a tailor who was a creative genus sounded expensive, and was afraid to ask.

Willy was braver or just had to know. "What's the approximate cost of that?"

"I'd estimate, based on the gentleman's size, about $9,500."

Hippo hoped his eyes didn't pop out when he heard the price, but a cool, collected Willy just responded with a thank you, and that they'd certainly think about it.

The man smiled at them, gave a slight bow, and the two of them headed upstairs.

In the elevator, Hippo said to Willy. "Holy crap, do people actually pay that much for a suit?"

"People with too much money," Willy said. "But how much did you expect to pay?"

"Um, $250."

"We might be in the wrong place. But we should look anyway. If we can find something in your big boy size, and it doesn't cost a fortune, we might want to get one here. The quality will be better, and they'll alter it for you." She paused. "Probably not by the creative genius."

"Not likely," Hippo agreed.

And they found suits for bigger men on the third floor. And they all had prices on them. The prices did not include a $75.00 alteration fee. They scanned the racks and ultimately found a navy suit that seemed acceptable. Hippo tried on the coat, and it mostly fit. Because of his build, it didn't seem possible to find anything not requiring extreme tailoring that wouldn't look like he was a sausage crammed into its casing, but it looked more than presentable. Hippo went into the dressing room to try on the pants and came out a few minutes later with a dejected look.

"I could never fit into these," he said.

A nearby sales associate apparently overheard him and approached and introduced himself as Roscoe. "And you are?"

"Derek and Wilhelmina," Willy answered.

"Nice to meet you. Don't worry about the trousers, sir. We can alter those to fit you. Why don't you put on the jacket, and I'll look it over. Then we can get to the trousers." He surveyed Hippo. "You're certainly a big fellow. But we've helped many people your size. A nip here, a tuck there, and you'll look great."

Hippo was about to grumble about the $75.00 alteration charge, but thought better of it.

"You know, that jacket looks fine," the sales associate said. "People with your build can be tough to outfit, but I think you found a decent fit on the jacket." He eyed the trousers that Willy held, and she handed them to the man, who took one look and said, "No, no, no. This will never do. Hold on a second. I don't even think these trousers belong with this suit. Give me a minute, and I'll fetch something else."

Hippo and Willy waited a few minutes until the man returned. He held a fresh pair of navy trousers out.

"Here, try these, and meet me just outside the dressing room." He looked at Willy. "Why don't you come with me? We can both give an opinion when the gentleman returns."

Hippo came out of the dressing room wearing the trousers, which had the top button unfastened.

"They're too tight," he said, a despairing tone in his voice.

"Oh, we can fix that easily. It's the legs and buttocks that the tailor will want to evaluate." Roscoe nodded at an approaching thin man wearing tiny round glasses. "Here he is. Derek and Wilhemina, meet Gerhard."

Gerhard gave a small nod, and motioned Hippo to a small, raised platform, pulled a tape measure out of his pocket, and measured Hippo's legs, then his waist. He wrote the figures in a small notebook. He had Hippo turn around, measured him from one side of his butt to the other, and again recorded the result. "Okay, please put on the jacket."

Hippo complied, and Gerhard stood back, surveying his subject with a critical eye. "Turn around, please." He took more measurements and again wrote them down.

Gerhard looked at Roscoe and nodded. He turned to Hippo and Willy. "We'll fix it right up for you. Give us four days."

Roscoe did a double-take. "Four days? That's fast."

Gerhard was already walking away, but he turned and said, "It's slow this week."

Hippo and Willy had not even agreed to the purchase, so Hippo turned to Roscoe. "We haven't bought anything yet," he said.

"Don't worry about that, sir. We'll take care of that paperwork right now. Gerhard won't start until I give him the go-ahead." He looked at them both. " Are you undecided? That suit will look great on you. Of course, you don't need to decide right now, but that four-day window Gerhard gave you is only because this is a slow week. Sometimes that window is as much as a month. Let me give the two of you a moment to talk." He stepped away. There were no other customers nearby. Although the other floor had a few people milling about, this one was empty. Willy made that observation when they were alone.

"What do you think that means?"

"This is not a popular floor. Or it really is an unusually slow period."

"Or the business is having financial trouble," Hippo

said.

"Or that," Willy acknowledged. "This store has a great reputation, but one only has to listen to the news to know that clothing stores are having trouble in this economy. But more to the point, do you want to buy that suit? The jacket looked really nice," she said.

"It's way more than my $250 budget," Hippo said. "And it will have a $75 alteration charge. Don't you think that's a lot?"

"As a flat charge, including both the trousers and the blazer? No, it's cheap. My experience doesn't include men's suits, but tailoring is very expensive for women."

"Oh, what the hell. It's only money. And I want to make a good impression. Once I have that job, I won't need to subsist on Bert's meager wages. I'll consider it an investment in my future."

They gave an affirmative answer to Roscoe, who wrote the sale up, and told them to expect a call in four days, and to produce the sales slip when picking up the suit.

They returned downstairs, and Willy took one look at the expensive merchandise and told Hippo they would shop for dress shirts and shoes in different stores.

"I have shoes," he said.

"Are they presentable?"

"I used them only twice. And they're newer and took less wear than my old suit."

"Good. We'll finish our shopping this morning, and have you looking spiffy for your interview."

"Thanks for helping me, Willy. Let's go out to lunch

after we're done here."

"Sounds good to me. And you're very welcome."

16

"It's our first day at our new jobs," I observed to a sleepy-looking Daze. "Time to get up."

"I don't want to," she replied, pulling the covers over her head.

I waited, and a moment later, a pretty face appeared. "Okay," she said. "Let's go kick Bachenko's ass."

We showered and dressed for work.

"Do you think khakis and these loafers would be okay for an airline inspector?"

"For your first day, maybe. Make a good impression and all. But I've seen those guys wearing cutoffs and T-shirts."

"I'd rather wear that," I said. "And I guess I don't really care whether I make a good impression. It's a short-term job."

Daze took a moment to think about it. "For our purposes, maybe a little less casual is a good idea. We want Bachenko's crew to take you seriously, to think you're the real deal that they actually have to answer to. We want them to jump when you speak. If they don't, we're screwed."

"Yeah, I guess you're right. Not really the way anyone

dresses in Florida, and not comfortable for me. It's like wearing a costume, I guess."

"Sure, if that motivation works for you. Go with it."

"What are you wearing?"

"I'm a grease-monkey. Jeans and long sleeves."

"Why the long-sleeves?"

"To avoid getting oil, gas, and other noxious materials permanently fused onto my arms."

"Good point."

"Another lesson learned after long experience. Look at my hands."

I looked, and I saw heavily callused hands, with a faint discoloration.

"You see this? It's almost impossible to get the stain permanently out. There are good solvents and detergents, and I have to use my hands for the precise work, but I'll be damned if I'll let my arms look like this."

I nodded. "The hair dye looks perfect. It's like you're a totally new woman."

"Do you like it? I mean permanently?"

"Heavens no. It looks good for the part you're playing. And to avoid detection, but I love the way you usually look."

"Correct answer, Mr. Steele."

I smiled. "Just telling the truth, ma'am."

"We have a problem," Daze said, suddenly.

"What?"

"We can't arrive together. And we only have one car."

I thought about it. "We don't want to pay for an Uber all the way to the airport. So why don't we drive together to just short of Jacksonville, where those highway hotels are all lined up? You'll take the car to the airport, and I'll grab a ride from a hotel. Or maybe sneak on one of their shuttles. Whatever option presents itself."

"Why me to take the car?"

"A mechanic is more likely to arrive in my crappy Duster than an inspector."

Daze smiled. "They probably pay a mechanic twice as much as an inspector."

"Maybe, but a mechanic is much more likely to have the skill to fix a car like mine than an inspector."

"You're very good at fixing that car."

"I am. I've always been good with cars. But the run-of-the-mill inspector might not be. Anyway, I thought you'd prefer taking the car to the extra hassle of getting a ride to the airport."

"I do. Thank you."

Breakfast eaten, and fully prepared for our first day, we boarded my Duster, and headed off towards the airport. It was about an hour's drive, so Daze took the time to quiz me on some of the terms I'd learned.

"Your knowledge of car mechanics will help, but there are distinct differences in airplanes."

"Planes can fly, for one."

"See, you've mastered a basic fact. Now let's hear your mastery of a few more complicated things."

"Are you going to remove an item of clothing for each five correct answers?"

"Not this time. You're on your own. And it's unlikely that your supervisor or co-workers will do so either."

"Or Bachenko's stooges," I said.

"Or them."

But once I learn lines, I retain them. It's a highly practiced ability, and not all actors can master it, but it's as much in my skill set as speaking them in a play. Daze looked pleased at my command of aeronautical terms. She added a few ways to respond to questions, and I think I nailed the ability to parry, stall, and deflect. So, I was as ready as I'd ever be by the time we reached one hotel situated a mile shy of the airport. I turned the keys over to Daze and wandered over to where the hotel shuttle sat waiting for guests to board. And caught a ride when the driver didn't check for a room key. Or more to the point, assumed that someone going to the airport had already checked out and had no key card to show. I cruised to the departures part of the airport and made my way on foot to the building housing the private plane terminal.

I walked into the small office housing the non-commercial airline inspectors, better known as the rich guy oversight office, or so I was told by Skip Turnbull, the boss of his merry little group.

Upon entering, I received a glare from a man sitting at a desk in an open space. That was the office. An open space with a few metal desks with big computer monitors sitting on them. There were three desks—one housing the man with the contemptuous expression, one with a man who turned out to be Skip, and an empty one, presumably destined for me.

Skip stood up when I entered. I judged him to be about fifty, around six feet tall, had an oval face, with a ruddy complexion, and a shock of tousled brown hair topping his head. His greeting was friendly. He introduced himself and shook my hand. My eyes cut to his hands, which were heavily callused and faintly stained like Daze's, but much larger. I realized he'd spent many years as a mechanic, and I involuntarily glanced down at my own hands, which looked more like those of an actor, or sigh, a food server. I wondered whether Skip noticed, but of course he did. The man's intelligent looking eyes portrayed perceptiveness.

Skip introduced me to the glaring man, whose name turned out to be Conrad King, or Connie, as Skip referred to him. He didn't leave his seat, and I wondered what his hostility was all about. But I shrugged it off. I just needed him to stay the hell out of my way for a short time. Then he could have his little world not upset by an officious newcomer.

"This is the control center of the inspection team. It's not glamorous, as you can see, but we get the job done." He looked over at the other man. "Connie and I have worked here together for about ten years now, isn't it, Connie?"

"Yeah, a decade of fun and games together," he said, and looked at his computer monitor.

"As you can see, your co-worker is an upbeat, sparkling conversationalist."

Connie looked up and stared for a moment at me. "Look," he said. "We're getting the job done. We don't need anyone else. And certainly not a guy dressed like that, with hands that never saw hard labor, pants that will get dirty in about two seconds, and, oh my God, are those loafers? You'll slip and fall the first time you do an inspection." He looked at Skip. "He's a plant from upper management. Bet on it." And to me, "Why don't you just leave us alone? Tell your daddy, or uncle, or whoever sent you here to stop bothering us. We're doing good work here."

Skip looked at me and said with a laugh. "Connie must like you, or he's getting tired. That was a pretty muted diatribe. But he has a point. I get it, you wanted to make a good first impression by wearing those clothes, but they're wildly impractical." He appraised me. "And you look like you hate wearing them, am I right?"

"Right on both counts," I said with a smile.

"You're not a mechanic," Skip said.

"No, I'm not, other than I worked on cars my whole life." I glanced at Connie, expecting a sneer, but he maintained a blank expression. "But I have a shitload of oversight experience, and I studied my ass off before the airport management interviewed me for this job, and I beat out at least a dozen other candidates. I know my stuff." I looked at both men. "Not as much as you do, I'm sure, but I'm eager to learn."

Connie gave a simple reply. "I was born and raised in Missouri," he said, and went back to staring at his computer.

"The Show-Me State," I said, but got no reply.

"Oh, he'll come around," Skip said. "We need an extra pair of hands, even if Connie doesn't think so. Let's do some paperwork and get you checked in." Skip examined my ID, jotted down the number, and had me sign a variety of documents so they could pay me. I looked at the amount, and figured it was more than I'd made from waiting on tables at Bert's for the last two weeks, but maybe only because it was so slow. Most of the time, I'd done pretty well there.

"Okay, why don't I give you a tour of the various hangars? You can meet some people you'll be overseeing, including each plane owner's staffs, and the mechanics servicing the aircraft. This well just be a general tour, but I warn you, it's also a test to see whether you know anything about aeronautical mechanics. I need to do that before I send you out in the field yourself, I'm sure you understand."

"Quiz away," I said, as cocky as I could manage. "And be hard on me."

"I will," Skip said. "I don't compromise on safety. Ever."

***

Daisy entered the little office and a heavy-set man bearing a clipboard greeted her. He introduced himself as Ben Cavendish, but that everyone called him Benny. He looked at her ID.

"Tracy Bell. Hmm, I knew a Tracy once. But he was a grizzled old guy." He looked at Daze. "But you're a girl."

"Acute observation," Daze said. "Tits and all."

The man threw back his head and roared at that. "Feisty, too. So, you're an aeronautical mechanic. We don't get many girl mechanics."

"No surprise there. If you treat great women mechanics like little girls, you'll miss out on some spectacular people who work hard and have terrific skills."

Daze knew enough from her past to never, ever show weakness in this traditionally male occupation. And her attitude scored with this guy, her new supervisor, who gave a wry chuckle at her rebuke.

"Okay," he said. "I deserved that. But I warn you, you'll get much worse from the others." He pointed out the little office window at the hangar outside. "You think I'm bad? They're a bunch of misogynist cretins."

"I'm used to it," Daze said. "But once they get a look at my work, they stop mighty quick."

The man nodded. "I hope so. We need quality mechanics. You have an A&P certification. They don't just give them out like hunks of cheese. Okay, let's see what you've got." He grinned. "Your mechanic skills."

They walked out of the office and into the hangar. A man, who Benny called Jimbo, was busy at work on an engine. He looked up at Benny's introduction, made a crude joke, and looked back at the engine. He turned to Benny. "I'm having some trouble with this. Can you take a look?"

"Perfect opportunity for our new mechanic to put another set of eyes on the problem." He turned to Daze. "Tracy, check this out, and give Jimbo and me an opinion."

Trial by fire, Daze thought, and at a glance saw the issue. But she went by the book. "Show me the blueprints and most recent diagnostic," she said. "I think I know what the problem is, but I like to get it right. Lives at stake and all."

"And all," Jimbo agreed. Daze could see his skepticism, but it faded right away when she described the issue and fixed it.

"She's got game," Benny said, and Jimbo nodded.

"No more jokes. You're the real deal."

Daze endured some mostly good-natured ribbing from the other mechanics, but her performance under fire abated the vitriol, at least after Jimbo and Benny told them about it when the coffee truck pulled up promptly at 11:00 am, and they all sat at a picnic table nearby sipping their java.

As they sat, Daze spotted Bachenko's Gulfstream outside of another hangar, and casually asked about it.

"That's owned by a super-rich industrialist. Mikhail Bachenko," a man named Vic told her. "You see those men around the plane? His security guys. Mercenaries, I hear. The airport prohibits carrying sub-machine guns in plain view, but I bet they have them stashed somewhere. And you can be sure they have multiple concealed weapons."

Another guy, Mel, cracked "This is Florida. Everyone has concealed weapons." After that, there was more joshing and kidding around, until their 15- minute break was up and they all went back to work in the various hangars.

Benny assigned her to work the rest of the day with Jimbo, who Daze had clearly won over. They worked well as a team, making sure they properly performed the maintenance, and the plane was safe to fly.

"Who services that guy Bachenko's plane?" Daze asked at one point.

"We do," Jimbo told her. "We service everything in the Private Aircraft Section. That guy is secretive as hell, though. We can't even enter the plane without one of his goons accompanying us." He laughed. "We service everything here, including that car over there."

He pointed to a classic Cadillac. "Most of us can work on cars, and the head of this lovely enterprise knows it. So, we service that car, too."

"Just another benefit to being a big-wig," Daze said. "I'm driving a late 1980s Plymouth Duster."

"Whoa," Jimbo said. "As an A&P certified aeronautical mechanic, you must make decent money. Hell, I don't have the certification, and I do okay."

Daze's immediate thought was that as a woman, she routinely received seventy-five percent of a man's wages for the same work, but decided that this was neither the time nor the place to say it.

"I spend a lot," she said.

"Ah," is all he said, and they went back to work.

Daze finished up her day, and, as pre-arranged, drove the Duster to the hotel to pick me up.

17

"How did it go?" I asked as soon as I got in the passenger seat.

She looked at me. "The usual misogynist hazing, of course."

"Oh, bummer. I assume you struck back in your usual way?"

Daze smiled at that. "Tough talk followed by a showing of outstanding competence."

"Same as always, or so you've told me. Did you use the "Tits and all" line?"

Another smile. "I did, and it scored. But I also got lucky. The supervisor, Benny, doesn't seem like a bad guy, but he wanted to test me. So, he assigned me to assist Jimbo, the unofficial pack leader. Long story short, I solved Jimbo's complex problem, thus winning myself his grudging respect, and muting the ribbing by the other mechanics, none of whom have my level of certification. So Jimbo endured being bailed out by a girl, and the teasing I received was mostly good-natured."

"Sounds like you handled them well, but a shame you

have to endure it all the time."

"Yeah, not only a girl, but a short one."

"I think you're perfectly sized," I said. "Hey, did you have time to scope out Bachenko's jet?"

"A little. During the coffee break, I spotted it. I asked a few innocuous questions, and was told what we already know—that he's security paranoid. From my vantage point, I could see four or five tough looking men milling around the plane.

"Were they armed?"

"No submachine guns hanging from their necks. But I asked my fellow workers about it, and one of them said there's an airport or Federal prohibition against unconcealed weapons. But the guy also told me he was sure they'd armed themselves to the teeth and probably had automatic weapons stashed somewhere easy to retrieve."

"Let me get this straight. You can only carry weapons at the airport if they're hidden? Kind of 'what I can't see, can't hurt me?'"

"Yes sir. Same as the rest of Florida. Stuff an M-16 into your underwear, and you're ready to go."

I shrugged. "Anyway, good information on your first day. I got nothing, not even a full tour."

"And I want to hear all about your wildly unsuccessful day, but I have two more things to share."

"Fire away," I said. "Oops, terrible choice of words, given your previous statements."

Daze gave me an indulgent half-smile and went on. "I found out that we, meaning the airport mechanic staff, service Bachenko's plane. We do all the maintenance and repairs. But apparently they prohibit entry inside the plane without one of

Bachenko's goons accompanying us."

"That could be a problem," I said.

Daze nodded. "Another thing that maybe we can exploit somehow, although I don't know how, is that the mechanics service the Cadillac owned by the airport chief."

"He gets aeronautical mechanics to change his oil and rotate his tires?"

"It would seem so. All the mechanics are good with cars." She paused. "You are, too."

"I've worked on cars my whole life. My Dad and I used to buy old cars from the salvage yard, and fix them up."

"That might be useful," Daze said.

"Well, it helped a little with the skeptics in the Inspectors' office."

"They quizzed you."

"They did, and not on my knowledge of aeronautical terms, but on the state of my hands."

Daze glanced down. "Ah, not completely callused and permanently stained like mine. I guess it's an unlikely badge of honor, and is hard to replicate."

"I might have tried, but I never thought of it. So, I'm branded as someone who may have book learning, but never actually touched a screwdriver. But working on cars helped a little. They think I'm a plant, sent by management to gather information about them. I tried to dissuade them, and maybe I did a little."

"Did you leave the office at all?"

"Not today. Tomorrow I get the big tour."

"That's what we're hoping for. A good close look at that plane. I don't know when, or if, I'll get a look. I don't want to be too forward about it and get anyone suspicious."

"Good plan. Let it play out. We have time. Probably not a lot of time, but some."

***

I felt a little weird at rehearsal that night. I was playing two roles at the same time. In my not so illustrious acting career, the good fortune of simultaneous roles had never blessed me. The famous actors and actresses did it all the time. I thought about that. Maybe they didn't. They performed many roles in succession, but few at the exact same moment. And right now, I had Feste, Terry and Tripper all occupying my brain.

Carleton noticed. The new and improved, not exactly kindly director. Okay, still acerbic as hell, and demanding of perfection, but with an affected air of paternalism. He must have been an actor himself once, to pull that off. Anyway, he observed something about my acting.

"Not quite up to your usual adequate performance today, Mr. Steele. You seem distracted. No trouble at home, I hope."

"No, no. Everything's fine. Just a little off today, I guess." I paused, then added, "And thank you for the unusual superlative about my adequate acting. I think I'll put it in a future publicity release. Noted director calls actor adequate."

Carleton was fast. I gave him that. His reply "I said you were not quite up to adequate, but thank you very much for the 'noted director' comment. I'll add it to my new PR release. Maybe it can say "Noted director brilliantly handles not quite adequate actor."

I couldn't help it. I laughed, and he did, too. The rest of the troupe looked on with uneasy smiles.

"Well played sir," I said.

Carleton smiled, and said, "Okay, enough fun and games. Let's get back to work. And bring up your game, Trip."

I nodded, but only staggered my way through the rest of the rehearsal.

When I returned home, I found Daze sitting at the kitchen table studying something.

I kissed her head and sat down. "Whacha got there?"

"Some schematics for two of the aircraft we're working on tomorrow. I asked for them, so I can apply half a brain to what I'm doing."

"Very studious of you. Taking your role seriously."

"It's more than that. If I'm the mechanic, I'm responsible for the plane's safety. I want to do it right, no matter what else I'm there for."

"Uh, oh," I said.

Daze looked up from the plans. "What?"

"I'll be the safety inspector for those planes," I said.

"Only for a little while. Inspecting a mechanic's work is not the same as performing the tasks of a mechanic."

"So, my job is ministerial? Just for show?" I said it hopefully.

"So earnest in your desire to be ineffectual. Adorable. But no, it's an important job. I'm the only A&P certified mechanic out there. And I'm the new person, not yet charged with doing anything by myself. Think about that."

"There might be some safety violations," I said.

"There probably are more than violations. Outright dangerous conditions. It's in everyone's interest that we get our actual job done as quickly as possible."

"Getting rid of a faux safety inspector, but it seems like you're improving the quality in your close-knit group."

"Uneasy with the new girl group is more like it. They have grudging respect for my skills and outright hatred of my gender."

"They hate women?"

"That's what demeaning people because of their sex means."

"I'm sorry," I said.

"No need for you to be sorry. I've never, ever heard you say anything disrespectful to women."

"I love women, and value their individual intelligence and talents. I hold many women in high esteem. Especially you."

"See what I mean? Very respectful. And very appealing." A suggestive wink followed the statement.

"We only have a week's leave of absence from Bert's Eats," I said, as we drove back to our new jobs. "Do you think we can wrap this thing up by then?"

Daze shrugged. "I hope so, but I kind of doubt it. We've only been there a day. We need to do some surveillance and get the lay of the land before we try to grab that jet. And we need a good plan to deal with Bachenko's security detail."

"We do," I said. "Any initial thoughts?"

"A few ill-formed ideas, but I'll know better in a few days. Who knows? I might even get to work on his plane. That would really help us figure out how to deal with the goon squad."

"I might get some information today. I'm getting the extensive tour."

"Take notes. They'll expect that."

I nodded. "My pad and pen are in the back seat. Don't let me forget them when you drop me off."

"You think you'll be able to finagle a free ride again?"

"Sure. I'm an actor. It's my job to convince people I'm someone other than myself."

"A freeloading weasel?"

"I think of it as income-challenged."

"Ah. That sounds much better."

"Yes, it does. I have my scruples."

"You have your credit card?"

I patted my wallet. "Right here. But I won't need it."

And I didn't. The shuttle driver waved me in right away, and I repeated the previous day's trek from one terminal to the other.

I sat down at my desk and scanned the papers that someone had placed there. It contained a list of aircraft, and a separate page, with descriptions, name of owner, and specifications and schematics for each plane.

Skip looked up from his desk and told me to get familiar with it, because we were going to view all the aircraft during the day's tour.

"This is just an introductory visit. We won't be doing any inspections, but you should look as carefully as you can.

We'll talk about your observations tomorrow morning. You brought a pad and pen. Good." He handed me a clipboard. "You'll need this."

I thanked him and went back to studying. This was a test, and I didn't want to fail, or he'd never let me do anything alone.

After an hour, we headed out to the hangars.

"Hold down the fort, Connie," he told my surly fellow worker.

Connie just grunted, which Skip seemed to take for assent.

We started at one end of the small terminal and worked our way to the other side. Skip introduced me to the mechanics working on each plane, and they all looked up, nodded, and went back to work. One by one, Skip asked the mechanics to stand aside so we could get a closer look, and the men complied. They were used to this drill. I recorded my observations on my pad and was grateful to Daze for showing me a lot of this stuff as part of my flying education. So, I wasn't relying just on book education and memorizing terms. I knew a lot already. I wasn't sure whether it was enough to convince Skip, but at least it was not confusing to me.

We arrived at the hangar in which Daze was working with a heavy-set man, and we repeated the procedure. Daze showed no signs of recognizing me, and I stayed nonchalant, even when the other guy referred to Daze as Tracy, the new girl. She has skills, though, the man said, as if in wonder that a woman could be an excellent mechanic.

We took our close-up look, and I jotted some notes. I was happy that the discussion with Skip would take place tomorrow, because Daze could give me a lot of technical information I could use in convincing Skip, and maybe even Connie, that I was the real deal, who they could trust to do an inspection. As we hoped that would happen soon, any edge I could get was valuable.

We met no owners on our tour, and I asked Skip about it.

"The owners are never here. They all expect their aircraft to be ready at a moment's notice. That's not possible, of course, because sometimes the planes are being serviced or repaired at the moment they want to take a joy-ride, or conduct important business. I'm never sure what these rich people are actually doing other than playing with their toys."

"Do they get mad?"

"Furious. Not usually at us, but at Benny, the maintenance chief."

I knew the name, of course, but for appearances' sake, I asked Skip.

"Benny?"

"Ben Cavendish. He was in the back office in the first hangar, um, the one with the girl mechanic."

"Oh, okay. I remember her. Benny didn't come out of the office, I guess."

"Nah, he had Jimbo out there with the girl. Jimbo knows the drill."

I filed away in my mind Skip's view of a woman mechanic, but made no comment. One plane we reviewed was that of Mikhail Bachenko. Skip warned me about the guards standing watch, and sure enough, I spotted at least five very alert-looking guys surrounding the aircraft, which was being worked on by a lanky man. The guards eyed me suspiciously, but the sight of Skip accompanying me seemed to ease their collective minds. He'd obviously accustomed them to his visits. Skip did not introduce me to the guards. I met Alonso, the mechanic, who offered me a grim smile. Working under the gaze of armed men was apparently stressful to him. But he assented to Skip's request for a closer look, and I took my notes, without any of the men shooting at us.

"That was a little harrowing," I commented to Skip when we moved on to the next hangar.

"He's a paranoid guy, that Bachenko fellow."

"But he lets the mechanics here service his plane?"

"He has to. Safety regulations. No privately employed mechanics allowed here. And he wants it available to him any time, night or day."

"Paranoid and demanding, too," I observed.

"That he is," Skip said. "A bit of a pain when we do an actual inspection, but we get through it." His eyes briefly gleamed with an affected evil look. "Maybe I'll assign you to do the inspection as kind of new guy hazing."

I gave a nervous sounding laugh. A pretty good one, I thought. Then I added "I've dealt with all types in my time. Bring it on."

Skip laughed. "False bravado, I love it. Oh, you might draw that inspection, but it's perfectly safe, I assure you. Too many people around for any mischief. And the guy really wants his plane to be safe. So, no worries."

18

"It kind of makes sense," Daze said on our way home. "Bachenko wants his plane available at a moment's notice, so that entails it being in working order and approved by…you, the inspector, as ready and safe to fly. We know he never lets anyone on the aircraft alone when he's not there, so it's safe to assume that he's onboard for every single flight. He doesn't want to die. So, he just wants to keep the plane safe."

"Maybe I should just approve an unsafe aircraft and we can all be done with the son of a bitch."

"It could hurt other people, too. And we don't do that kind of stuff. It would make us as bad as him."

"Oh, I know. I can dream, though."

"Keep dreaming. But we can accomplish almost the same thing by figuring out how to abscond with the plane. Any thoughts on that?"

"I got my first look at the layout today, and I don't think it's impossible. That's a start."

"He has armed guards surrounding the plane."

"Yeah, I saw them. But while I could see their suspicion

of me, they seemed comfortable seeing Skip, and they didn't interfere with our inspection. And from what you were told, only one of them accompanies the mechanic onto the plane."

"I'm not big enough to overpower one of those guys."

"I looked at them, and I doubt I could either. Or even both of us together. We'll need either to get one of Abby and Jeff's Swedish giants onto the plane with us, or we'll need something like a Taser."

"Jabbing a mercenary with a Taser might not be easy. They're trained in hand-to-hand combat, I think. I vote for the Swedish giants, Lars and Liam."

"Sure, me too. But getting them in place might be a problem. They know we're permitted to be in the hangar and even expect it. But Lars and Liam?"

"We'll figure something out," Daze said.

I nodded. "We will. How did your day go? Any new information?"

"None, I'm afraid. I'm still working on the plane you saw. Me and Jimbo bent over an engine. Oh, what fun."

"It was the highlight of my tour, seeing you and Jimbo," I said.

"Made my day," Daze said. "But I was too afraid to ask about Bachenko. There was no need to make him think I care. I'm hoping, of course, to get assigned to a different hangar, and be on my own. I think that will happen tomorrow. Maybe it will even be the Gulfstream."

"Too bad we can't coordinate when we get assigned to it. We'll have to work on that issue, too."

We were both dead tired when we arrived home, but I still had to go to rehearsal.

"The show must go on," I said.

"Break a leg. I'm going to watch TV a little while, and go to bed."

"I'll try not to disturb you."

"I'm so tired, I doubt I'd hear an alarm clock blaring in my ear."

Despite my exhaustion, the rehearsal went pretty well. Afterwards, Carleton asked me when my dermatology appointment was, and I drew a momentary blank. Thankfully, I quickly remembered my cover story, and told him I expected to hear soon. That seemed to mollify his expressed concern that because the actual performance was fast approaching, rehearsals would have enhanced intensity. "More intense than now?" I teased, and he met me with the expected solemn glare.

"Take this seriously, Trip. You have experience, unlike the rest of the troupe. They look up to you, so please set a good example."

"No worries," I said cheerfully. "We'll all be fine. We'll have a wonderful performance. Just wait and see."

"I wish I could share your optimism," Carleton said. "Some actors show glimmers of promise. Others, I don't know."

"Isn't that always the case? Even in the finest production companies?"

"Oh, I guess so. This is such a rag-tag group, though."

I decided to pump Carleton up. He'd been mostly nice to me lately.

"We have a fine director whipping us into shape. We'll have a stellar production, largely because of you."

Carleton gave me a suspicious look. "That was a

gracious thing to say."

"Oh, I mean it," I said. "You're an excellent director. You must be to put up with the likes of us. But don't get a big head. I still think you're an asshole."

That drew a grin. "That's more like it," he said. "I was afraid you pitied me."

"Not a chance."

When I arrived home, Daze was already asleep. I tiptoed in, quietly shed my clothes, and got into bed. She stirred briefly, mumbled something unintelligible, and went back to sleep. I was bushed and joined her in a deep slumber.

The next day, we headed out in the Duster. We discussed potential avenues of accessing the Gulfstream and decided that we needed more surveillance time before any plan could take shape.

"I'm hoping to get out of Hangar 1 today. Jimbo is mostly inoffensive, but I'd like to work solo somewhere. I think it's too much to expect that I'd get to work on Bachenko's plane, but you never know. I'm the new mechanic, and working there cuts both ways. It's unpleasant enough to work under the eyes of a bunch of armed thugs, but also to endure one of them accompany me if I need to enter the jet. Which of course is a regular occurrence, because I often need to check out the instrument panel, and other technical issues accessible only from the inside. Benny might consider it the type of undesirable work he assigns to the least senior mechanic. Alternatively, it could be a sensitive situation that Benny would want handled by a more experienced mechanic."

"No way to tell," I said. "Just like me, we'll have to wait and see. But if I were to hazard a guess for both of us, when we get assigned to the Gulfstream, our respective supervisors will want someone else coming along. At least for the first time."

Daze nodded. "That's a good guess. And that will make

it harder to fly that thing out of there."

"At least the first time we're there. And there's no telling when or if we'll get assigned to it again, and even less chance that they'll assign us there at the same time."

Daze sighed. "All true. We have some figuring to do."

"We do. But one further thought. You need Benny to send you there, but maybe I don't. I can go to any hangar, and just walk over to that one at the right time, and pretend to be doing an inspection. At least as long as no one else is already there."

"I can just give you a signal," Daze said.

"Might work," I said. "We'll keep thinking."

"Another thing I was pondering last night. That car."

"The Cadillac owned by the airport boss? What about it?"

"We're supposed to service it. But you're great with cars. Maybe we can fit that into our plans somehow."

"Interesting thought. I also wonder if Lars or Liam is good with cars."

"Abby and Jeff said they're smart. What do you have in mind?"

"Just the hint of an idea. What if I get asked to look at that car, and I break something in an unusual place? I tell them I know a skilled mechanic who can fix it in a jiffy."

"And that brilliant mechanic would be one of our Swedish allies, placing him near our little project."

"That's the idea."

Daze looked doubtful. "I suppose it could work, but it

presupposes both you working on that car, and the airport authorities allowing an uncleared guy into a sensitive area."

"Could be a problem," I acknowledged. "One of many."

Daze dropped me off at the hotel, and I waved at the familiar shuttle driver, who let me ride again to the airport.

"I'm assigning you to Hangar 3," Benny said to Daze when she arrived. "You'll be working with Carter today."

Daze looked over at Carter, who nodded.

The two walked together to Hangar 3 without speaking, and they began working.

"You're the new girl," Carter said. "Let me show you a few things. Watch and learn."

Daze was pretty sure she couldn't learn a damn thing from Carter other than the correct way to demean a woman. But she remembered why she and Trip were doing these godforsaken jobs, and just grunted at the man's statement. And she watched, as directed. Watched the man totally screw everything up. Daze didn't know what to do. An obviously incompetent mechanic was creating a safety issue on a plane on which she was the…she guessed…assistant mechanic. And aside from it affecting her career advancement, which she had no interest in, it was a safety issue. So, what to do? Get everyone mad at her, affecting her ability to gather information for their real purpose, or let a safety issue go unchecked? Daze gave a long, inward sigh, and ventured a question.

"Um, Carter, I'm watching you and trying to learn. So, I want to write this down. Do we always attach the blue wire to the yellow terminal, the red wire to the green terminal, and the green wire to the blue terminal? And it looks like someone pushed that slider to the left. I want to get it straight in my head."

Carter looked, muttered something, and told Daze to attach the wires correctly, and to push the slider to the right.

"I was just testing you," Carter said, but they both knew he'd screwed up. Daze was grateful it was an easily correctible mistake, but wondered whether Carter messed up in more serious ways on other aircraft. She shuddered to think that people actually flew in planes he'd worked on. But at present, she hoped she hadn't caused a problem in her gathering information. She didn't need to worry. No insights were likely to come from Carter, who kept his mouth closed for the remainder of their work together.

To her great relief, Benny assigned her to work with Alfonso in Hangar 5 after lunch break. Daze liked Alfonso and sat next to him during breaks.

"Hey Tracy, we're working on Mr. Porter's jet. He's a good guy, we might even meet him, because he seems to enjoy hanging around here. Don't ask me why, 'cause I don't know."

"A nice rich guy," Daze said. "Unusual here, isn't it?"

"Some of these people are real jerks, sure. And some, like that guy Bachenko, oh my goodness. You've never met someone as bad as him. He's the guy with all the armed guards. In Hangar 4. Next door from where we're working today."

"You met him? Most owners seem to not show up here at all."

"Oh, I met him once. I was working on his Gulfstream when he showed up. He ranted and yelled a lot, not just at the mechanics, but at the other staff, his own guards, everyone. He's a real prick, that guy."

Daze tried not to show much interest, but casually asked whether Alfonso worked on the Gulfstream often.

"Oh sure," he said. "I think Benny likes me working there. As you might have seen, I have a pretty even disposition. Nothing bothers me much. So, working under the watchful eyes of a bunch of overgrown, steroid infused mercenaries is all in a day's work."

Daze chuckled at that. "I doubt I'd mind much either," she said. "And honestly, I could put up with a lot to get to work on a Gulfstream."

Alfonso looked at Daze. "Really? You're not running away from that gig? No one wants to deal with that crap. The rest of these guys want nice and quiet, no distractions."

"And you don't?"

Alfonso smiled. "I'm good at ignoring my surroundings. But I'd welcome a partner like you. If you want to work on a Gulfstream, I can show you a few things." He paused. "You're probably fine without any advice from me. I doubt I have anything valuable to share with someone as qualified as I'm told."

"Who told you I was qualified?"

Alfonso smiled. "Benny. I asked, and he told me you're A&P certified, and he watched you school Jimbo. And Jimbo is pretty good. Benny said, and I quote 'she's got game,'"

"So maybe you can show me a few things," Alfonso said with a smile.

"How about we learn from each other?"

"I'd like that."

They worked well together for the rest of the day and chatted easily. Daisy could see right away that Alfonso "had game" himself.

19

"Let's go," Skip said to me a few minutes after I arrived.

"Okay," I said. "But one question. Do you live here? No matter what time I arrive, you're already here." I pointed at an empty desk. "Connie's not here yet."

"Connie is an arrive late, leave early guy. I'm just the opposite."

"Arrive early, leave late," I responded.

"You got it. Five in the morning to eight at night."

I gave a low whistle. "That's a fifteen-hour day."

"You can add very well. That skill will come in handy on our inspection today."

I dwelled on his hours for a moment more. "I hope you're getting paid much better than I am."

"Oh, way, way better. Or not. But I get the big title. See that on my desk?"

"Chief Aeronautical Inspector, and in tiny print, 'Jacksonville International Airport, Private Aircraft Section.'"

"That's me. The damn title takes up most of the stupid nameplate, but it earns me maybe five percent more in pay than you."

"But I'm the new guy," I said.

"Yeah, go figure. I'm only making about three percent more than Connie, and he's been here for years. Maybe he's right, you're a management stooge."

"I'm no such thing. And my pay would be much better if I was, wouldn't it?"

"I don't know. They're clever bastards in upper management. Maybe paying you more on the side."

"I'm driving a 1987 Plymouth Duster," I said. "And I loaned it to my girlfriend to get to work. She drops me off and takes the car."

"Between the two of you, an ancient Plymouth Duster. That's just sad."

"See what I mean? I'm pretty sure being a whore to upper management pays enough for a decent ride."

"Okay, okay," Skip said. "You're not a plant. You're a charity case, but not a management stoolie."

"What are we inspecting today?" I asked, the unpleasantness behind us.

"Hangar Ten. An Embraer Phenom 300X owned by Catalytic Corporation. Are you familiar with it?"

Fortunately, that was a jet on the list Daze had me study. Because of its range and size, it was a likely candidate to be in the Private Aircraft Section.

"Yeah, I said to Skip. "Brazilian made, single pilot, light business jet. Top speed a tick under 600 miles per hour. Range about 2200 miles."

Skip just looked at me. "What are you, an encyclopedia?"

"I just have an excellent memory. And I told you, I studied my ass off to ace the interview."

"Well, okay. That's great. But inspecting an aircraft involves more than memorization of facts."

"I know. But I always figured that the more I have committed to memory, the better able I will be to look at blueprints, schematics and diagnostics."

"I guess I should have given you all that stuff to review before we headed down there. But I figured your first inspection, you could just observe. You seem prepared for that, so let's check out this jet."

We headed out of the office, and while we walked, I asked Skip if the inspections were a surprise.

"No, they know we're coming," he said. "And the mechanic assigned to it today is Mort Sands. He'll have it all gussied up for us."

"A mechanic charged with keeping a plane safe has the name Mort?"

"Yeah, ironic, huh? But Mort's a good mechanic. Some guys down there are a horror show, but Mort's okay."

And he seemed okay. And a pretty nice guy. I observed Skip's safety inspection, and had to admit he was very thorough, peppering Mort with questions, and writing the responses down on his clipboard. We peered into the engine compartment, checked out the baffling system, and took multiple measurements. We boarded the plane with no one else accompanying us, and checked out the instrument panel, and made sure it was working properly. The entire process took about an hour and a half. And this aircraft passed its safety inspection. We shook Mort's hand, transferring the grease on his hands to ours, and headed back to the office.

"That's why you wear the coveralls," Skip said to me. "To wipe your hands after shaking hands with a mechanic."

I chuckled at that. "Also, to get the grease off from our hands-on inspection."

"That too. Anyway, that's today's lesson. Questions?"

"I have some, thanks. But I've committed the wearing coveralls lesson to memory."

"If that's all you take away from today's inspection…"

"We're all screwed," I said. "And no, I learned a lot. Thank you."

***

"I think I got some useful information today," I said to Daze as we drove home.

"Yeah, me, too. But tell me yours first."

"I went on my first actual inspection today. Skip wanted me to observe, and it actually seemed very thorough."

"That's been my experience," Daze said. "Most inspectors don't do a lot of messing around. They have a job to do, and don't really give a crap about the sensibilities of the mechanics."

"Skip didn't behave that way with the mechanic today. He seemed to think today's mechanic was good at his job."

"Who'd you meet?"

"A guy named Mort."

Daze smiled. "I've met him. He's one of the guys who has coffee with our little group during break time."

"What do you think of him?" I asked.

"I know nothing about his skill as a mechanic. But he's okay as a fellow worker. Pretty quiet, actually."

"Unfortunate name for a mechanic," I said.

"Like a football player named Dropsy," Daze said.

"Yes, like that. Anyway, the significant piece of information I gleaned, other than wear overalls to do inspections, is that we board the plane to check it out. And we do it alone."

"That could be useful," Daze said. "And nothing would stop you from needing the input from the mechanic on your inside inspection."

"Correct," I said.

"And together with my information, we might even have the beginning of a plan," Daze said. "I worked with a mechanic named Alfonso today."

"You like him, right?"

"Yes. He never tried to haze me like the others. And here is the kicker. He is often the mechanic working on Bachenko's Gulfstream. And would welcome me as a partner the next time he's assigned there."

"Whoa, that's helpful. Of course, we'd need to get around him to do what we have in mind."

"I was thinking about that. Maybe the first time I'll have Alfonso working with me, but if I can show that I can do it alone…"

"The guards will be used to you being there, and

Alfonso might be just as happy to let you deal with that craziness alone.”

“That’s my thought. It will take a little while to get to that point, and I don’t know our timeframe on this project.”

“I don’t know, either. We’re making progress pretty quickly, but we’re clearly not ready to grab the plane yet. And we only asked Bert for a week off.”

“I know. But our vacation might have to be extended. I’ve been meaning to check in on Hippo, anyway. Maybe he has an idea about how busy it is there.”

“And update you on his preparations for his big interview,” she said.

“That’s the idea,” I said.

“We’re supposed to check in with AbbJeff,” Daze said.

“Did you hear from one of them?”

“Abby texted me today. Very cryptic, presumably to protect against prying eyes.”

“What did she say?”

“Stop by on the way home tonight. We have pizza.”

“You think they really have pizza?”

“It wouldn’t surprise me, and I’m hungry.”

“Yeah, me too. Inspecting is hard work.”

“Poor baby,” Daze said. But she was smiling.

20

We stopped off at AbbJeff on our way home, and when we entered the office, we smelled pizza.

"I hope you like pepperoni," Abby said when we arrived. "But we have a plain cheese pie, too."

"We like pepperoni," I said.

We sat at a table in a little kitchenette and ate pizza while we reported to Abby and Jeff what had transpired in our few days of work at the airport.

"You've made a lot of progress," Jeff said. "Very impressive in such a short time."

"I think our biggest problem right now is that neither of us can yet control where our bosses assign us on any day. We think we'll need Lars and/or Liam at some point, but we don't know when. Ideally, Daze and I are both assigned to the Gulfstream and without our respective guardians. Earning our bosses' trust is paramount, or we'll never get to do anything alone."

"I think I might get free at some point," Daze said. "I'm the only A&P certified mechanic in the place, other than Benny. And he's the supervisor. He doesn't work on jets himself. But I admit I don't know when he'll set me free."

"I might get free myself at some point," I said. "Not because I'm more competent than anyone else, but because we're woefully shorthanded. And my co-worker Connie, he seems to go through the motions. I can't imagine him wanting to inspect a jet with a bunch of armed guards watching his every move. And those guards have now seen me once, on my initial tour. They're trained professionals. They'll remember me for sure. And figure I'm okay."

"This all sounds promising," Jeff said. "So, let us show you what we've done to help."

"You might as well just turn your laptop around and let them look," Abby said. Jeff nodded and turned it around for Daze and me to put our heads together and huddle over the screen, which showed a spreadsheet.

"Holy crap," I said.

"We thought you might like that," Abby said. "It's what you think it is. Bachenko's full flight schedule. You see the date highlighted in red?"

Our heads bobbed in affirmative nods. We had a specific date to make our plan work. A sort of D-Day for absconding with a Gulfstream. G-Day.

***

I called Hippo as soon as we arrived home. I wanted to catch him before I had to head to rehearsal, which was fairly soon.

"Business is slow, no doubt about it. Bert had this week pegged as a down week, and as usual, his prognostication was spot on. It's dead in the dining room. At least has been all this week. Other than that, this would be a great week for you and Daisy to come into the kitchen and schmooze, thus easing my profound boredom. No one has missed you at all."

"You miss us," I said.

"Okay, yes I do. But I don't think Bert does at all. The two new kids, Ollie and Dax, are doing fine waiting on empty tables."

"What do you think Bert would say if we needed to extend our week off by another week?"

"Hard to say about what next week will look like, but I bet Bert has already made a guess as to our lunch and dinner traffic. But from what I've seen this week, I doubt it will be a problem. Why? How's everything going at the airport?"

I gave Hip a blow by blow account, and he seemed impressed.

"That's a lot in just a few days," he said.

"Hopefully, the pieces will come together. And sooner rather than later. It's hard to keep up a fake persona for weeks on end."

"It's what you do," Hip said.

"On stage. Not in life."

"Point taken. How's Daisy doing?"

"You can ask her yourself. She's right here." I put the phone on speaker, and Daze gave a response to Hippo's question.

"Okay, I guess. The biggest thing to me is that I'm not flying at all. I'm kind of in withdrawal."

"Can you fly on Saturday without blowing your cover?"

Daze looked at me with pleading eyes, and I nodded.

"If we stay away from Jacksonville, which we always do anyway, we should be fine. I'm certainly not going to ask

Abby or Jeff."

Daze brightened at my response. "We'll stay far, far away from Jacksonville."

"What the hell," I said. "If I can rehearse for a play, you can fly. No one will ever find out."

"Our secret identities will be safe," Daze said solemnly.

I asked Hip about his upcoming interview.

"We leave for London next week," he said. "My interview is next Thursday, but they paid for us to stay for three days. If I get nothing else out of this process, Willy and I will have a nice vacation."

"You'll get the job," I said. "I guarantee it."

"And your guarantee is worth…."

"Maybe not much, but I'm sending good vibes."

"Me too," Daze said. "Good vibes have to help."

Hippo chuckled. "They help me, anyway. Whether they affect the decision makers at the network is another thing altogether."

"Optimism, my boy, optimism."

"Oh, I'm optimistic. Like I said, the worst thing that could happen is that we get an all-expenses paid vacation, complete with spending money, to London. That's the worst. Or, we get that, and I have a new job. One that gets me as far away from Bert's kitchen as possible."

I disconnected and quickly dressed for rehearsal. A rapid jump from Aeronautical Inspector to Shakespearean actor. Quick costume changes are part of my business, so I'm practiced in doing it swiftly. Daze watched the process with amusement.

"You could do that in a telephone booth, just like Superman," she said.

"You've been watching reruns of the original Superman. I'm not sure I've ever even seen a telephone booth."

"Sure you have, admittedly a long time ago. But wasn't that quick change from Clark Kent to Superman cool?"

"It was. Removing his glasses and shedding his outer clothes. And you never saw what he did with that Clark Kent suit. Did he leave it in the telephone booth?"

"It was an imagination thing," Daze said. "Maybe they were magically zapped back to his Clark Kent apartment."

"Maybe so." I kissed Daze and zapped myself out of the apartment and down to the Duster. Another rehearsal awaited.

***

The next morning, during our drive to Jacksonville, Daze talked excitedly about flying on Saturday.

"I'm coming along, right?" I asked. "You're not using your flying day up on one of those rich dudes with the stray hands?"

"Heaven forbid. No, it's you and me up in the air."

"Where are we going?"

"I'm still thinking about it. Right now, I just want to get back in the air and fly somewhere good."

"Why don't we make a day of it? Fly somewhere nice, and bring a picnic lunch, stay a few hours and fly back?"

Daze clapped her hands. "I love picnics."

"Good. So now the only thing we need to decide is

where we're going."

"The big work issue is still how to get us both in that hangar with no one else accompanying us. And how to orchestrate it without looking like that's what we're doing."

"We're going to have to be patient. Get the training wheels off both of us. Right now, we're the new kids in town," Daze said.

"You seem to be a little further along than me in that department."

"Because I'm actually what I purport to be. You're not."

"Yeah, you're an actual mechanic. I'm an actor pretending to have skills I'll never have."

"Oh, you know things. You kind of have to know things if I'm the one teaching you to fly."

"True enough," I said. "Almost as much classroom as cockpit."

"How about Fort Lauderdale?" Daze asked me when we arrived at my hotel shuttle stop.

"We'll have to refuel there," I said.

"So we refuel."

"Okay, Fort Lauderdale it is," I replied before closing the car door and walking over to mooch my latest ride to the airport.

The driver dutifully let me aboard the shuttle, but said this time, "I know you're not a hotel guest."

"So, why are you letting me ride?"

"Look around. Do you see anyone?"

I didn't.

"You're good company. And you must be desperate if you get dropped off by a woman in a late 1980s Plymouth Duster."

"Well, thank you. It's a big help."

Daisy parked the Duster in the employee parking lot and arrived at work a tad early. Benny was there, but no one else.

"Hey Tracy," Benny said. "Alfonso told me you're willing to brave the craziness at Hangar 4 when he next gets assigned there. How does today sound?"

"It's fine with me to go wherever you need me. I don't give a crap if there are people watching, even a bunch of armed guards. Ignoring the noise and doing my work has served me well."

"Good, that's what I try to do, too. Alfonso is a master at it and wants you along. So, review the schematics and latest diagnostics." Benny handed Daze some papers. The rest of the data you can pull up on this iPad." He handed her a tablet. "Bring this with you."

"I'll do that, thanks."

Daisy and Alfonso walked together to Hangar 4.

"Don't make any sudden moves," he said. "I move almost robot-like. Slow, deliberate moves. Nothing to arouse the sleeping beast."

"They sleep on the job?" Daze asked.

"Just a figure of speech. They don't sleep on the job. I'm not sure those guys ever sleep at all. They have laser sharp attention spans. Poised like cobras to strike at a moment's notice. Scary dudes. Just ignore them, and you'll be fine. Probably," he said with a little grin.

Daze responded with her practiced 'nothing bothers me, I just do my job' line, and Alfonso shrugged.

"That's a wonderful skill to have. I'm mostly like that, too. Ignore them and they'll ignore us. I haven't had a problem with them. As the new person, they'll scrutinize you for any sign of a threat, but it's not likely you'll worry them much."

"Because I'm a woman, and short, you mean?"

"Sure. That's their conditioning. Truthfully, someone like you might pose the greatest threat, but those misogynistic morons would never know."

Daze guessed that what Alfonso said was true. And maybe it would work to their advantage.

They walked into Hangar 4 and headed over to the jet. It was a beauty, Daze thought. Every bit as spectacular as she remembered. She put her iPad on an adjacent table, and she and Alfonso gave the jet a once-over. As Alfonso had warned, Daze felt the gaze of four men upon her, watching her every move. She'd thought there were five men, but only four were there. Was one of them somewhere else? She needed to know. It was certainly possible that one was out sick or something, but his absence worried Daze. She didn't want to ask Alfonso, because she'd made a big deal of ignoring distractions. But she'd noticed and made a mental note. One of them might join the others a little later, too.

A thunderous voice rudely interrupted Daisy's thought process. A security guard barked a command at her.

21

"We need to see that thing you placed on the table. What is it?"

Daisy turned toward the speaker. "It's an iPad with access to the technical specifications of the Gulfstream. The boss just gave it to me. Look at it. Even children have these now."

The man walked over to the table, picked up the iPad, turned it over, and even sniffed at it. He had Daisy turn it on, and when she complied, seemed to conclude that it was an iPad. He put it down, gave Daisy a hard stare, presumably memorizing her face.

"You're new," he said, stating the obvious. "What are you, this guy's gopher? Fetching stuff for him?"

"She's a first-rate mechanic," Alfonso said.

"You don't look like a mechanic," he said. "And you're a girl." He looked at Alfonso. "Scraping the bottom of the barrel these days," he said, ignoring Alfonso's denial as he went back to join his fellow mercenaries.

Daisy knew enough not to give an angry response. It

was better for her they underestimate her, but she was a little shaken by the guy's stare. Vowing not to exhibit fear, she simply turned back to Alfonso, and they discussed a strategy for accomplishing the day's work. The guards listened intently to their conversation, but seemed to grow bored. Daisy smiled to herself. Listening to technical aeronautical terms could serve as a sleep aid. Not to her, of course, but their discussion clearly caused the men to go from Defcon 1 to more like Defcon 3. And paved the way for a future visit to Hangar 4.

***

"You tell me you've worked on cars your whole life," Skip said to me after I'd settled at my desk. Connie's station was empty, as it seemed to be most of the time.

"Sure, I said. "Helped my daddy when I was five years old. He loved taking wrecks and fixing them up. And so do I," I said. "Not much chance to do that now, unless you count my Plymouth Duster. That needs all kinds of fixing up to keep on the road. And when you're as financially challenged as I always am, that's pretty much what I work on now."

"How would you like to work on a Cadillac?"

"For what? Changing the oil? The owner can go to Jiffy Lube. They don't need me."

"It's a 1975 Coupe de Ville."

"Whoa."

"Exactly. Interested?"

"Anyone with an interest in cars would drool over that. It's not a '59 Series 62 convertible, but the '75 Coupe de Ville was a magnificent car."

"Is a magnificent car. Our illustrious airport chief owns one. Had it over to one of our hangars earlier this week for our mechanics to work on it. But they're airline mechanics. You obviously know your cars."

"He has a classic Cadillac. Why doesn't he just bring it to an auto mechanic?"

"Says he can't find a good one. And to be honest with you, he's cheap. He wants someone competent, sure, but free. You know how much a classic car mechanic charges?"

"More than I can afford. But he's screwing up a true gem by entrusting it to amateurs."

"Like you?"

"I'm an amateur, yes, but I know the car. My daddy and I worked on one once."

"You worked on a 1975 Cadillac Coupe de Ville?"

"Yes sir. With my father. He was a master mechanic, and enjoyed taking wrecks and fixing them up. And one wreck was a 1975 Coupe de Ville. In horrible shape. What does this guy's car look like?"

"It's not a wreck. It's a beauty. Must have cost the guy a pretty penny."

"If he's looking, count me in. I'd love to work on that car again."

***

I told Daze about it on my way home.

"Did you really work on a 1975 Cadillac Coupe de Ville with your daddy? And was he really a master mechanic?"

"Oh, geez, of course not. I don't know shit about working on a Cadillac. My dad and I worked on a few old cars, and it's true I know my way around an engine, but I never did that."

"So, you lied to him?"

"I acted," I said. "My role demands that I worked on Cadillacs, so ergo, I worked on Cadillacs."

"It could be helpful to us," Daze acknowledged.

"My initial instinct was to grab the opportunity, without thinking about the rest. But I know enough to not embarrass myself if the owner watches me. I can study up on the actual engine in the '75 Coupe de Ville. And I know the car. It's a true classic. Not something to be owned by a cretin who will get any free mechanic to service it. I'm sure he thought, wow, what a cool car. I'll buy it, knowing nothing about its proper care. Or he inherited it. I suppose that's possible. But take one look at that car, and you know you need professional help."

"And you're not it," Daze said.

"No, I'm not. But I know an opportunity when I see one. And this is a golden chance to get Lars or Liam, or both into the airport, mere yards away from Hangar 4."

"By telling the airport chief that you need help to do a terrific job, and know a guy, maybe brothers, who are veritable geniuses with Cadillacs."

"You got it."

"This could be the break we're looking for, if you play your cards right, and carefully."

"I plan to," I said. "Now let's hear about your big adventure today."

Daze told me the entire story. I cringed a little when she described the big, muscular guy getting right in her face with a cold, menacing stare.

"That must have been scary," I said.

"Yeah, it was. But I was determined not to show fear, and I think I pulled it off. I tried to project that I was just a simple mechanic trying to do her job. No threat, no devious motives. And I think it helped big time that he viewed me as a girl, who probably was just there to fetch stuff for Alfonso. He even used those words. Alfonso told the guy that I was a skilled mechanic, but I know he didn't believe it."

"I think the guy's attitude sucks," I said. "But he's just playing right into our hands. Underestimate you. And if I can pull off the same thing on my next visit there, something like I know nothing, I just do whatever Skip says, we might have a perfect setup for the ultimate goal."

"You said they didn't watch you too closely when you did your tour with Skip, so maybe you're halfway there already."

"Oh, they scrutinized me at first, but I guess they're just used to seeing Skip, so they thought I posed no issue. A new guy, that didn't look tough or otherwise threatening."

"The real question is how we'll get everyone into the hangar at the right time. We'll know any changes to Bachenko's schedule in advance. Abby and Jeff will take care of that. We can't very well grab the plane if Bachenko flies it off early."

"Unless we stowaway and overpower him in flight," I said.

"I'd rather just fly it away right from the airport. I doubt we could pull off the overpower thing."

"No. Not likely. But we can't work at the airport forever, either."

"No, but we've made a lot of progress in the time we've worked there. We have the pieces in place. We just need to pull them all together."

"I agree. Getting the two of us flying solo, so to speak at Hangar 4 without Bachenko showing up, and figuring out a way for Lars or Liam to get on the plane with us, without arousing the suspicion of the guards."

"I'm more confident of getting us there together than getting one of the Swedish giants to evade the security guys."

"Yeah, I agree. I bet I can get them close, but the last part is tough. Unless…"

"What?"

"Unless we get Lars and Liam to overpower all the guards."

"Tall order," Daze said. "Those security guys are big and armed."

"Lars and Liam are bigger," I said.

"Like mountains," Daze agreed. "We'll just have to see how this all plays out. We need Benny and Skip to set us free to work alone."

"You know, I think that might happen soon for me. Connie seems to never show up. I don't know what his story is, but it makes us shorthanded."

"Almost forcing Skip to send you out on your own. I love it."

"Are you thinking about Saturday?"

"Almost every waking moment. I have withdrawal symptoms."

"Are we still going to Fort Lauderdale?"

"I was thinking about that. I'm not sure we can find a quiet picnic spot there. It's more known for pandemonium."

"We need somewhere with a nearby airport. Preferably a small local one. Fort Lauderdale airport is way bigger than we need."

"It is, but it also has easily available ground transportation."

"We'll think about it. We have until Saturday to decide and file a flight plan."

22

"Let her hang me: he that is well hanged in this world needs to fear no colours."

"Cut. That was good Trip. Do it that way. The way you did it before sounded stilted."

"Okay, I will."

Carleton looked at his watch. "I think we'll stop there. Leave on a high note, so to speak."

Some weary actors breathed sighs of relief and filed out.

I hung behind to chat with Carleton.

"Your real opinion," I said. "How is this ragtag band doing?"

Carleton sighed. "Better than I expected. Not where I want to be."

"I think Beatrice is coming along well," I said. "Lindsay, too."

Carleton nodded. "I agree. But Allison, I just don't know if I can salvage an adequate performance out of her. Nor Greg."

"Have you considered their understudies?"

"I have. But I'm not sure they're even as good. That's why they're understudies."

"I don't know about that," I said. "I've been an understudy, and at times I've wondered why the actor who got the part was on any stage. Sometimes, directors get it wrong, or an actor auditioning has a bad day. Just a suggestion, mind you, but in particular, you might take another look at Brendan and Alyssa."

"You've noticed something?" Carleton asked.

"Just a hunch. But I think those two have more potential than Allison and Greg. And more than a hunch. Allison and Greg might not be upset if they're pulled from the play."

"I won't ask," Carleton said. "But I might take you up on your suggestions. Alyssa and Brendan can't be much worse than what we have now. And I can't have the production brought down by awful acting." He sighed. "If I'm going down, I want to go down with the best group I can assemble."

He paused. "Don't you dare abandon me."

"I won't. I'm in it for the long haul."

I hoped that was not a bald-faced lie.

***

"You're early," Daze said when I returned.

"Yeah, I think Carleton was a little demoralized about two actors. I said my 'well hanged' line for the third time, and he liked the third rendition so much he ended rehearsal on a high note."

"The 'Let her hang me' line?" Daze had listened to me practicing my lines so many times, she could probably recite them herself. She also put up with reading various female lines. Daze was a good sport about it. If it was important to me, it was important to her. One of the many reasons I loved her.

"That's the one. I guess I finally got the cadence right." I said it again to Daze, and she smiled.

"I think you've got it," she said in her best British accent.

"Hey, that's not bad. You should teach that to Hip and Willy. They'll sound just like the natives."

"You pick up all kinds of totally useless stuff hanging around with you," she said.

I puffed out my chest with shoulders back and said, "I am the very embodiment of a purveyor of finely honed, carefully considered useless stuff."

"Yes, you are."

"Hey, have you given any thought to where we're going on Saturday?"

Daze flashed a dazzling smile. "I have just the place. Fairly close, good airport, only 51 nautical miles, so plenty of room for pre-landing acrobatics, no need for refueling, easily available ground transportation, and lots and lots of quiet green spaces for a picnic."

"Sounds perfect," I said. "And 51 nautical miles is equal to…um…"

"Ninety-five kilometers, and fifty-nine of what you'd call regular miles."

"Exactly. I knew that."

"You're supposed to know that as an exalted aeronautical inspector."

"No one's asked that question yet."

"And now you'll be ready if someone does. I think I have a conversion chart around her somewhere, so you can study."

"In the morning. I'm tuckered out."

"You go to sleep. I'll join you soon. I still have some reading to do."

"What are you reading?"

"Just some technical manuals I want to be warm on. I'm just finishing up now. I'll be along in a few minutes."

I nodded, brushed my teeth and went straight to bed.

***

"Did you stay up late?" I asked Daze as I sipped my morning coffee.

"Maybe an hour after you went to bed. I don't have personal experience with the new line of Embraer executive jets, and it seems like they take up almost half the hangars. I figured I'd better look like I knew enough about them."

"Do mechanics have personal familiarity with all the jets they service?" I was genuinely interested.

"No, we don't. There is some specialization, like the Bombardier guy, the Northrop Grumman guy, the…" she paused and flashed a grin… "the Embraer gal. It's not much different from auto mechanics, right? Most mechanics will service any vehicle you bring in, even if they don't know shit from shinola about the car. And there are computer diagnostic tools that are specific to a particular car. So, some mechanics work directly for different car makers, and develop expertise in a single kind of car. The 'I do all cars' mechanic doesn't have the right tools to do the job well, but he takes it on anyway, and does a substandard job, or maybe gets it done well almost by accident. Aircraft are the same thing, but in our case, we all have access to the particularized software diagnostic tools, so with a little study, we can service the jets pretty well. But I emphasize the study part. You can't just bludgeon your way into an engine. You must review the schematics, the latest diagnostics, and you have to know what the hell you're doing."

"Hence the late-night studying."

"Yeah. I've worked on Embraer jets before, including the other day, but I have no experience with their new line. Of course, no one else does, either."

"One night of studying, and you're the expert."

She gave me a slight bow. "At your service. Now finish your coffee, the Duster chariot awaits."

I walked into the office to find Connie sitting at his desk. Skip was sitting on mine, chatting with him. They turned to look at me, and I said, "Did I miss a meeting?" I wanted to ask Connie why his royal-ness had graced us with his presence, but I wisely kept my mouth shut. But it bummed me he was there, because our plan likely depended upon the office being shorthanded.

Skip turned to me.

"Connie's moving back to Missouri. So, it looks like it will just be you and me for a while. I don't know when they'll hire another inspector."

Connie looked up, and surprised the living daylights out of me by saying, "Hey, sorry, man. I know I was a little frosty to you. Skip tells me you're a standup guy, and willing to learn and to work. Not some know-it-all management plant." He paused and gave me an inscrutable look. "Not sure I believe him, mind you, but I am truly sorry to leave the two of you alone to handle all the inspections. If you're ready to learn and work, there's no better way than a trial by fire. That's how I learned, as Skip can tell you. But I have some important personal stuff to attend to, and it isn't in Jacksonville. I need to move back to Missouri, at least for a while."

Skip rose, and Connie emptied his desk. Once finished, he shook our hands and walked out, carrying his box of personal effects.

I couldn't believe my good fortune. Shedding a toxic fellow worker and clearing the way for our plan to take shape, all in one fell swoop. Then I glanced over at a dejected-looking Skip, and felt bad. He'd been nice to me, and now I was rejoicing in the disaster he was facing. But I'd do my best to be a great inspector, or at least someone he could count on, but alas, only for a short time.

Skip watched Connie shut the door, sighed, and handed me some files.

"Lots to do today, so look at these files. We'll do these inspections together today, but you'll be on your own tomorrow."

I scanned the one-page summary of the files on the top.

"These are all scheduled for 11 a.m. And later. What are we doing this morning?"

"We're looking at a classic Cadillac," he replied. "Before I knew Connie was leaving, I offered you up as a mechanic."

"You did what?"

"You heard me. And from what you've told me, my blatant attempt to curry favor with the airport chief was a perfect gambit. Imagine his delight when I told him that one of his employees had worked on his very car."

"Well, yes, I said. It was a long time ago, but to be honest with you…I'd absolutely love to get my hands on one of them. Thanks Skip." I stopped, as if taking a moment to reconsider. "But I can't promise anything. Like I said, it's been a long time, and he should really get a specialized mechanic for such a special automobile."

"He knows, but he's the definition of a cheapskate. So, you're it. Don't let me down."

"I'll do my best," I assured him. "Lead the way."

We walked down the little staircase, and over to Hangar 1. The Cadillac sat in a small cul-de-sac about fifty feet from the hangar.

"He leaves this outside? Oh my God, he doesn't deserve such a precious jewel."

"I know, right? I think he used to have it garaged, but ever since he enlisted the aircraft mechanics to service it, it's sat right here. Dopey, if you ask me."

"Criminal. What have the other mechanics been doing with it?"

"Nothing. They pretend to look at it, claim lack of knowledge, but I think they're afraid to screw something up and be responsible."

"And I'm not afraid of that?"

Skip laughed. "Apparently, you aren't smart enough to be afraid."

"This little baby needs help," I said. "Proper care. So, if Mr. Cheap won't hire a real classic Cadillac mechanic, I'm going to give her the attention she needs."

"Good boy," Skip said. He handed me some keys. "Take an initial look this morning and assess what the car needs. I'll check back with you in an hour."

I nodded and gave an inward cheer. Skip was leaving me alone with the car, and its owner was an ignorant dunce. I could say almost anything at all was wrong with it, and say I needed to consult with an expert to do a good job. A Swedish expert, and his equally knowledgeable brother. I just needed to work out the timing. Not a minor task.

23

"I hear you got a little hazing from the security staff in Hangar 4," Benny said a while after she and Alfonso returned.

"Nothing I couldn't handle," Daisy said, as nonchalantly as possible.

"So I hear. Alfonso said you were rock solid, in a nothing bothers me kind of way."

Daisy looked at Benny for a moment. "It bothered me. I get annoyed at cretins like that. But there was no percentage in a nasty response. It's not like I could kick the guy's ass, so ignoring him seemed like the best option."

"It's my option, too," Benny said. "Alfonso's as well. Fighting with those guys makes no sense, and I'm glad to see that you have the brains to avoid it. They're a fact of life in Hangar 4, and we have a duty to service that Gulfstream, so we have to put up with some crap. The good news is that they don't seem to keep it up. You're a known quantity now, so they'll likely leave you alone in the future." Benny gave Daisy a long look. "Will there be another visit to Hangar 4? Because I need your skill set, so if that place is not for you, I have plenty of work away from there. No shame in it, either. Most of the mechanics try to avoid that duty."

"I told you before, I go where I'm needed. If you need someone to service the Gulfstream, I have absolutely no problem doing it. I don't run away from anyone. I won't fight them, because that's just stupid. But I'll put up with a lot of misogynist crap, because I've done it my entire work life." Daze paused. "People respect hard work and outstanding skills, and I think I show both. So, the hazing, if you want to call it that, rarely occurs after people see what I can do."

Benny nodded. "Like here," he said. "Everyone gave you a hard time on your first day. Now you sit at the coffee break table with all of them, and many ask you for advice. Big change in a short time."

"The guards at the Gulfstream will do their thing. My job is to focus on the aircraft, and ignore the noise. So, bottom line, if you need me there, I'm all in, with Alfonso or without. Up to you."

"Good to know," Benny said. "But not today. Today, I have you working with Todd in Hangar 7."

"The Embraer Legacy 450," Daisy said.

"Good memory. You warm on it?"

"Yeah, I know that jet. And truthfully, I did a little studying last night on the Embraer and Bombardier jets that populate most of our hangars."

"You remember all the jets we have, and studied them at home?" Benny's tone was one of disbelief.

"I didn't remember them. There's a list in the first-day packet you gave me. Daisy went to her designated locker and pulled out the list. See?"

"I'd forgotten about that. I thought you were some kind of savant."

"Oh, I am that," Daisy said with a smile. "If savant means study, hard work and practice, I'm definitely a savant."

Benny chuckled. "Okay, you got me."

Daisy was fine working with Todd. He was a big kid, maybe 20 years old, with red hair, a freckled face and a boyish, shy smile. The two of them walked together to Hangar 7, and Todd peppered her with questions about the Legacy 450.

"I never worked on her," Todd said, charmingly referring to the jet as female. "I'm new here, just like you…well I don't mean I have your experience…I just mean…"

Daisy flashed a sunny smile at the lad. "You mean we're both new employees? We're co-workers. We learn from each other. Did you review the schematics of this Embraer jet?"

"I did," he said, his face reddening almost as much as his hair. "I mean, I looked them over. The latest diagnostics, too. But they were unlike anything I've seen before, so I doubt you can learn anything from me."

"You'd be surprised," Daisy said. "I needed to review the specs on this jet myself. And we'll run diagnostics ourselves to figure out what's troubling her. And we'll figure it out together."

***

I was all alone, with the keys to a classic Cadillac. In case anyone was watching me from the nearby Hangar 1, I put on a show. First, I walked around the entire perimeter of the vehicle, touching the chassis in various places, and dutifully writing things down in the little notebook I always carried. I had it to record acting notes, but no one else knew that. The automobile notes included such things as mild abrasion at location L-4; tiny convexity R-6 (repainted?).

The locations referred to left and right. But the numbers were a figment of my imagination. I just wanted to have data to discuss, so it was logical to start on the outside and work my way to the engine.

After completing my perimeter study, taking up about 15 minutes of my allotted hour, I unlocked the driver's side of the car and sat down. I turned the key in the ignition and the engine rewarded me by roaring to life. I let it idle for a few moments, while I jotted down some notes I designated as auditory—such as the imaginary intermittent catch in the engine noise, the faint whining hum—not a good sign—check out. Possible safety issue. I made a few more cryptic notes that meant nothing, but all related to questionable sounds in the engine. I spent some time with that, because I knew for a fact that sounds are the most difficult tissues to diagnose, and I needed things like that. Visual problems you need to point out. If someone doesn't hear what you hear, you can suggest they don't have a practiced ear, that from experience you know what even a faint whir means. And engines will always have sounds. They may be wonderful sounds, but not everyone knows what an engine should sound like. And the owner of this car clearly did not.

This engine sounded almost perfect. Whoever had been working on it knew his or her stuff. Probably one of the aeronautical mechanics drafted to service the car. So, I wondered why he wanted me to look at it. Maybe a sound that he heard that the other mechanic told him was not a problem. Because hello, it wasn't one. But the guy didn't trust an aircraft mechanic, so he enlisted…an actor.

I popped the hood and took a gander at the engine. I poked and prodded and jotted down notes. And from what I could tell, whoever preceded me in servicing this vehicle had skills. The car was almost fifty years old, and it looked like this? With an ignorant owner who had no clue what a treasure he had? Or maybe knew it was a classic, but entrusted his baby to a random aircraft mechanic rather than a specialist in classic Cadillacs. But he'd been lucky, because the mechanic he chose knew cars. No doubt about it. And that presented a difficult problem for me. How to get him to accept the help of a faux expert if the car was in fine working order?

But I knew how. I'm an actor. I make up a problem, that is just too vexing even for my wonderful skills. The car deserves the best, and all that. But I also knew another card to play with this cheapskate. It will cost nothing, because the Swedish brothers owe me a favor. And I'd even say this with a straight face: "Consider this an unabashed attempt to curry favor with my bosses. Yes sir, I'm sucking up by bringing in these fine experts." With the right tone, I knew I could pull it off. And I had to, because this car was in fantastic shape, inside and out.

When Skip returned, I still had my head under the hood. I made it a point to mutter a lot close to the time when I knew he'd return, and when he tapped me on the shoulder, I lurched in apparent surprise, and almost hit my head. I stepped back and took a hopefully sad looking back glance at the engine and then faced Skip.

"How's it look?" Skip asked.

I paused for a long time, staring at my feet, then looked up and said, "It's a beautiful car. But it needs love and attention, which I'm afraid has been mostly absent." I paused, and as if remembering something, I added, "I don't mean that the prior mechanic wasn't well meaning, or didn't know engines. Please don't think I'm criticizing anyone. I meant no disrespect. I'm sure every single mechanic here has great skill. We're inspectors and it's our job to make certain that's true. It's just that this requires specialized attention. It's not a jet, it's an automobile. Both have engines, but of course, all engines are not the same. Even our aircraft here have many different manufacturers and engines." I pointed to the Cadillac. "This little lady needs the right type of attention."

"Okay, I get it," Skip said. "Can you provide it? Or do I have to tell my boss I've let him down? That the car needs help, but I have no one to fix it."

"I'll spend some time with the car," I said. "In between inspections. I think I can help, but before I operate, I need the right tools, and more than the hour you gave me."

"Understood. We'll figure that out. But we have inspections to do, and this will be the last time we do them together. With Connie headed back to Missouri, we need to both go solo."

"I can handle that," I said.

"I sure hope so. Otherwise, we're screwed."

I handed him the keys to the Cadillac, and closed the hood, and we headed back to the office.

24

Daze told me about working with Todd.

"Sweet guy," Daze said. "Very deferential to the old lady he was working with."

"You're an old lady?"

"I am to him. He's maybe 20. Pretty good natural mechanic, and eager to learn. That's an excellent combination."

"So, you took him under your wing," I teased.

"Yes, I did," she said. "But the importance of that is I'm now free to work alone. Benny trusts me to serve as a mentor to Todd, so he doesn't think I need supervision anymore."

"I think I'm in the same position," I said, and told Daze about my day with the Cadillac, and Skip's comment that today was the last day we did inspections together "So, I'm on my own, too."

"Perfect," said Daze. "And I love how you set the stage for a Liam and Lars' appearance."

"Things are coming together," I said.

At Abby's texted request, we stopped by AbbJeff for a

short briefing.

"No pizza," I said with a smile.

"Not today," Abby said. "We can order Chinese if you're hungry."

"No need," Daze said. "He's just teasing."

"I figured this as a very brief visit, so you can tell us where you stand."

We told her and Jeff about the current status, which pleased both of them.

"You've done a lot more in four days than we could have imagined," Abby said.

"It's all set up," Jeff added. "We just need to figure out timing."

"Some of that will depend on where we get assigned," I said. "We're free to work alone, but we don't control when we're working in Hangar 4."

"Any thoughts on how to manipulate the schedule?" Abby asked.

Daze and I looked at each other. "We talk about that all the time," Daze said, "but we haven't figured that piece out yet. Even if one of us could get assigned to Hangar 4 on the appointed day, we don't know how to arrange simultaneous assignments. We can text each other, of course, but that's still depending on fate. We need something concrete."

"We also need to have Liam and Lars on site when that happens," I said. "And I keep thinking that the answer to our scheduling issues revolves around that Cadillac."

"Tomorrow's Friday," Jeff said. "Hopefully, we can get a coherent plan ready for a Gulfstream takeoff next week. This can't wait forever, and I imagine the two of you want to get back to being Tripper Steele and Daisy Wilson."

"We would," Daze said for both of us. "And I can't wait to get rid of this awful dark hair."

"Maybe you can wash it off on the weekend," I suggested.

"Be careful," Abby warned. "This may sound trite, but there are eyes and ears everywhere. You don't want to be recognized as a blonde. Too many questions."

"We'll be careful," I said. "I don't want anyone to recognize me as an actor, either."

"We're monitoring Bachenko's schedule," Jeff said. "Any change in his plans may involuntarily hurry us along. We don't want the plane to leave Jacksonville unless it's piloted by you," he said to Daze.

We bid the two of them goodbye, grabbed a bite to eat at one of the many restaurants lining A1A. On the way home, we discussed strategy.

"Maybe we need to take a test flight, requiring both the inspector and a mechanic. Or something like that."

"Sure, why not? How can I inspect without checking it in flight? I wonder whether the inspectors ever do that. I'll ask tomorrow."

"I'll ask around, too. Not Benny. One of the other mechanics might know."

"And after Friday is done…"

"Weekend flight and picnic, yay!"

"We'll grab some fixings for our picnic on our way home tomorrow. Do you have a cooler?"

Daze nodded. "I do, but not the goodies to put in it."

"Grocery shopping tomorrow evening," I said. "Picnic food shopping."

"I think I have one of those water-proof on one side blankets, too. I'll look tonight."

***

I called Hippo to get a status in the restaurant.

"He's fine with you two being out another week," Hippo said in response to my inquiry. "You need to ask Bert yourselves, but I tested the waters for you, and I think he'd be glad to not have to pay you anything. It's not like you can ask for another week of leave with pay. You'll be saving him money in a lean time for his business."

"Thanks, Hip," I said. "We'll call him in the morning. And the leave without pay thing is a cold reminder to Daze and me. We've received no pay yet from our fake jobs, and rent to pay. We'd better get results soon from what we're doing, or we'll be out on the street."

"How's your project going?" he asked.

"Pretty well," I said, and gave him a brief rundown.

"That sounds good," he said. "And on the lack of income thing—I can lend you some money to cover the rent."

"No need for that," I said hastily. "We have time. But thanks anyway."

"You said those two, Abby and Jeff, claimed they had money. Maybe you should ask for an advance. Like a good faith deposit on the work you're doing."

"Not a bad idea," I said. "I think we're okay so far, but thank you for the idea."

I told Daze what he'd suggested, and she smiled.

"He's a prince," she said, and I nodded.

"We each still have a little money. It doesn't have to be much, but they talked big. They should at least cover our expenses."

"Maybe so," Daze said. "I've given up both my waitressing money and my flying lessons income. Neither was much, but it paid the bills. I don't want to run through all of my savings."

"I don't either. I have little, but I'm earning nothing right now."

"Aren't we supposed to get paid for our new jobs?"

"Yes. I checked. Every other week they pay us a ten-work day paycheck. I suppose we could wait for that."

"We're supposed to wrap this whole thing up next week," Daze pointed out.

"Before payday," I said.

"We're working for nothing," Daze said. "Unless we pull off the reclamation of the Gulfstream."

"And even then, all we have is promises from two people we just met, and a man running a business we know nothing about."

"Are we being foolish?" Daze asked. "Pie in the sky and all that."

"I wish I knew. They talked about a lot of money, but no dollar figure, and it's not like we have a contract. We have promises."

"We're in it now," she said. "All we've done is work four days. We can bail out if we want."

"Do you want to?"

Daze gave it some thought. "No," she intoned. "Let's play it out and see where it leads us. But I hope they all pay up if we accomplish our mission. And I hope we can get Bachenko out of my life."

"Repo of the Gulfstream might not do that. But finding the data AbbJeff is looking for—that might do it."

"Do you think it will be evidence of criminal activity? Or just sharp practices to get Abby and Jeff out of their company?" Daze asked.

"It could be both, or neither. We just don't know."

"Accessing the data might itself be criminal," Daze said, a worried look creasing her face.

"Yeah, I thought of that, too. The two of them hacking into Bachenko's software, to get us a schedule, can't be exactly legal itself."

"We'll just repo the plane," I said. "And leave the safecracking and data mining to AbbJeff and Lars and Liam."

"If we get that far," I said.

"We will. That Gulfstream is as good as in the air, heading for London."

"Funny how we're going to London, just like Hip and Willy."

"We're not being put up in the Savoy," I said. "Unless we are. No one has talked about that."

"We have some details to work out with AbbJeff," Daze said. "We only have an outline. Repo the plane and fly it to London. Heathrow or Gatwick? They don't say. Where we'll stay when we get there? They don't say. How much money are they going to pay us? Again, nothing more than a lot of money. Not a specific sum."

"I have one more," I said. "Do we have a signed piece of paper allowing us to repo the plane, so no one accuses us of stealing it?"

"We need to ask these things at our next pizza meeting."

***

The next morning, Daze drove us to Jacksonville. En-route, I called Bert, and luckily caught him in a good mood.

"Oh, that's no problem. Very slow this week. But I expect the following week to be huge. I'll need all-hands-on-deck."

"The regatta," I said. "Nice nautical reference."

"I thought you'd like that. Yes, and it brings plenty of hungry boat race spectators. It's a very profitable week for us, so make sure this extended vacation you and Daze are on doesn't interfere with you showing up then."

I was going to say it wasn't a vacation, but decided it wasn't worth the effort. So, I just thanked him and told him we'd definitely be there for regatta week.

"We're good to go," I told Daze.

"I heard. Regatta week is a moneymaker for the restaurants, and servers like us. Lots of tips from intoxicated and hungry people."

"We'll show up that week no matter what happens with this project. We owe it to Bert. But maybe we'll make a lot of money on this, and not have to wait tables anymore."

"I'm hoping we get a little more useful information today. If our target date for flying that plane out of Jacksonville is next week, we'll need to get our plan to take shape."

And we did, almost as soon as I entered the office.

Posted on the office bulletin board was a schedule of all the inspections we needed to get done the next week. Nine, and number 7 on the list was the Gulfstream in Hangar 4.

"I saw the schedule," I told Skip.

"Good. We each need to do at least two a day, now that Connie has departed to a better place."

"You sound like he died. He's in Missouri."

"Sometimes I think anywhere is a better place than here. Two inspections a day? We can do it, but we'll need a third person in here soon, or we'll go nuts. And you probably saw that one inspection is Hangar 4, with all those military guys looking over your shoulder. Ugh. I'll do that one, of course. Don't worry, I'm not the kind of supervisor who sticks the new guy with the hardest jobs."

I knew I needed to react fast to this. Skip had just served up a perfect opportunity on a silver platter, but he'd gobbled it right up before I could leap at it.

"I'll do that one," I said. "I'll consider it a great opportunity to prove my worth to you. What better way to curry favor than to take an unpleasant chore away from your boss?"

Skip smiled. "As you saw on your tour, those guys watch everything. If you blink the wrong way, they'll be all over you. They were mostly well-behaved when we visited, but it wasn't a full-blown inspection, just a tour. They're not always like that. Sometimes, they're downright scary."

"As you've probably noticed, not much bothers me. I'll just do my job in the most non-threatening, robot-like way and get the hell out of there."

"Well put. Okay, against my better judgment, you'll handle that one. I've put it down for next Thursday. The owner hasn't notified us he's taking a trip next week, but with this guy, that could change in a heartbeat. If he wants to fly before

Thursday, we'll have to move up the inspection."

I nodded, pretending to have moved on to things that actually interested me. But I was elated. Now to figure out how to get Daze there on Thursday, and Lars and Liam to be invited to work on the Cadillac that same day. I waited a little before raising the issue with Skip. I definitely didn't want him even subliminally linking the two together.

25

Benny assigned Daisy to Hangar 11 on Friday, to work on a Bombardier Challenger 350. And for the first time, she went alone. A good sign, she thought. She wondered how to get him to send her to Hangar 4. Although she assumed he'd do so at some point, they didn't have the luxury of waiting until that happened. As she evaluated her current engine, she received a text from Trip, reporting that Skip had assigned him to inspect Bachenko's jet on Thursday. Good news, but the plan required both her and Tip there at that time. Benny had not set a weekly schedule. He seemed to go day by day. She'd have to work on that problem after lunch, and just focus on the Challenger 350 in front of her.

***

"Hey Skip, before I head out to today's inspections, do you want me to look in on the Cadillac?"

"Not today. We're too busy, and I have heard nothing from upstairs, so maybe he's happy right now. He's a little baffling. First, he needs it to be checked out immediately, then he seems to forget all about it. He'll probably think of nothing else over the weekend, and want you back there on Monday. But for now, let's just do our actual jobs."

That's just what we did the rest of the day. I took

comfort knowing that Thursday was the day, and it would be all over soon. And I still had plenty of time to work out bringing in Lars and Liam to give their expert advice about the Cadillac. I'd ask for their help as a personal favor to Skip, I thought, with a little laugh to myself.

But that turned out not to be the major problem. When Daze picked me up at the hotel, she told me that right before quitting time, Benny had asked to speak with her.

"What did he want?"

"By itself, it's not a bad thing. It might even be good, but I'm not sure. A lot depends on your supervisor."

I listened a little impatiently and finally broke in. "What did Benny say?"

"Oh, I guess I didn't text you. Bachenko's jet needs to be ready by Thursday, so Benny asked me if I was still willing to do what's necessary to clear it for takeoff then. And of course I am, because that's the day we intended to move anyway, but the wrinkle now is…"

"We won't be alone. I mean alone with all of those goons. And Bachenko there, too, with his pilot and crew. We can't do it Thursday."

"No. G-Day is now Wednesday."

"Skip didn't tell me about it," I said. "Probably because no one told him. But my understanding is that Bachenko will need the inspection before he takes off for parts unknown. So, we're probably good. On Monday, Skip will move the inspection up to Wednesday, when you're there, and we'll grab the Gulfstream then. I'll figure out a way to get Lars and Liam there, or at least a few hangars down, on Wednesday. If the airport chief doesn't specifically request it, I'll just invent a reason. Something I forgot to check out, a real safety issue that I'd be horrified if anyone was hurt because of my oversight. Something like that."

Daze looked over at me. "Sometimes your ability to lie at the drop of a hat scares me."

"Oh please," I said. "I'm an actor. And I've never even told you so much as a fib."

"No, you haven't. But still…"

"I might have played too many roles in my life than is good for me," I allowed. "But I know the difference between roles I assume and the real world."

"Oh, I guess you do," she said. "And this is a wonderful time to have your acting skills on our side. We need to pull this off and move on with our lives. You need to act, and I need to fly."

I nodded. "Hopefully, we both get to do that next week. I'm looking at this whole thing as a role in a dramatic production. A bad one, but I'm no stranger to those."

"We need to report our latest information to AbbJeff."

"I think they were expecting us to drop by tonight, anyway. End of the work week and all."

"Tomorrow we get to fly again. And have a picnic."

"Pretty excited, aren't you?"

"I am. I almost can't stand waiting until tomorrow."

"I feel that way, too. We'll get an early start."

"Up at five a.m.," she said.

I smiled. "Maybe. Is Dennis there that early?"

"The place opens up at six-sharp."

"And six-sharp, we'll be standing there."

Daze just beamed.

We stopped by and briefed Abby and Jeff.

"We were going to tell you that when you got here," Jeff said. "I spotted the change in schedule this afternoon. He's definitely scheduled to fly out on Thursday." He looked at me. "Daisy is all set, it would seem. Do you think you can get your boss to reschedule for Wednesday?"

"No problem. I assume he'll get a call or email, or however he gets this kind of news, on Monday. We already agreed I'm handling Hangar 4. I just need him to still assign me there on the changed date. And figure out a way to get Lars and Liam nearby at the same time."

"You've got your work cut out for you," Abby observed. "Anyway, enjoy your weekend. You'll be busy next week."

***

We flew both days of the weekend, and thoroughly enjoyed our temporary respite from the tense operation in which we'd embroiled ourselves. And we made a pact not to speak about it until Monday morning. Both days included plenty of time for Daisy's aerial acrobatics, and a fabulous picnic in a quiet spot in Gainesville. But the peaceful good times ended when I landed the Cessna at our home airport. Next week, Daisy and I were flying a Gulfstream to London.

26

"**G**ood morning, Terry," Skip greeted me on Monday morning.

"Hi Skip." I made a show of looking around the office.

"What are you looking for?"

"A cot, a sleeping bag, maybe a camp stove. You are always here, no matter how early I arrive."

"You're not early," he pointed out.

"Well, you know what I mean."

"Yeah, I do. Another slave to his job. That's me. Hey Terry, are you still game for Hangar 4?"

"Sure, live dangerously, that's me."

"No, seriously."

"Sure," I said. "I told you I would do it. I haven't gotten cold feet. Maybe after I'm dumb enough not to be scared this time, my tune will be a little different next time, but right now, I'm ready, willing and able to charge into battle."

"You're an odd bird," Skip said.

"So I've been told. Truthfully, the bluster keeps me sane."

Skip chuckled. "Okay, you seem up to the job, and no way to really know until you do it. And they moved it up to Wednesday."

I feigned surprise. "Really? Why?"

"The owner needs it on Thursday. I'm surprised he even gave us this much notice. Sometimes he just shows up, and we have to scramble to get the Gulfstream cleared for his majesty."

"Tough being you."

"Sometimes, it's a living hell. And trust me, at times, you'll need more than that quirky sense of humor of yours to keep from going bonkers."

"That bad, huh?"

"Worse. Anyway, here's your data sheets for today's inspections. You're on your own. Make me proud."

"Yes sir," I said, eschewing the snappy salute I really, really wanted to give. Over the top, and not helpful.

I donned my overalls in the little bathroom/dressing room in the back of the office, grabbed my clipboard, and headed out. But before I opened the door, Skip called me back.

"What's up?" I asked.

"The Cadillac. The boss says something is wrong with it. Some sound he didn't like." Skip offered a cross between a baying hound and a whinnying horse. "I think that's what he told me. Close to that, anyway."

"Are you sure it wasn't more like this?" I asked, emitting a whirring sound followed by a clank.

"No, I don't think so. Maybe he meant more like this."

Skip gave off a deep sounding, quick whistle. "But no clank, I'm sure of it."

"No clank is good," I said. "Very good. But the…" I whistled like an owl… "is troubling."

Skip started laughing. "This is crazy. You're crazy. Just go look at it and listen for yourself." He checked the calendar. "After you finish up with Hangar 1. Here are the keys."

I nodded. "Will do. I'll get to the bottom of what actual sound is coming from that Cadillac."

Skip sighed. "And maybe figure out how to fix it?"

"Yeah, that too." I gave him a backward wave as I headed out.

I was in a state approaching euphoria going down the stairs. I had everything set up on my end. Skip had assigned me to Hangar 4 on Wednesday, and he had asked me to check out some problem with the Cadillac. A problem I was already certain I'd need the expert help of two Swedish brothers to fix.

I finished up my inspection of the Bombardier jet in Hangar 1 and wandered over to the Cadillac, which someone had moved. The owner had obviously driven it. I gave it a once-over, then turned over the engine and listened. And damned if I didn't hear a noise like a whinnying horse. I popped the hood and looked over the engine. I pulled out something clinging to the fan belt, closed the hood, and turned it over again. It roared to life and purred like a kitten. Oh shit, I thought. There's absolutely nothing wrong with this Cadillac. Now what?

Knowing what to do is not the same as feeling good about it. I hated my next action, but duty called. Popping the hood again, I retrieved the piece of unknown material, and carefully clung it again to the fan belt. After re-closing the hood, I turned it over again, and lo-and-behold, the engine exuded a whinnying sound. I threw up my hands in mock frustration, and pretended to be befuddled, in case anyone was watching. I carefully locked the car, and walked over to Hangar 6 for my next inspection.

When I completed the morning's inspections, I returned to the office just as Skip was returning from his own. He asked me how they went, and I said I had no problems. Everything went fine, I told him.

"They must have," Skip said. "No one called me to complain about you. I think when Connie started out, I had maybe five calls. An hour," he said with a laugh.

"Really?"

"No. Connie was a good inspector. Very thorough, but also didn't piss anyone off."

"Hopefully, I did it as well," I said.

"Oh, I'm sure you did fine. And hey, what was up with the Caddy?"

"Oh," I said, with my best dramatic showing of woe.

"Bad?"

"Well, maybe. Maybe not. Definitely whinnying. No clank, thank God, but maybe beyond my skill set."

"He should take it to a specialty mechanic," Skip said. "I told him that."

"Well, that would be best, I suppose." I said with sheer terror in my head that he'd report that to the airport chief and place our plan on life support. "But maybe I have an alternative that won't cost him an arm and a leg."

"Really? He's a cheapskate. What's your idea?"

"I don't know if they'd agree," I said.

"Who?"

"Well, they owe me a favor."

"Terry, I swear I'll smack you if you don't tell me what you're talking about."

"I know a guy," I said. "Actually, two guys. Brothers. Sheer geniuses at classic car repair. But they only work on cars that interest them. They're very much in demand, so they can pick where they work. They do charge premium prices, but I think they'd waive it if I brought them a real classic. And this is a classic 1975 Coupe de Ville. It might interest them, if I ask nicely."

"Can you get them on short notice?"

"I don't know. It's possible, but only because they owe me. Well, at least Liam does. I set him up with a woman he later married, Annika Nilsson, who was a friend of my girlfriend."

"And you'd call in a favor for this?" Skip seemed skeptical.

"Like I said, it will have to be a gem. And the Cadillac sitting out there, owned by an absolute idiot, might appeal to them. But be aware, they'll probably try to buy it from him."

"I don't think he'll sell," Skip said.

"No harm in letting them make an offer," I said. "As long as they fix the car."

"Good point. Okay, call them. I'll work it out with the boss. But I'm sure he'll agree, especially if he doesn't have to pay much."

"Up to them," I said. "But maybe nothing at all. It all depends on how much they love the car."

***

I told Daze about the day's events, drawing a smile from her.

"So, it's all set for Wednesday," she said. "I assume that Lars and Liam will magically and coincidently be available on Wednesday," she said.

"Amazing that they can come so soon," I said. "But they're eager to get a look at a pristine 1975 Coupe de Ville."

"We still have to figure out how to get one or both of them over to Hangar 4," Daze pointed out. "And then one of them, at least on the plane. I mean, he doesn't have to stay on the plane when it takes off, but he'll need to overpower Bachenko's security guy. The one who accompanies us during the inspection."

"Yeah, another logistical problem. We have until Wednesday morning to figure that piece out."

"We're stopping at AbbJeff?"

"Yes, we have some questions, and so do they. They're ordering Chinese takeout."

"Good. I'm hungry, and don't feel much like fixing dinner."

When we stopped in, we all sat for a while in the conference room. We had some things to report, and some things to ask. And one of those things on our minds was just how much money we were being paid for this escapade.

Jeff answered it right away. "Imperial is paying $500,000 upon delivery of the Gulfstream. Abby and I will take none of that. It's all yours. You're doing the work, and you should get the payment. But we'll also match that, no matter what happens with finding the hard drive. So, we guarantee you one million dollars, to split anyway you want. And if you find the hard drive, and we're able to access the information in it, and if it gives us the information we need, we'll give you a one-million-dollar bonus."

"Who decides whether the information is what you need?" I asked.

Jeff smiled. "We do. But if it's what we think, believe me, we'll gladly pay you your bonus. And it might just get Bachenko off your back, Ms. Wilson. And help a lot of people in the process. But all we want is the company bearing our names back in our control. After we're done with that hard drive, we'll turn it over to the British authorities."

"Fair enough," Daze said. "And since we seem in business together, you can call me Daisy."

"Call me Trip," I said.

"Okay, let's get Lars and Liam in here to talk strategy." Abby rose and went to the next room, and returned with the two Swedes.

They joined us at the conference table, and we briefed them on what we had in mind.

"This is no problem," Lars said. "We can both pretend to be mechanics, but Liam here actually can work on cars. He fixed my uncle's Volvo last year."

"Fixed might be an overstatement, but I know some things. We'll both look like mechanics, no problem."

"Great," said Jeff. "Now we have to figure out how to get at least one of you on that plane with Daisy and Trip, without arousing suspicion."

"Maybe we need help on the plane with something that takes more strength than we have?" I speculated. "We could even pretend to ask the security guy to help, but you know he'll refuse, because he can't just abandon watching everything we do. So, we yell down we need some help, and…."

"The airport chief knows about this," Daze said suddenly.

"Sure, that's how you got your identification."

"Can we get official outfits for Lars and Liam?"

"Maybe not in their size," Abby said with a chuckle. "But shirts with badges, I'm sure we can get that. What's your idea?"

"Do Trip's plan, and a burly mechanic's helper with proper credentials, just happens to be right outside when we need help. I'll bet they'll let him on board, but probably assign another security man to watch him. I suppose they might refuse, but then Bachenko won't have a cleared plane, and there will be hell to pay. And if they send another security guy to accompany Lars or Liam…"

"It will be me," Lars said. "Liam will do a better job of pretending to be a mechanic. He keeps working and making noise, and I slip off. And if there are two security guys to overpower, I like those odds. Three would be tougher. But two? And they won't expect it."

"Oh, one thing I forgot," I said. "I told Skip that Liam owes me a favor for setting him up with his wife, Annika Nilsson."

Liam just laughed, but Jeff had to ask. "Did you just make that up on the spot, including a Swedish name?"

"Um, yes, I guess so."

"Pretty fast on your feet," Abby said.

"Oh, he's an accomplished liar," Daze said with a half-smile.

"It's called improvisation," I said. "It's what I do for a

living. Well, used to do. Now I'm a food server. Oh, enough of this. That's the story I told, so if anyone asks, you'll know."

"What does everyone think of the plan?" Abby asked, looking at all five of us and receiving nods.

"Okay, we're ready," she said. "Wednesday morning."

"One thing," Daze said.

"What is it?"

"You can't just fly a jet out of the airport. We need to file a flight plan, contact the tower for takeoff instructions, things like that."

"We'll get the flight plan filed," Jeff said. "London. Gatwick Airport. Getting clearance from the tower is up to you."

"Will Lars be accompanying us on our flight?" I asked.

"Ideally, he overpowers the Bachenko's security guy, and takes him off the plane somewhere between leaving the hangar and taxiing to the runway. But if he's unable to do that, well, you'll have Lars and the security guy as company for your transatlantic flight."

"I hope he's able to get them off," Daze said. "It will make for a more peaceful flight."

"We do, too," Abby assured her.

27

"What time do you need to get to rehearsal?" Daze asked me.

"No rehearsal today, Carleton texted me. He has some unavoidable engagement. Very sorry, and all that."

"I wonder what it is," Daze said. "Very mysterious."

"Yeah, that's Carleton, man of mystery."

"Why don't we use your newfound evening to have a little impromptu going away party for Hip and Willy?"

"Hey, that's a great idea. They're leaving on Wednesday."

I called Hip, and we set a time to meet at an outside eatery along A1A Beach Boulevard.

When we showed up, we spotted them sitting with Margaritas set before them. I hailed a server and pointed to their drinks. He nodded and returned a short time later with drinks for Daze and me.

"You guys all packed?"

"I am," Hip said.

"I have a few more things to get ready," Willy said. "Including figuring out what Hip forgot."

"That's probably everything but his underwear," I said.

"Hey, I forgot underwear," Hip said with a laugh. "No, I didn't. I'm so revved up for this interview, I've probably checked everything three times."

"Nervous?"

"You know, I don't think so. Excited is a better word."

"He's looking at this like the interview is a quarterback he's aiming to sack."

Hip grinned at the characterization. "She knows me well. The only thing to figure out is bull rush, or spin move."

"I'd go with the finesse," I advised.

"That's what Willy said. But sometimes, sheer power puts a signal caller on his back."

"Still," I said.

"Yeah, I know. They're hiring my smarts, not my brawn."

"They're hiring both," Willy said. "The total package. And your confidence is adorable."

"That's what I always said about him," I commented. "Adorable."

We all chuckled at the thought of this giant, goateed man as adorable.

"We're leaving on Wednesday, too," Daze said.

"So, it's all set?" Willy asked.

"If all goes well, and there are a million things that could go wrong, yes. Wednesday Trip and I fly that Gulfstream out of Jacksonville on a flight plan to Gatwick."

"I'd say we'd see you in the airport, but we're flying into Heathrow."

"Imperial must have a terminal at Gatwick," I surmised. "But I looked it up. There is an express train from there right into Victoria Station in London. Maybe we can meet for lunch or something."

"How about high tea?" Daze suggested. "I've always wanted to do that."

"That sounds lovely," Willy said. "Keep in touch. We'll figure out a time and place, assuming we are both there."

Having settled that, we enjoyed the rest of the evening together. As we all had to get to work the next day, we limited our alcohol intake, and parted ways shortly after dinner.

***

The next morning, I gave the good news to Skip.

"I talked Liam into coming to look at the Cadillac," I said.

"That's great, Terry. I still need to clear it with the boss, but I think he'll be happy about it. I'll call him this morning, after we do our pre-inspection prep."

I nodded. "He can't come today, but he and his brother Lars will be here tomorrow, early."

"Oh, okay. Great. Let's do our prep, and I'll call the boss."

After finishing up our preparations for the day's inspections, Skip called the airport boss directly, told him about the visit from the Swedes, and disconnected.

"He's thrilled. Even arranged for uniform shirts and badges for them. I hadn't even thought of that, but they'll need some official status to even be here. That's why he's the boss, I guess. He's always thinking ahead."

I thought that Alistair Brooke had put the fix in, but of course I said nothing, and we went about the day's business without further talk about Cadillacs or enormous Swedish mechanics.

***

Daze's Tuesday was uneventful. The one hiccup came when Alfonzo asked her if she wanted him to accompany her to the Hangar 4 inspection on Wednesday.

"I'm sure I can arrange things with Benny," he said.

Daze tried to give the appearance of nonchalance. "Oh, no need for that. I'll be perfectly fine. If I get any crap from those security guys, there's like a million people around here. Anyway, I relish challenges."

Alfonso looked at her for a moment. "Yeah, I think you do. Okay, just offering."

"Thank you."

Daze reported the exchange to me when she picked me up.

"Seems innocent enough," I said.

"I think it is. He was there during my first encounter with those security guys, and obviously heard and saw their attempt to intimidate me."

"They might try it again," I said.

"Oh, probably so. But I'll have you there, and just around the corner, two of the biggest people I ever saw. Those guys are bigger than Hippo."

"They are," I said with a smile. "More like buildings than people."

"We still haven't really figured out the best pretext for getting anyone else on board."

"No, we haven't. But we're really far along. And Alistair Brooke arranging for Lars and Liam to have official status with badges and something approximating uniforms helped a ton. They have a reason for being in the area when we need them. So, it will be a simple matter to get their help, for a made-up reason."

"Even better if the security guys ask for their help," Daze said.

"What do you mean?"

"Say I need a big person's help on something inside the plane. I turn to the security guy and ask him for his help. He, of course, says no, so I give an enormous sigh, and exit the plane, ostensibly to find someone to help. I ask the remaining security guys to help, and of course they say no, too. But Lars is conveniently walking near the hangar at that moment. Maybe the security guy corrals him and tells him to help me."

"Do you really think a security guy would do that?"

"I don't know. But if he doesn't, I will. It's just better optics for it to be his idea. And I think there's little chance they let Lars or Liam aboard with only one security guy."

I nodded. "Not likely."

Our rough plan determined, we stopped by at AbbJeff for a final briefing.

All six of us assembled around the conference table and discussed our respective roles. The four of them all approved of our methodology, but cautioned that things often go wrong, so we should be prepared to change course if needed.

We knew that, and said so.

"Keep in mind that if we need to have a bigger physical confrontation, we can handle it," Lars said. "But it will draw unwanted attention. Your way is best if you two can pull it off."

I wasn't sure I'd yet heard that many words from Lars, but the implication was clear. He was smart as well as big.

"Thinking optimistically," Abby said, "once you're in the air, if no one refueled the Gulfstream, go to this airport." She showed us where she meant on a map.

Daze nodded. "I know the airport. It can handle a Gulfstream. And it won't be a place Bachenko is watching."

Abby nodded. "Right."

"Good to know," Daze said. "We won't have the time to get it fueled up, and that would raise suspicions, anyway. But I think it is ready right now. When I worked for him, Bachenko always wanted the jet fully fueled, so it could fly at almost a moment's notice. And he's leaving on Thursday. I bet it has a full tank, and we can go straight to London."

"That's good," Jeff said. "And once you're on your way," he added, looking at me, "can you leave the cockpit and search for that hard drive?"

Daze answered. "Yes. Planes these days almost fly themselves. Obviously, we can't both go simultaneously, but we can search separately. Whomever stays in the cockpit will go on oxygen." Daze explained that the high altitude might make the air thin and a cause a pilot to pass out. It's an FAA regulation. And in case you were wondering, Trip is more than competent to take over for me while I'm absent. He's an excellent pilot."

"I've never flown a Gulfstream," I cautioned.

"No, but you've already studied everything about its operation, and I can show you anything else in the air, and I'll take over whenever we see turbulence up ahead, or when any other issue arises."

"Hopefully, you're not absent long," I said.

"I don't plan to be. But it's a long flight. You'll be the primary searcher, though."

We shook hands with the four of them and headed back home. We were all set. G- Day was tomorrow, and we felt mostly ready.

***

Daze fidgeted nervously as I drove to Jacksonville. Usually she drove, because I still jumped out at the hotel and rode on the shuttle to the airport. The shuttle driver made a point of waiting for me. He knew full well that I was a freeloader, but seemed to enjoy my daily company. Almost like a bartender greeting a regular at the corner bar.

The evening before, Daze and I suddenly realized a giant omission in our plans.

"Clothes, toothbrushes, necessities when traveling," Daze said.

"Oh, crap."

"Yes. We need to figure out how to get some of those things on the jet before we leave."

"Maybe not everything," I said. "I assume they have department stores in London?"

Daze smiled. "Of course. Some of the most famous ones in the world, like Selfridges, Harrods, Fortnum & Mason, and Marks & Spencer."

"How do you know that?"

Daze gave a coy smile. "I'm a woman going to London."

"Ah, of course."

"I plan to do some shopping," Daze said, then looked down at her customary outfit. "Even though as a pilot living near a beach in Florida, I have few chances to dress up."

"Maybe at the opening of my play," I offered. "You'll be the belle of the ball."

"Accompanied by the handsome leading actor, of course. All the ladies will be jealous."

I chuckled at her comment. "So, let's not sweat it too much. I always carry a knapsack to inspections, and you have that very attractive fanny pack along with your tool belt."

"You know, if I could reach over there, I'd smack you one for the 'very attractive fanny pack' comment. It might be the worst fashion statement of all time. But a pocketbook just gets in the way for a pilot or mechanic."

"True enough," I said. "But between the two of us, we have room under the usual implements of our jobs to fit a few items, like fresh underwear and toiletries."

I arrived at work and saw Hangar 4 assigned to me that morning. So, nothing had changed on my end. I prepared for the inspection by viewing the schematics of the plane, which I had already almost memorized, put the sheaf of papers in my knapsack along with various testing equipment, and common implements like protractors and rulers. Tools of the trade, as Skip liked to say.

Daze had given me a long briefing on the controls to the Gulfstream, and I felt as good as I could about it without actually ever flying the plane. And there was no substitute for actual flying experience. But such air training was not possible, so book study and briefing were the best I could do.

I checked in with Skip before I left, and in response to his inquiry, told him that the two mechanics, Lars and Liam, arrive at 8:30. I looked at my watch and added, "Right about now."

Skip tossed me the keys, and asked me to take a minute and brief them on what I needed before I went to Hangar 4 for the inspection, and I agreed. Then I was off.

I met Lars and Liam near Hangar 1. They were examining the car with feigned great interest. Or maybe it was real. I couldn't tell. I greeted them, handed them the keys to the car, and left them alone. They already knew what to do.

As I neared Hangar 4, I spotted Daze near the entrance. I entered a few moments after her and took pains to introduce myself to her as a show for the security guys.

I caught up with her, extended my hand, and identified myself. "And you are Stacy Bell, right? I met you earlier this week, albeit briefly."

Daze shook my hand and corrected me. "It's Tracy, and yes I remember you, Inspector Rogers."

"Terry is fine," I said, and we both headed toward the plane, where the familiar security guys assembled, listening to a tall man in khakis and a polo shirt, with another shorter man.

I heard Daze let out a quiet gasp. We were too close to the men for me to inquire, but I guessed. We were looking at Mikhail Bachenko.

28

Oh crap, I said to myself, but there was nothing to do but brazen it out. Maybe they wouldn't recognize Daze, with her hair dyed and scrunched up in her baseball cap.

We tried to ignore the assembled group, but Bachenko turned towards us, a genial smile on his face.

"Excellent, the mechanic and the inspector." He looked at his watch. "Right on time."

"Yes sir, Inspector Terence Rogers," I said. "And you are?"

"Mikhail Bachenko, the owner of this fine jet." He nodded toward the other man. "And this is Justin Lake, one of my assistants."

"Pleased to meet you, sir."

"I want this plane ready to fly tomorrow morning," he said to me. It was a command, not a request.

"I don't think that will be a problem, sir. I've found that the mechanics keep these jets in tip-top condition. But safety first. This inspection will make sure it is safe to fly."

Bachenko shrugged. "Then get with it."

I nodded and turned toward the plane. I hoped like hell he wouldn't try to speak to the mechanic, whose back was to him at present. She was examining the engine. She'd avoided the introductions, because a lowly, greasy mechanic should never presume to greet a rich owner. But alas, our luck had run out.

Before I could get five steps away, Bachenko asked me to tell the mechanic he wished to speak to her, and would I mind terribly asking her?

Again, stated as a question, and impertinent as hell to ask an official inspector to serve as his messenger, but I just nodded, reached Daze, who had heard Bachenko's request, sighed quietly and turned around to accompany me back to where Bachenko and his group stood.

"You wanted to speak to me, sir?"

"Yes. I make it a point to speak to all the mechanics. I haven't met you yet. Is my jet in good working order? Is this man going to find anything that will unacceptably delay my departure tomorrow?"

"It's in great working order, sir." She glanced at me. "The inspection will go like clockwork."

"Good. I need to be in the air at 9 am tomorrow. No delays."

"No, sir." Daze began to turn away, but Bachenko stopped her.

He looked straight at her. His eyes flew to Daze's dark hair, then back to her face, and looked into her eyes.

"I'm certain we've met before," Bachenko said. "But not here." He thought for a moment and tapped the side of his head with his palm.

"Daisy Wilson," he said.

Daze shook her head. "My name is Tracy Bell, sir. I don't believe we've ever met."

"No, I'm certain." He looked at me. "This is Daisy Wilson, the best damn pilot this side of the Atlantic."

"I met her as Tracy Bell, sir," I said. "Are you sure you're not mistaken?"

"I'm not mistaken," he said, turning to his associate.

"Justin, isn't this Daisy Wilson?"

Justin peered at Daze. "It's her, boss. No long blonde hair, but the same size and weight."

"And those eyes," Bachenko said. "Beautiful eyes."

"Daisy, why on Earth is an ace pilot working as a mechanic in this place?"

Daze gave up. "Daisy Wilson was my stunt pilot flying name. And you know I am a skilled mechanic. So, when you got me banned from all the airlines and any stunt pilot jobs, I needed employment. So here I am, back to being Tracy Bell, mechanic."

Bachenko stared at her. "I don't even know how to answer that. But I'll try. With great reluctance, I fired you, because you took my jet on a joyride to Hawaii. Any owner would have done that. And I'll admit to a certain amount of vindictiveness on my part in using my connections to get you a one-month ban. But that's all. It would have been almost criminal to stop a talented pilot like you from flying, and word of honor. I did no such thing. What makes you think it was longer than a month?"

"That's what I was told. That it was permanent. I'm not sure I tried after the first couple of months. I kept getting the same answer."

"I would never do such a thing," Bachenko said. He turned to Justin. "Make sure that Ms. Wilson is free to fly at any job she chooses. If there's any opposition to that, let me know."

"You let me know as well," Bachenko told Daze. "And if you want your old job back, I'd welcome it. I'd even bump up your salary a bit. I never could fly with you, but Justin here tells me you're the best he's ever seen."

Justin nodded. "I don't know if you remember, but I was the one to vet your flying skills. I'm still proud of myself that I didn't throw up during some acrobatics you demonstrated that day."

"I don't know what to say," Daze told the two men. "But I have a job to do today at least, and this nice inspector is waiting patiently. So, if you don't mind, let's get this jet inspected."

Bachenko nodded. "Yes, please carry on. I need it ready by tomorrow. And Ms. Wilson, or Ms. Bell, whichever, please consider my offer. And again, please let Justin know if anyone, I mean anyone, prevents you from any job as a pilot. But I hope the job is back with me." He paused. "Provided, of course, you promise not to take any more joyrides."

Daze nodded, but said nothing, and we walked over to the plane, as Bachenko and his assistant walked out of the hangar.

"We need to talk privately," I whispered as quietly as I could, when we got far enough away to be out of earshot.

Daze nodded.

"I'd like a private word with you," I growled. "An explanation would be a good start. Let's step outside, away from prying ears."

The security guys looked over and shared a laugh among themselves. The mechanic was in trouble, and they loved it. So we stepped outside, and there was no one close by. I could see Lars spot us and walk our way, but I put up a hand, palm facing him, advising him to stop, and he complied. So, we were alone.

***

"We should abort," I whispered.

"That was a shocker," Daze said, not responding directly to my suggestion.

"We should abort," I repeated. "You have your life back. And, wait a minute, when did you last check to see if the prohibition was over?"

"That's the problem," she said. "Bachenko said it was a one-month ban. But it definitely wasn't. I periodically check. I guess the last time was about four months ago. I just put out feelers, nothing more than that, and believe me, it was not a month."

"Oh geez," I said.

"Yeah. So, I don't know the answer to your question. He was lying to me, for sure, but maybe he's prepared to lift it."

"And we might never get another chance to repo that plane. We lined everything up. But I think we should abort, anyway. The most important thing here is getting your life back. And pissing off Bachenko will kill any possibility of that, in the off chance he's telling the truth."

"I know, and we can't stay out here talking much longer, or those security guys will get suspicious."

My mind was racing as she talked. Maybe…if we actually do this, maybe… "I have an idea," I said.

"I'm all ears."

"Why don't we set this up so that those guys, and by extension, Bachenko, think I'm forcing you to do it."

"How would that work?"

I explained my idea, and Daze nodded. "If we do it at all, that might be the way. And if Abby and Jeff are right, we might help stop him from further evil acts."

"And it won't endanger a restoration of your flying opportunities."

"It might work," Daze said. "But I have another quick question, with no answer. What do we know about Abby and Jeff, and Imperial Reclamations? Could they be playing us?"

I grimaced. "Yes. And if so, we might be in deep do-do."

"Let's hope they're the good guys," Daze said. "Here comes Lars. Give him a quick whisper about the change in plan and send him away for a few minutes."

I nodded, and said loudly, "I'll be right back in, Ms. Bell or Wilson, or whatever your name is. My report will include this outright deception. I expect the jet to be ready for an enhanced inspection."

Daze gave a meek sounding answer. "Yes sir, Mr. Inspector. I'll have it ready right away."

When Lars approached, I looked around, saw no one, and whispered in his ear about Bachenko recognizing Daisy, and the change in plan as a result, and what I needed him to do. He asked no questions, and just walked back towards the Cadillac. He was smart, and I was certain he would perform precisely as instructed.

I strode back into the hangar and walked right up to the jet, to begin my inspection. "This will be an enhanced inspection," I declared, loud enough for the security men to hear. I'm not happy about how this has proceeded to this point, and I'm way behind schedule. But the owner made it crystal clear that he needed this jet first thing tomorrow, and I'm going to be damn sure it is in tip top flying condition."

My speech over, I walked toward the security men and spoke to their chief. "This inspection will include rolling this jet out of the hangar to determine whether it can taxi properly. I don't want you to shoot at me while I do so. But there is no way on Earth I will pass this aircraft without that step. Unfortunately, I can't have it test flown, because there are no test pilots available, but I will make sure the owner is safe in his jet." I lowered my voice and said, "Not the least because he scares me a bit."

The security guys just guffawed at that. "He's not to be trifled with," the chief said. "Okay, thanks for the heads up."

I made a great show of putting Daze through her paces, showing impatience at times, and nodding approvingly at others. When it came time to board the jet, I looked over at the security staff and nodded. "Time to look inside," I said.

The chief tapped one of his men on the shoulder. "Go up there with them," he said. But he showed no sign that he thought this was anything more than the dozens of inspections he'd seen before.

Inside the cockpit, Daze showed me many of the items I needed to inspect. I measured everything and checked circuits with a multimeter I pulled out of my knapsack. The guard looked on with apparent disinterest, almost bored. The two of us obviously posed no threat. Finally, we got to an overhead compartment containing—I noted for my audience—the wiring for the entire instrument panel. And lo-and-behold, the panel was stuck. Pretending to pry it with a screwdriver didn't help at all. I was going to take brute force, which neither Daze nor I possessed in abundance. I looked at the security guard.

"Can you give us a hand here?"

"Not happening," he said. "I'm not taking my eyes off of you."

I gave a big sigh and walked down the steps to the floor of the hangar. I approached the remaining four security guys and asked whether they could help with the brute force needed to open a stuck panel, and received the expected declination. Again the "Not happening," comment. I looked at the ground, back at the plane, and grumbled, apparently to myself, about having to tell my boss and that owner that I needed to delay the inspection, at least until I could find someone to help open that panel. And to my unspoken glee, the security chief pointed to the entrance to the hangar.

"That guy looks like a strong one. Get him to help you."

"I don't know…oh wait, he works here. Hey Lars, can you come over here for a moment?"

Lars looked up and strolled into the hangar. "What's up?" he asked, with all appearance of innocence.

"Can you help me pry open an overhead hatch? The one containing all the wiring for the instrument panel?"

"Oh sure," Lars said. "That thing gets stuck all the time. One of us has to slide the screwdriver or pry bar, and the other, that's me, yanks it down. They need to make those better. But I know exactly what you need to do."

We walked toward the jet, and the security chief said, "Stop."

29

We turned around, and he said to one of his men, "Calvin, go with them. Watch the big guy."

Calvin immediately got up and followed us up the steps into the jet.

We walked into the cockpit, where Daze and the other security guy were waiting. Daze did not look happy, so I assumed the guy had done some hazing of the "girl" while I was gone. But they both remained silent as we approached.

Lars made a good showing of yanking the balky panel down, then turned to exit. But before he did, he grabbed one guard around the neck and squeezed, while kicking the other one in the face. Both crumpled to the ground in seconds. I went to the hatch, called out to the guards that we were going to move the jet out of the hangar, jettisoned the stairs, and the jet moved.

By this time, the security guys had awoken. They were groggy, but alive, and alert enough to spot Lars pointing one of their Berettas at them, and pointing the other one at Daze.

"Get this jet moving," I barked at Daze. "That guy Bachenko said you're an ace pilot. I am, too, but right now, I want you to prove those skills if you want to stay alive. I don't need you, but having a co-pilot is never a bad thing. Now get this jet moving."

I thought Daze did an Academy Award-winning performance as the scared pilot as she taxied the jet out of the hangar. Before we arrived at the runways, Lars took the two security guys off the plane, waved goodbye, and we contacted the tower for the go-ahead to complete our flight plan to London, Gatwick. We moved from Number 3 in line to number 2, then number 1, and finally we gathered speed, and took off in Bachenko's Gulfstream. We were all alone on the jet, which was a little eerie, but Daze and I were together, and that's all that mattered. Mission accomplished, almost.

After we were underway for a few minutes, Daze turned to me and said, "We may have a teensy little problem."

"What? Low fuel? Instrument problem?"

"No, this jet is running like a dream. No, I mean, our plan to have you force me to fly the jet, to not have Bachenko think I'm borrowing his jet again."

"Why? Do you think he suspects the truth?"

"I don't know. I wonder about that, too, and I'll get to that after we discuss a bigger problem."

"What could be bigger than he finds out you're involved?"

"When we arrive in London," she said.

"We use our credit cards until we collect our payment, and maybe bonus."

Daze chuckled. "The credit cards that are almost maxed out."

"Almost being the operative word. But what's the problem?"

"Well, I might use my almost maxed out credit card, but it's possible you won't use yours."

I was getting a little impatient. "Enough stalling. Out with it. Why won't I be able to spend money, too?"

"Because you'll be in jail for kidnapping," she said.

"Oops. I never thought of that."

"Neither did I, but when you have to make split-second decisions, sometimes you make mistakes."

"That's a pretty big mistake. I don't want to go to jail. Jail is bad. And not a role I'm playing, the real thing."

"You won't go to jail," Daze said. "I'll tell them I went along willingly, and that it was part of a charade to repossess the jet, which we're fully authorized to do."

"But that will blow your cover," I said.

"That's pretty likely," Daze said. "But maybe not definite."

"Why not?"

"Don't you wonder a little why the tower didn't stop us from taking off?"

"The fix was in with some bigwig in the airport's administrative office. That's how we got our aliases and brought Lars and Liam into the airport."

Daze shook her head. "That part of it, sure. But permitting a takeoff when someone was being kidnapped? The administrative office doesn't control the tower. That's strictly regulated. It's totally different people."

"But maybe no one notified the tower that there was a problem on the jet before we took off."

"Probably not," Daze said. "Which brings me to another question. Why didn't anyone notify them?"

I thought about it for a moment without answering. "Lars disabled those two security guards while we were still in the hangar. They were in no condition to report anything. Nor were they in a position to do so after they woke up, and we did the little play acting with their guns. And then Lars took them off the jet just before we reached the runways. I'm sure he didn't let them call anyone, at least not until we were clear. So when would anyone know a kidnapping had taken place until after we took off?"

"You're right about the kidnapping part. The tower couldn't have known, even if someone spotted the three men leaving the jet. No way they'd know the details. But Bachenko had to know the plane was leaving, because his security staff would have notified him. Reluctantly, but they would have called the moment the plane left the vicinity of the hangar. Yet the tower did nothing other than clear us for takeoff, and we've heard nothing but normal chatter since that time."

"That is strange," I acknowledged. "Wouldn't the authorities at least try to contact the jet if they knew a crime was being committed? Maybe not scramble fighter jets, but at least direct us to return to Jacksonville?"

"They would," Daze said. "No doubt at all. We might ignore it, but they'd figure they could arrest us in London. If we actually went to the place set forth in our flight plan."

"We're not going to London?"

"Of course we are. I was speaking of a hypothetical criminal. We're not criminals. But the only thing that makes sense here is that Bachenko didn't contact the tower. Because we weren't even first in line. We waited for our turn. So, he had plenty of time to stop the jet if he wanted to. Remember, he even has contacts within the FAA. No, he didn't stop us."

"He didn't want police scrutiny," I murmured.

"Maybe. Or maybe something totally legitimate. Could be anything, but it is notable."

"Yeah, it is. And one more thing."

"What?"

"We need to ditch this gun somehow."

"Good point. We really, really don't want the London police to find a firearm in our possession."

"How do we get rid of it?"

Daze smiled. "We're above the ocean. Best place in the world to dispose of stuff you don't want anymore."

I got up, and took the gun to a disposal chute Daze identified, dropped in the gun, pulled a lever, and away went the firearm into the vast expanse of the ocean.

When I returned to the co-pilot seat, Daze told me someone's radar might pick up the object, but would likely disregard it once it hit the ocean and made such a minuscule splash.

"We need to look for that hard drive," I said.

"Plenty of time for that. It's a long flight."

"How long?"

"On this baby, maybe nine and a half hours."

"So, we arrive at Gatwick…"

"Two-thirty a.m. London time. Six-hour difference."

"Both of us will need to fly this thing," I said. "That's too long for just you."

"It is," Daze said cheerfully. Even ace pilots need to go

to the lavatory sometimes. But I'll handle it most of the time, and when we have turbulence."

"Good," I said. "I've never flown this big a plane."

"You've flown nothing other than the Cessna," she said. "As you can see, there are some differences. But you pick things up quickly. Autopilot helps a lot. You'll be fine. But maybe we should use some of our nine hours on some instruction."

"I think that would be a superb idea," I said. "Same rules as last time?" I asked.

Daze smiled. "Maybe not at 30,000 feet. That kind of training is a home activity."

"Safety first," I said.

"Always. But I'll think of some way to reward an exemplary performance. Okay, here are the ground rules for this new and not as fun training. One, you need to repeat the instruction and demonstrate it back to me."

"That seems reasonable," I said.

"And way too easy," Daze replied. She retrieved a flight manual from a compartment and handed it to me. "Have you read this?" I nodded.

"I'll show you several things. We'll wait a half hour, and then you can repeat them back to me, and show you understand the action or concept."

"That sounds harder," I said.

"It's called learning," Daze said sweetly.

Daze rattled off about a dozen things about the Gulfstream, together with demonstrations of the jet's systems. All of it was in the cockpit, so it was easy for me to watch while also monitoring the instrument panel. And I noticed Daze did the same thing. No matter what else she did, she knew exactly what was going on with the jet. Long experience makes a difference, I thought.

"I can't show you much about the inner workings of this jet from the cockpit, so I won't try. You already memorized it, anyway."

"I did," I said.

"And there's not much to learn in the cabin itself," she added. "But you'll see the cabin for yourself when you search for Bachenko's hard drive, if it really exists."

"Do you doubt it exists?" I asked.

"Yes. The whole thing is feeling wrong to me. Maybe it's my premonition, but something feels wrong."

"I know," I said. "Bachenko inviting you back as his pilot was strange."

"It was," Daze said. "And not stopping our takeoff, when he had ample time to do it."

"And what do we really know about Abby and Jeff?" I asked rhetorically.

"Nothing," Daze said. "They seem to be hackers. Manufacturing websites for a software business and a repo company would be a piece of cake for a hacker, or at least that's what TV shows portray."

"What have we gotten ourselves into?" I asked, throwing my hands up in despair.

Daze looked around. "Well, at present, a pleasant joyride in a Gulfstream. Again."

"Good point. Let's just enjoy the ride."

30

We flew quietly for a while, then Daze glanced at her watch, and fired a question at me. It jolted me out of quiet thought, but I reacted quickly, answered her question, and rose to demonstrate.

"Very good," she said.

I waited for the next question, which Daze posed right away.

Again, I responded correctly both in words and actions, and she rewarded me with a smile and praise.

"Now for the trick question portion of the exam," Daze said.

"I didn't know there'd be a trick question portion."

"You want to learn, you have to work," Daze said with a grin.

"Oh, I want to learn," I said, "and earn that unspecified performance reward. Bring it on."

Daze posed a hypothetical situation and asked me how I'd handle it.

"No fair," I said. "This wasn't part of the training."

"You've taken lessons from me," Daze said.

"Yes, of course. You know that."

"How do I teach?"

I hung my head. "By making me deal with real-life situations, that could be the difference between life and death."

"You got it. It's not just memorization. It's applying the lessons to the real world. And no matter how many hypothetical situations I pose to you, there is always something unexpected when you fly. Tell me what you'd do in the situation I just described."

I gave a thoughtful answer, and Daze smiled at me.

"That's what I would do, too. Of course, there might be other approaches that would work as well."

We flew silently for a little while, until Daze turned to me and said, "I guess we should look for that hard drive."

"If it exists," I said. "I'm not convinced. And who uses a hard drive now, anyway? As I understand it, you can put oodles of stuff on a little tiny flash drive."

"Oodles?"

"You know what I mean."

"I do. A little piece of plastic that holds various sizes of information. Like one oodle, five oodles, or ten oodles."

"Right. I don't have the lingo down, I know. But the point is, I don't think anyone uses one of those clunky big hard drives."

"You have a point. But Abby and Jeff described it as a hard drive, and they're the technology experts."

"Maybe they're not," I said quietly.

"We have too many questions, don't we? Ones that we should have looked into better before we took off in a possibly stolen jet."

"At least they'll only arrest me," I said.

"You know I won't let that happen. We'll explain the whole thing, including the fact that we staged the kidnapping. The most they can charge us with is theft, and even that is questionable, because we have no intention of doing anything with the plane except turning it over to Imperial."

"And if Imperial is bogus, too?"

"Another joyride, with no harm to the jet, and taken under a misunderstanding."

"You're good at explanations," I said. "They even sound plausible."

"Reality sometimes is different," Daze acknowledged. "But let's just enjoy the ride, and take turns searching for the data Abby and Jeff described. They even said they weren't sure whether it was on the plane, or even what form it would take. So, it could be a hard drive, a laptop, a flash drive, or even paper. Let's just see what we find."

"Okay. I'll take first crack at it, back in the cabin. Sometimes crooks on TV store things in the freezer, or in the toilet tank. I'll check both."

"There's no freezer," Daze said. "But there is a refrigerator."

"Okay, I'll look in whatever is in the kitchen."

Daze donned her oxygen mask, and I left the cockpit. I completed a quick survey of the passenger seats, but left a closer examination for last. It was an unlikely spot for Bachenko to store anything. I went straight for the first lavatory, near the entry to the cockpit. Searching everywhere, including the small storage cabinets, and even in the bowl itself, yielded nothing other than the expected items. My next stop was the second lavatory, and I performed the same search, and came up empty. Looking up, I noticed what looked like drop ceiling panels, and pried them open. I regretted not having a flashlight with me, but remembered Daze's tool belt, and walked back to retrieve one. I aimed the light into the opening, while feeling around with my hand, and found nothing but dust, which I wiped off on a towelette in the lavatory. Then I headed back to the first lavatory and performed the same check, to no avail.

I sighed heavily, and headed to the kitchen, and looked absolutely everywhere, including in the drop ceiling panels. I knew that what I was looking for could be tiny, so I was extra careful, but I couldn't find anything out of the ordinary, so I sat down in one of the very comfortable passenger seats to give it some thought.

"This is the way to fly," I said out loud. "Way, way better than commercial, where you barely have enough leg room to sit with your knees up, and none to stretch out. These even recline," I said. Leaning back. Suddenly I felt exhausted, but jumped to my feet before I fell asleep right there. I needed to get back to the cockpit and give Daze some relief. And it occurred to me that if I was hiding something on a plane, I'd keep it there, not in the place where many passengers sat. Unless…Bachenko had a particular seat assigned only to him. I looked at the seats and decided that one in particular in front had to be Bachenko's personal spot. And he'd let no one else sit there. It was a seat near the cockpit, and had a few extra luxuries, including a kind of glove compartment.

I hurriedly searched the seat and the compartment, but found nothing interesting.

I returned to the cockpit, and told Daze about my revelation, and failure to discover anything. She thought it was a good idea to look again at Bachenko's personal seat, as I described it.

"Were there any others with compartments?" she asked.

"Maybe," I said. "I left the seats and the cockpit for last."

"Take over for a bit. I'm going to look over Bachenko's seat."

"Sure." I looked at the instrument panel and affixed my oxygen mask. "It's under control."

"You probably won't need to do anything," she said. "But holler if anything funky comes up."

I saluted and pulled up on my mask. "Aye, aye, sir… er… ma'am."

"Kind of lame ass correction there, co-pilot," Daze said with a smile. "Work on the proper show of respect for the captain."

"Will do, ma'am," I said, and lowered the mask.

"Better."

Daisy wandered back and studied the prime seat, which obviously was Bachenko's chosen location. She'd never actually flown with him onboard, so she didn't know it for sure, but a quick view left little doubt. She ignored the compartment for the moment, and ran her fingers along every inch of the seat, feeling for…she didn't know. A crack, a soft spot, a hidden compartment…anything unusual. The high quality, expensive leather seats showed no signs of mobility or alteration. She turned her attention to the compartment, which, as Trip had told her, was empty. She repeated running her fingers along the inside and sides of the compartment, but again felt nothing amiss. In front of the seat was a wall that contained a panel that included many connectors for plugging in electronic devices, including several a/c outlets, USB ports, network cables, and even a round port that looked like a cable television port. Again, Daze felt around the panel, to no avail. She'd hoped that something would click, like a switch opening a hidden compartment, but alas, no click, and no secret panel. She doubted that the hard drive Jeff and Abby referenced existed at all. Maybe a tiny flash drive, but not a big, clunky hard drive. She was not tech savvy, but even she knew small jump drives that contained enormous amounts of data had largely replaced them. But Abby and Jeff, who were ostensibly experts in computers, had specifically mentioned a hard drive. If they meant a flash drive, wouldn't they have said so? But they'd be the first ones to know the difference between the two. And they didn't seem lazy in their speech. More doubts crept into Daisy's brain about the whole adventure that, in a whirlwind had swept up her and Trip. And her premonition remained as strong as ever.

At that moment, the plane lurched and swayed. Daisy almost fell down, but steadied herself on the top of a seat. She held herself there for a moment, but when she started back to the cockpit, the plane shook again, and she had to stop. Her only thought was of Trip, and how she never should have left him alone in the cockpit.

31

The turbulence ended as quickly as it began, and Daisy hurried back to the cockpit to find a very rattled Trip, hands glued to the yoke, eyes straight ahead.

"It stopped, Trip," Daisy said. "You can let go now. I'm here."

I heard and saw her, but my mind didn't register right away. I gradually came out of my locked-in brain, and gratefully acknowledged her takeover of the controls. I removed my oxygen mask, turned to her, and said a single word.

"Thanks." Then a torrent of pent up terror and self-doubt invaded my brain. I looked at Daisy and said, "I had wrongly believed a few hundred hours of flying and a license made me a pilot. But oh my God, I am no such thing."

"Nonsense," Daze said after listening to me. "Of course you are. You handled an unfamiliar and much bigger jet perfectly. We didn't see this turbulence coming. Usually you do, but sometimes you need to deal with the unexpected. The mark of an excellent pilot isn't one that's good at going through the motions, or memorizing stuff, but one who can do what you just did."

"Okay, thanks." I said it without fully believing Daisy's expression of praise. And absent an emergency, there was no way I'd let her conduct any more searches.

After a while, I said "I'll go look again."

I tried to be methodical about it. I started at the first set of seats and worked my way back. I used Daze's technique of feeling along all the seats and areas around them for hidden compartments, or frankly, any sign of tampering. But I doubted Bachenko would hide something important in a seat he didn't frequent. And I found nothing amiss. If Bachenko had hidden something in the passenger area, I sure couldn't find it. I went back to the cockpit and reported my non-findings.

"Nothing?"

"Nothing. I don't think Bachenko would hide something in one of those seats, anyway."

"No, probably not. And I wonder…."

"What?"

"Um, why would he hide it in the plane at all?"

"I know, right? If it's a small flash drive like you think, and I agree, he can hide that anywhere. Is he afraid of someone searching his home or office? Does any of this make any sense to you at all?"

"Trip…I'm scared. What have we gotten into?"

I put my arm around her. "I don't know. But I suspect we are two of the most gullible people who ever lived."

Daze looked at me, and I could tell she was trying not to laugh. But she did anyway, bursting out into raucous laughter. "We are, aren't we?"

I joined her. "I mean, other than the two of us, who would believe the crazy story they all told us?"

"I know," Daze said. "We even went undercover and took jobs at the airport. I'm actually a mechanic, but you as an airline safety inspector? If there was any doubt about your acting ability, that settled it."

"I think Abby and Jeff might be better than me," I said, sobering a little.

"If this is a giant con, what do you think they're after?"

"I don't know. The plane, I suppose. Probably other things we don't know."

"Do you think this is an actual repo? If Abby and Jeff are frauds, what about the repo company?" Daze wasn't laughing anymore, and neither was I.

"Probably fake as well. Our big payday is rapidly going 'poof.'"

"Right now, my only goal is to get out of this fiasco as unscathed as possible."

"Yeah. Good goal. Let's shoot for that."

Daze nodded, but obviously her brain was still working things out.

"You know," she said. "The thing that bothers me the most about this mess we've bumbled into is that Bachenko had his goons removed from the plane at gunpoint, his beloved plane has been, um, taken away from him, and he raised no alarm at all? The tower cleared us for takeoff without a hitch, and no one has told us to return to Jacksonville. In fact, no one has told us anything at all. Everything points to this trip to London as an ordinary flight. I mean, WTF?"

"Nice use of an acronym," I said. "And I agree. It makes no sense. Bachenko threw a fit when you borrowed his plane for a joyride to Hawaii. And you returned the jet in good condition."

"Better condition," Daze corrected. "So why the change of heart this time?"

"I don't know. I suppose we should keep searching. Maybe we'll get lucky."

"I define lucky as escaping without going to jail."

"Not going to jail would be good."

***

Hippo and Willy settled into their first-class seats on a jet for an overnight flight to London. They had half expected to hear chatter about the commotion in the airport regarding Bachenko's plane flying away over his loud objections. But they'd heard nothing.

They didn't expect to hear anything from Tripper and Daisy right away, because they'd have their hands full until they were aloft for a while. And even then, who knows what might go on in that plane? And they didn't even know if, in fact, their friends had taken the plane.

As they waited for their jet to taxi to the runway, Willy turned to Hippo.

"I don't like this one bit," she said.

Hippo knew exactly what she meant and had the same thought. But he tried to divert them both.

"Flying first class or going to London?"

Willy grimaced. "You know what I mean."

Hippo sighed. "I do, honey, and I don't like it either. I wish I had dissuaded them from the whole thing. We all have a nice, quiet life. Shooting for the proverbial home run might not work out the way they want."

"And there's Daisy's premonition."

"There's that. And I've just had an unsettling thought."

"More than worrying about Daisy and Trip?"

"Yeah. Am I doing the same thing as they are?"

"No, you're not. You've wanted to be a network color commentator for as long as I've known you."

"I have. And way longer than that."

"Following a dream is not the same thing as trying to win the lottery, which is more or less what the two of them are doing."

"I know. Do you really think what they're doing is trying to win the lottery? Those people approached them. And the repo company seems legitimate. I don't know about those Abby and Jeff characters, but they seem to have a connection to the repo company. And the repo company seems to have enough influence with the airport authorities to arrange those jobs."

Willy shrugged. "I don't know. I just don't want them to get hurt. I hope it's all on the up and up."

"Me too. Hey, how do you like flying first class? Have you ever before?"

"Never. And try to fit into a commercial flight when you're my size. Oops. You've tried to do it too. Not fun."

"Worse for fellow passengers, I suppose."

"Have you ever flown first class?"

"Never. They used to charter planes for us when we traveled for away games at UF."

"Are those better than commercial?"

"They are. At least the ones I've traveled on. We were not small people. They had to accommodate us. Maybe they don't do that for all football programs, but I'm sure they do it for all the big-time college sports teams."

"This is nice. And hopefully, we leave London with you having a job offer."

"That's the plan."

***

I glanced at my watch. "Almost four o'clock Jacksonville time. Hippo and Willy are probably at the airport by now."

"Yes. I don't remember the exact takeoff time, but it's an overnight flight. I guess they schedule all the European flights that way, so that tourists arrive in the morning."

I nodded. "I knew that. Must have read it somewhere. It's not like I've flown to Europe before. Have you?"

"I have. I flew an international route for about a year. Went a lot of places. Spent almost no time anywhere. That's the life of a flight crew, pilots included."

"Maybe we should have tried to reach Hippo and Willy," I mused out loud.

"It wasn't a good idea, and still isn't. They need to remain blissfully ignorant. The British authorities may arrest us. Our friends don't need any phone or radio records tying them to our crimes."

"Alleged crimes," I corrected. "We did nothing wrong. We have a piece of paper allowing us to repossess, um, reclaim this jet. That's our story and we're sticking to it. But I take your point. No contacting Hippo and Willy. We meet in the agreed upon place and time in London."

"Do you still have that paper?"

"From Imperial Reclamation? Sure." I fished the document out of my pocket, unfolded it, and handed it to Daze.

She studied it. "Very official looking. Raised seal and everything."

"Even has a red ribbon coming out of the seal."

Daze nodded. "This might be our get out of jail free card, so to speak. We didn't steal the jet, we just reclaimed it for its rightful owner."

"Maybe this will work out," I said hopefully.

Daze didn't seem convinced, but she nodded and handed the document back to me. "Keep it safe. It might be the only thing standing between us and a British prison."

"It might also be our ticket to a big payday," I said, stubbornly.

"You keep dreaming, Trip. That's one of the many things I love about you. You dream big things."

I changed the subject. "Should we keep looking for a hard drive, or a flash drive?"

"I guess so, but we're running out of obvious places to look. Maybe we should give some thought to less obvious places."

"Where?"

"Oh, I don't know, maybe up there," she said, pointing to the panel above us.

"That's the panel we pretended to need help with," I said. "It just has a bunch of wires in it."

"And maybe a tiny item wedged in there."

"Okay, no harm trying." I reached up, and easily removed the panel, and felt around among the wires. "I hope I don't electrocute myself doing this," I grumbled.

"Not likely," Daze said. "Remember your schematics?"

"Obviously not."

"They're not connected to any electrical current at the moment."

"I'll take your word for it. And place my life in your hands. But I felt nothing in there."

"Worth a shot," she said. "Let's look around for other places like that. But not ones that will kill us. We'll avoid those."

"Good plan," I agreed. "Any ideas?"

She had some, and none panned out. We were striking out on finding the elusive hard drive Abby and Jeff hoped was on this jet. But it looked like they were wrong. Or lying to us. That seemed more and more likely as we continued our inexorable voyage to London, England.

We found nothing more than a few dust-balls. This convinced us that no hard drive, flash drive or any other similar object was anywhere on the plane. We didn't know whether Abby and Jeff were wrong or lying, or whether we were incompetent at finding it, but we both leaned toward the whole thing being a sham. I fully expected the British authorities to arrest us the moment we made it through customs. If we made it that far. Daze already had a passport, but I had to scramble to get one before we left. Alistair Brooke had somehow expedited it for me. He'd also arranged for accommodations for us for three nights, and Abby and Jeff had given us a small amount of spending money each. Once they paid us, of course, we'd have plenty more. If anyone paid us. And I hoped like hell that at least Imperial Reclamations paid us, if Abby and Jeff did not.

And if we stayed out of jail. The hour of reckoning was fast approaching. We'd find out our fate in less than an hour.

32

We landed at Gatwick Airport at 3:00 a.m. London time. Instructions from the control tower directed us to a particular gate, which clearly was far away from the commercial area. We taxied to a stop, deplaned and walked with some trepidation toward a small security area. Customs for rich people with private planes.

We cleared customs without incident, and a short, stocky man met us just beyond the security desk and directed us to a tiny office. He was very gracious and even thanked us. He produced a receipt for the Gulfstream, which correctly identified its make, model, and tag number, and I put it carefully in my pocket. We needed to keep it secure. Without it, we had no proof we'd returned a $70 million jet.

"When do we receive payment?" Daze asked the man.

"I have no authority to do that. I'm the night manager." He pointed to a large clock on the wall. "As you can see, it's well after business hours. My instructions are to arrange transportation for you to the pre-arranged hotel, and to ask you to please present yourselves at the main Imperial office in Piccadilly Circus." He handed us a card with an address, then picked up a phone and requested a car to take us to the hotel. He also handed us small British bills, adding up to about two hundred pounds.

Following his direction to wait outside in a particular spot, we soon saw an old -fashioned British cab approach. We put our small duffels in the boot, as the driver called it, which was in the car's front. We then headed to our hotel. The driver said little during the trip and waved away the tip we'd proffered. "It's all covered."

We thanked him and carried our bags into the lobby of a modest hotel directly across from Green Park. As it was dark, we had no opportunity to see its apparent greenery. We checked in without incident. They had our names, and our prepaid status was in their system. We went up the "lift" to our room, which was nicely furnished. It was clean and comfortable and had a quiet elegance. But it did not feel snooty at all. And the front desk clerk couldn't have been nicer. We were both exhausted, and even though we were also starving, we just tumbled into bed. The thought of trying to find an all-night restaurant at this hour seemed too daunting to even make a meager attempt.

But we both woke up after just a few hours. We were excited to, we hoped, collect our payment. We'd heard nothing from Abby and Jeff, although they'd had little chance to reach us. But Imperial was right here in London.

"I know this is a stupid question," I ventured to Daze. "But it's been bothering me since last night."

"What is it?"

"Um, why is an office in a circus? It's a British thing, right?"

Daze smiled. "It is a British thing. One I never understood, either. But it's not a real circus. It's a big, giant, busy, traffic filled intersection."

"Ah, that, um, still makes no sense."

"No, it doesn't. Welcome to London."

"We need to find a place for breakfast," I said, "and I have one errand to attend to down at the front desk."

At Daze's expectant look, I said, "I want to visit their business center. I spotted it last night. I'll check out what means they have for communicating with Abby and Jeff, use the computer to check out local restaurants, and make a few copies."

"Wait up. I'll go with you. We can go right out, get a bite to eat, and return here to shower and get ready to go to Imperial's office. We can go by cab or the Tube."

"The Tube?"

"Subway."

"Tube. I like it."

"And I'm pretty sure our cell phones work overseas."

"As I've never been overseas before, I didn't know that."

"Well, it's a wee bit more complicated. You either have to use wi-fi here, which they have in this hotel, or activate international calling before you leave the U.S."

"I didn't do that," I said. "It never occurred to me. I'll just use wi-fi."

"I will, too. It's cheaper. But I thought of it, so I can use my phone anywhere."

I made my copies and went to the hotel desk to request a stamp.

In response to the desk clerk's inquiry, I told him I wanted sufficient postage to mail an envelope home. I held up a hotel envelope provided helpfully on the desk in our room. He reached under the counter and retrieved two stamps bearing royal pictures.

"Royal Mail stateside," the clerk said with a smile.

We walked out of the hotel to grab a bite to eat at a restaurant Daisy identified on the computer while I was buying my stamps.

I spotted one of the iconic red post boxes and dropped my letter into it. Daze, who uncharacteristically had made no inquiry about why I wanted copies and was mailing a letter, asked now.

I smiled at her. "Covering our asses," I said, to which she shrugged and asked nothing more.

I eschewed the bangers and mash menu option in favor of some fresh fruit, pastries and awful coffee. Daze had the same, but substituted tea, which was a better choice.

"It's a tea drinking country," she said. "Although you can get better coffee than the rock-gut you're drinking. Just not here, apparently."

"This place is not bad, though," I said.

"No, it's pretty good," she agreed. "So, should we head right over to Imperial, or try to reach Abby and Jeff first?"

I sighed. "We have very little to tell them," I said.

"Other than we found nothing. I guess our chances of a double reward have gone up in smoke."

"They promised compensation," I said. "Maybe not a half a million dollars, but something."

"They did," Daze agreed. "But it's not like we have that in writing."

"We have nothing in writing, except the paper authorizing us to repossess, um, reclaim the Gulfstream. And I'm glad you thought to ask for that."

"If we didn't have that, the authorities could charge us with stealing the plane, and we'd see the inside of a British prison. And we have the receipt they gave us at Gatwick."

"Now all we need to do is collect our cool half million."

We returned to the hotel to take much needed showers and get ready for our big visit to Imperial.

While we were undressing, I noticed a tiny black speck on Daze's forearm.

"Hey, what is that?" I said, pointing to her arm.

"What?"

"Right there, on your arm."

She looked down and brushed at it, but it remained there.

"Is it a scab? Too perfectly round for a scab."

We put our heads together and examined the spot.

"It's not a tick," I said.

"No, not that. I don't like it there. I'm going to just pick it off."

I grabbed an envelope from the desk. Aim it in here. We can look at it better than if it ends up on this carpeting."

Daze nodded. "I hope it's not a scab covering a puncture. Maybe you should grab a tissue, in case there's blood."

"Okay, just a second." I retrieved a couple of tissues, but I seriously doubted a puncture this small would cause any blood.

"Okay, here goes," Daze said, and picked at the speck on her arm. It came right off, and flew directly into the envelope.

"Perfect aim, and no blood."

"No puncture either," Daze said, examining her arm. "Okay, time for a shower, and after that we should get right over to Imperial to collect our giant payoff."

I nodded. "This little mystery can wait. Our newfound wealth is a Tube ride away." I sealed the envelope and stuffed it in the back pocket of my jeans, which were draped over a chair. We completed our ablutions and headed out. We took the Tube to Piccadilly Circus, which was easy, because it seemed all lines went through there, before branching off all over London. Piccadilly Circus is enormous, with about a billion fast-moving cars speeding through.

But we found the offices of Imperial Reclamation after only a few meandering wrong turns. It had an impressive-looking sign in front, but the office itself was less opulent than we'd expected. It wasn't dingy, just…ordinary. I'd expected something more elegant for a company that dealt with extraordinarily wealthy people, and such expensive items as a Gulfstream.

A polite gentleman greeted us in the small waiting room and inquired about our business. I explained we had reclaimed a jet and were there to receive payment.

"Oh, reclamation agents," he said. "You'll want to see Mr. Owen. I'll tell him you're here. It should only be a few minutes. Please sit down."

"We thought we'd see Mr. Brooke. Alistair Brooke."

The man looked at us for a moment. "I'm sorry, but I don't know that name."

Daze and I exchanged a quick glance.

"Is there another Imperial office?"

"No sir. This is it. You must be mistaken." He hurried off.

We waited for about twenty minutes before the same man returned and ushered us into a small office occupied by a short, swarthy man. He had a pockmarked face adorned with a mustache that resembled a caterpillar. He rose, hand extended. We all shook, and Daze and I sat down in the proffered chairs in front of his desk.

"You did a repo," he said, looking at us. "You don't look like you could repo anything. It's a tough business."

"Um, I thought you folks called us reclamation agents. And Imperial recruited us for this job."

"Oh, the fancy name," the man said. "My mistake, the two of you are 'reclamation agents.'" He used his chubby fingers to make quotation marks in the air. "Very fancy repo agents. What did you repossess, someone's pet bunny? Maybe a dog?"

"A General Dynamics Gulfstream G650," Daze said, rattling off the manufacturing year and the tail number, adding that it uses two Rolls-Royce BR725 engines. "I can give you all the specs, if you require them."

The man looked at her. "Okay, you memorized some stuff. Very impressive."

"Look," I said. "She knows her aircraft, pure and simple. She memorized nothing. But none of that matters. We brought in a $70 million jet for Imperial, and we want our payment."

The man glared at me, but I didn't care. We'd worked hard, and at substantial risk, to bring Imperial that jet, and that entitled us to payment.

The man held his stare for a moment too long, but I returned it without flinching. At last, he broke it off.

"Let's see your receipt," he said, and I proffered it.

"We were told we'd receive a fee of $500,000," Daze

said.

The man's head whirled to look at her, and then he exuded a giant guffaw. "Five hundred large? Whoa, you two have big cojones, asking for crazy money like that."

"That's what we were told," I said, feeling kind of stupid we didn't have any such thing in writing. "Alistair Brooke said it was the standard fee for reclamation of a Gulfstream."

"Who the hell is Alistair Brooke?"

"The chief executive officer of Imperial," I said. "We saw his title on your website, and we spoke to him. He made many of the arrangements for us."

The man looked genuinely puzzled. His angry demeanor vanished.

"Look," he said after a moment. "Someone is playing a terrible trick on you. We don't have a website. Our business is, um, under the radar. We don't want to be seen. Our clients come to us on reputation, not because we advertise. And I have never heard of anyone named Alistair Brooke. We don't even use the term chief executive officer in the UK. Our managing director is Oliver Harris." The man sat back in his chair. "Either someone conned you, or you're trying to con us. Either way, we're not paying you $500,000."

33

“**S**how me the proof of delivery. If you really completed a repo for us, maybe we can work something out based on our actual payment schedule.”

I handed him the receipt, and he studied it, then turned to a computer monitor, presumably checking the details against Imperial's records. I braced for the news that Bachenko's jet was nowhere in Imperial's records, in which case we had a big problem. But Mr. Owen surprised us by turning back to us and nodding.

“Looks like you two captured a big fish. That jet has double stars next to it. Give me a few minutes. I'll be right back.” He left the room, and Daze and I looked at each other.

“This might work out,” Daze whispered, and I nodded. I wasn't so sure, but I kept my thoughts to myself. We'd know for sure soon enough.

Mr. Owen returned a few minutes later and sat down.

“Now what can I do for you?”

“Let's cut the crap,” I said angrily. “We gave you a receipt for the return of a $75 million jet. You looked at your computer, and confirmed that it was not only your lease, but a 'big fish.' It's time to pay us for our work."

"Do you have a receipt?"

"Oh, so we're playing that game. You keep the receipt and pretend you never saw it."

The man just gave us an infuriating smile, and I wondered if there was in fact a big payoff, but this guy was determined to keep it for himself. I didn't know how, but this was a tough business, and Daze and I were rank amateurs. But maybe not so much.

"You mean this one?" I said, producing a copy of the receipt. "Or perhaps this one?" I said, producing another copy. "And just so you know, I mailed a few as well. Now, can we stop this nonsense?"

The man just laughed. This must be his usual routine. He turned serious.

"Look, we are not paying you $500,000, or anything close to that. But as you've pointed out, and proven, you brought back a very valuable jet that we leased to someone who we believed would meet all the obligations imposed upon him in exchange for leasing the jet. He failed to do so, and we have a right to repossess it. You've saved us a ton of money and aggravation, and Imperial will pay you the standard fee for two-star items, 50,000 pounds. Not $500,000, but not a paltry sum either."

I looked at Daze, and she nodded. "Okay," I said. "It's considerably better than nothing. But we'll still consider it a down-payment on the full amount."

"As you wish," he said. "But I don't think you'll be successful in getting more. I'm not lying to you. It's the standard fee."

"You'll forgive us for not taking you at your word," I said.

"Fair enough. I've given you no reason to do so. But we won't renege on this payment. What are your wire instructions?"

I had no idea what he meant. I don't know what I'd thought. That they'd give us a suitcase filled with cash. Maybe handcuffed to my wrist. I just didn't know, and was unprepared for the question.

Fortunately, Daze responded, and gave Mr. Owen routing and account numbers. "Please give us a thousand pounds in cash," she said, and the man nodded his assent. He retrieved the cash from a drawer in his desk and handed it to her. He then tapped a few keys on the computer keyboard, and looked over at Daze. "Okay, it's done. 49,000 pounds Sterling. He printed a receipt and asked her to sign the accompanying release. She handed it to me, and I skimmed it, then added "down-payment on believed $500,000 agreement. All parties' rights reserved."

Mr. Owen looked at it and smiled. "I'm comfortable with that," he said.

Daze pulled out her phone, tapped a few keys, smiled, and put it away. "Deposit confirmed."

***

We walked out into a cloudy day, with small droplets of rain softly pelting our heads. Dreary to two Florida residents, but commonplace for London. Most people in the pandemonium that is Piccadilly Circus carried umbrellas. Not the silly portable ones found in every convenience store in America. Big, black umbrellas which would no doubt survive a hurricane. Funny irony. Our umbrellas invert in the slightest wind and are useless in a tropical storm. Theirs would survive a tornado, yet they only seem to use them for a drizzle.

We walked aimlessly for a while, then found one of the ubiquitous parks and, after wandering around, found a gazebo to stand in to get out of the rain. We brushed the water off our heads and gazed at each other for a moment.

"We're rich," Daze said finally.

It was true. We hadn't received the promised amount, but to two people living paycheck to paycheck, Imperial had paid a fortune—enough to not worry much anymore about paying the rent.

"We are," I agreed. "Maybe we'll even get more from Abby and Jeff," I said.

"I don't care," Daze said. "I just want to enjoy the rest of our time here and go home, hopefully with my flying opportunities restored."

"Good plan. What should we do now?" I asked. "Go back to the hotel?"

"We're in one of the greatest cities in the world," Daze said. "Want to explore a little?"

"Sure," I said. "But the place is unknown to me, so lead the way. The rain is even letting up."

"We should probably call Abby and Jeff," Daze said. "But let's wait a bit."

So, we walked out of the gazebo and, hand-in-hand, strolled around the fabulously green park. And for the first time in weeks, I felt myself relax. Daze's hand felt warm and comfortable in mine, and she periodically turned to train her thousand-watt smile on me. That gaze could melt away the densest London fog, and made me feel like I was walking in sunshine.

"I wonder what Hippo and Willy are up to?" she asked suddenly.

"I can't even remember the date," I said, and then it came to me. "Hip's interview is today."

"Ooh, I hope he gets that job," Daze said. "I can't stand the suspense."

"He'll get the job," I said, maybe more confidently than I actually thought. "He has to. I want to be best friends with a network star. Free game tickets."

"Oh sure," Daze said indulgently. "That's the reason."

"He's my friend. I want him to be happy."

"That's more like it. But what if he needs to move to London?"

"I won't like that. But I still want him to get the job. It's his lifelong aspiration."

"Willy won't enjoy moving," Daze said. "But she will. Those two are inseparable."

"They are. Kind of like us," I said, planting a kiss on her cheek.

Daze smiled. "We've had our periods of separation," she said. "But not anymore."

"No. Not anymore. We're in this crazy life together."

We had no desire to call Abby and Jeff right away. Imperial had given us some payment, and we were frankly both tired of the whole mess they'd pushed us into. We both seriously doubted that they'd pay us anything, much less the big money they'd suggested was forthcoming. So, we abstained, at least for the moment, from any further involvement. And they hadn't tried to reach us at all. That was fine with the two of us, as we strolled out of the park, and headed for the Tube, to take us to our first sightseeing destination——Westminster Abbey and the impressive clock tower, Big Ben. We spent the rest of the morning shopping and visiting various tourist stops, then retired to one of the many pubs for lunch.

"I guess we should call Abby and Jeff," I said.

Daze didn't answer. She was looking over my shoulder,

presumably at someone in the pub.

"What's up?" I asked.

Daze held a finger to her lips, then whispered, "I think that man in the gray sweater has been following us."

I instinctively started to turn my head and Daze stopped me. "Don't turn around. We don't want to tip him off."

"Tip him off about what?" I whispered.

"That we know he's following us," Daze whispered back.

"Why would anyone want to follow two people visiting common tourist spots?"

"No one. That's what's suspicious," Daze said.

"I guess so." I was unconvinced. "We're almost done with lunch. When we get up, we'll see if he follows."

Daze nodded. "Good plan."

When we finished, we rose and headed for the door. Out of the corner of my eye, I spotted the man do the same.

"He's pretty obvious," I said to Daze as we exited to the street. "Shall we confront him?"

"No, I don't think so. We're visitors here, and not anxious to have police involvement until we know we're in the clear."

"Okay. Should we try to lose him?"

Daze thought about that for a moment. "No, I don't think so. Let's go walk along the Thames for a while. If nothing else, we can try to bore him to death."

"I love it. And we might as well wait to call Abby and

Jeff until we return to the hotel, which our shadow probably knows about anyway."

We walked along the water for a good hour, then headed for the nearest Tube to return to our hotel.

Upon entering our room, we were met with complete chaos.

34

Someone had uprooted everything. An intruder had emptied the contents of our small bags on the floor, and apparently pawed through them. He or she had pulled the mattress off the bed, and cut it open, as was the box spring. The clothes drawers were all pulled out, and the contents emptied. The contents of the desk drawer, which contained the nice hotel stationery and envelopes, had been dumped on the floor. Someone had conducted a very thorough search of our room, looking for…who knows what?

"Probably looking for the hard drive we never found," I answered the unspoken question.

"What did they think?" Daze asked. "That we found it and secreted it in a hotel room?"

"Kind of explains our gray sweater shadow today, doesn't it?"

"Sure it does. His job was to watch to see if we visited any super-secret hard drive depositories. Perhaps in Westminster Abbey."

"Time to call Abby and Jeff," Daze said. "But first, we tell the hotel staff we didn't do this. Maybe someone will have seen our intruder. And we don't want to pay for the damage."

"They might want to call the police," I said.

"I suppose so, and we're trying to avoid that. Although it might be for the best."

"It might," I agreed. "But maybe not yet. Why don't we spin it as a common attempt a petty theft, and they found nothing to steal, so we're not concerned. The hotel should of course make certain the thief had burglarized no other rooms, but if we lost nothing and didn't want our holiday disrupted, did they really want the adverse publicity arising from police involvement?"

"Works for me," Daze said. "Should we start cleaning this mess up?"

"Let's wait to show the hotel manager," I said. "Then they can help us. And maybe give us a different room."

Daze nodded. "If one's available. This hotel is pretty crowded right now."

When the hotel manager came to our room, he put his head in his hands, then looked up at us.

"A bloody grim sight," he managed.

We nodded.

"We've never had this kind of thing here. It's a respectable hotel." He glared at us. "Are you two up to something?"

"Hey, we're the victims here," I responded angrily.

"Oh, I know. Forgive me. I'm a bit narky. I'm just cheesed off by this. We think we have a nice place to stay. When the constabulary arrives, it will cause all sorts of commotion, disrupt our guests, and damage our reputation."

"Do we need to involve the police?" Daze asked quietly.

The manager stared at her. "You wouldn't mind leaving them out of this. Keeping this quiet?"

"We like it here," Daze said. "And you've been nice to us. As far as we can tell, they took nothing from us, so there's nothing for the police to recover. And we'd rather sightsee than spend our time filing reports with the police."

"You might want to be sure that no one burglarized other rooms," I added. "But I'm sure you can do that quietly."

The manager nodded. "I can do that. And I will send two people to help you clean this up and replace your mattress. I'd move you to another room, but we're full right now."

"Won't the people you send to clean up gab about it?"

"Gab?"

"Talk to everyone. Tell them a room was burglarized. Gossip. Cause the exact problem you want to avoid."

The manager smiled. "Not these people. They're family. One of them is my son, the other my daughter-in-law."

"Ah," I said.

The manager hustled off, and we started cleaning up. Not long after, two people, a man and a woman, both sturdily built, arrived at our door, greeted us and immediately lifted the damaged mattress off the bed and carried it out. They returned for the box spring and again carried it out. Subsequent trips resulted in a fresh mattress and box spring placed in the vacated spot. They both helped us pick up, and they replaced the bedding and pillows. They cleaned the bathroom and restocked it with toiletries, and vacuumed the rug. Before they left, we thanked them profusely, and they smiled at us, and the woman handed me a card.

"What is this?" I asked.

"Papa wanted you to have this. It's a certificate for a free dinner."

"He didn't need to do that," Daze said. "He shouldn't have, really."

"This is a place to stay for you," the woman said. "But it's our home. And you two could have as you Americans put it, raised hell. But you didn't. And we all thank you for that." They both gave slight bows and left us alone in our fully refreshed room.

"Well, that was… surprising," I said.

"I know, right? We didn't want police involvement, but they wanted it less. And we have a free dinner for doing what we wanted, anyway."

I nodded and turned serious. "Are we sure they were after the hard drive?"

"What else could they want?"

"But we don't have a hard drive. We spent hours on a plane, searched everywhere, and found exactly zero."

"I know that. You know that. They don't know that."

"Who's they?"

"Bachenko."

"Yeah. Who else?"

"I just want him out of my life. Is that too much to ask? I don't believe for a second what he said in the hangar."

"That you're already free to fly anywhere? No, you've already shown that he lied about that. We'll get him out of your life."

"How? We found nothing. No way he's going to jail if there's no evidence."

She had a point. Our whole rationale for the jet repo was to find evidence to put Bachenko away. And we had nothing. Which was why we had felt no urgency to call Abby and Jeff. But we needed to now, and I told Daze that.

She nodded and handed me her phone. "You call. I can't do it right now."

"You want to wait more?"

"No. We have to call."

So, I placed a call. And it went straight to voice mail. And not one with Abby or Jeff's name on the recording. Just a computer voice announcing that the person owning that phone number was not available, and to leave a message. Upon hearing that recording, which I'd never received before when calling them, I hung up. I didn't know what message to leave anyway, and I was afraid to say anything. So, we had nothing more to do, but try to enjoy London, and wait anxiously to hear word from Hippo and Willy.

***

At that moment, Hippo was talking amiably with three network executives and one former NFL player. The tough stuff had ended, and the football talk had begun. All four of the men in the room loved talking sports, and football in particular. Hippo had survived everything from intense questioning about his knowledge of college football to familiarity with the players, not only from the University of Florida, but across the nation. Everything Hippo knew about the people he might one day be discussing on air. And Hippo knew a great deal and had little trouble talking about what he knew. He was careful to clarify that he didn't know about everyone, or even everything about the ones he knew about. And the network guys ate it all up. At least to Hippo's eye, that part of the interview went well. They actually gave him an IQ test, and while they never told him the results, they seemed pleased. A screen test similarly extracted smiles, with the caveat that he should "lose the goatee." Other than that, they said he cut a fine figure. And they particularly liked his ad lib anecdotes. He candidly stated he knew little about broadcasting, but the network guys clearly expected that.

"We have people who can teach you," one said. "We can't teach your vast knowledge of college football players and how they think. And we can't teach intelligence."

"So…"

The men all smiled. "We'll talk details later, but if you want the job, it's yours."

He named a starting salary, and Hippo tried not to let his eyes pop. But he doubted he succeeded. Almost anything was better than being an assistant chef at a glorified diner, but this combined both his dream job and a salary that was enormous to him.

"I want the job," he said. "And I guess we let the lawyers do their jobs at this point."

"You learn fast. Yes, we'll let them finalize our deal. Welcome to the team. I'll bet you have a thousand questions."

Hippo grinned. "At least. But I'll start with one, very near to my girlfriend's heart. Will I have to move to London?"

"Ah, the lovely and very talented Wilhemina Deathtrap Danvers. She wants to stay in Florida, I assume?"

"She does."

"That's good. Because we have no intention of locating you in London. We need you exactly where you are, very close to both Gainesville and Tallahassee."

"UF and Florida State."

They nodded. "And not that far from Alabama and

Georgia. Very close to a huge chunk of the best college football teams and players in the country. And I know there are phones in London, but we don't need you here. We need you in Florida."

Hippo asked other questions, but the major obstacle to taking the job had vanished. He was dying to tell Willy, who was waiting for him in a plush waiting room, but he figured that talking football for a while was a good idea. And he truly enjoyed talking football with former Florida linebacker Blake Perry, a Gator legend from long before Hippo's time at UF.

But he ultimately emerged to share the good news with Willy, and to reassure her that they could remain in Florida.

"Deathtrap lives," he joked.

"Oh, that's great, but I'm so proud of you, Derek. I knew you'd get the job. You've trained for it for so long. I doubt anyone knows more about college football than you."

"I bet they do," Hippo said. "But I think I held my own. One thing: I know you love my goatee, but I have to shave it off."

"I hate that thing," Willy replied.

Hippo chuckled. "You know, I don't think I like it much anymore either. Looking fierce is no longer necessary."

"We have to celebrate," she said.

"We do. I wonder what Trip and Daisy are up to?"

"They haven't called," she said. "I'm a little worried about them, but we were so focused on this interview that I put them out of my mind. I know Daisy has her phone set to receive calls here. I'll call her."

35

We didn't have to wait long, as Daisy's phone played the first few bars of Steve Miller's Fly Like an Eagle.

Daze looked at her phone and glanced up at me.

"It's Willy."

She answered with obvious trepidation, then broke out in a big smile.

"He got the job? They want him in Florida? That's great. Better than great!"

Daze looked at me, and told me the good news, which of course I could hear as I was sitting next to her on the bed, our legs extended and thighs touching. I almost couldn't believe it. My best friend had the job of his dreams and wasn't moving away. I couldn't be happier than I felt at that moment. I wanted to give Hippo an enormous hug and firm handshake, but satisfied myself by leaning over and hugging Daze from the side while she kept talking to Willy.

She hung up, and told me we were all meeting at the little Italian restaurant named in the gift card. The network had apparently offered to treat Hippo and Willy at one of the finest restaurants in London, but they'd demurred, with thanks.

Neither of them was a gourmet restaurant person, and they wanted to meet with us to hear all about our big adventure.

His new employers expressed disappointment, but said they understood.

"You'll have to get used to wining and dining at the best restaurants to impress the college athletes," one warned, but with a smile.

"No doubt," Hippo told them. "But some of those athletes would feel more comfortable with burgers and beer."

The man had nodded. "Good point. That's one reason we need you. You have an excellent feel for how athletes think. Very helpful for color commentary."

"I hope that's true." Hippo said. "I want to do a good job, and I'm ready to learn. But I owe it to my friends to meet them tonight at some restaurant where they have a gift card. A place called Giorgio's."

The man laughed. "Your friends received a delightful gift. That place is small and exclusive. And has the best Italian food in London. But no burgers and beer."

"Good to know. I love Italian food. And I wouldn't want to celebrate my great new job over a burger."

Daze and I continued to sit on the bed when she disconnected.

"We're meeting them at 7:00 pm?" I asked.

"Yes. That's the time specified on the gift card."

"Pretty specific gift card," I observed.

"It is," she said. "But I don't mind. We avoided the hassle of finding a restaurant ourselves. We're all set to just show up." She pointed to a few shopping bags on the chair. "And I'm glad we picked up some clothes and accessories at

Marks & Spencer."

I nodded. "We really didn't plan that plane hijacking well, did we? We only had a few things in a bag you'd stowed in the plane and my knapsack. At least we had some toiletries, and a few wrinkled items. But now we can look presentable at the restaurant."

"What should we do until it's time to get ready to go out? It's a little late to go out in the big city before dinner."

Daze looked down at the bed, then looked at me, and we simultaneously began disrobing.

By the time we concluded our entanglement, it was time to get ready for dinner. We showered and dressed in our new clothes, nicely ironed, with the provided implements Daze found in the closet. We looked like a fine, upstanding couple of yuppies.

"Hippo and Willy won't even recognize us," I said.

"We're in London, not at the beach," Daze said. "I think we look nice."

"You do. Did I say how happy I was that you shed that awful brunette disguise?"

"Several times," Daze said. "And I like my blonde hair, too."

I pulled my wallet out of my jeans and draped them over a chair. Daze and I looked at ourselves in the mirror, and I commented on how pretty she looked, to which she responded with the comment that I looked pretty dapper myself.

***

We met Hippo and Willy at the cute little intimate Italian restaurant. The place only had six tables, spread out so that diners could have quiet conversations. Which is what we did after we completed our exuberant greetings and hugs.

Neither management nor the other diners seemed to mind. In fact, they all appeared to enjoy the brief show. We of course appeared to other people as a somewhat odd group, dominated by two enormous people. I wondered whether they thought we were American celebrities, but decided not. A professional wrestler and an ex-college football star probably didn't rise to that level.

So, we settled down to a wonderful dinner and great conversation. In between visits by the servers, we filled Hippo and Willy in on our escapades, and I think their mouths literally fell agape. It was quite a story we had to tell.

"And you found nothing?" Hippo asked.

"No hard drive. And we looked everywhere on that jet. We had almost nine hours, obviously searching separately."

"At least someone paid you. Not what you thought, but payment. You won't go home empty-handed. After all that effort."

"I figure I came out ahead by not getting arrested," I said, dryly.

"You did nothing wrong," Willy protested. "You had authority to repo that jet. And they paid you for doing it."

"They did," I acknowledged. "Not what they promised, but they paid us. And Imperial denies even having heard of Alistair Brooke, the Imperial guy who their website listed as the head of the company."

Daze spoke up. "There's something strange about how they all handled this. I mean, that guy Brooke arranged everything—our, our jobs at the airport, our um, secret identities there, even expedited passports. That's difficult to do, isn't it?"

"It is," Willy said. "None of it is easy to do. And you are well-qualified as an airline mechanic, so that was an easy sell, but Trip knew nothing other than what you taught him.

And they trusted him to ensure all those jets were safe?"

"Seems kind of hard to believe, doesn't it?" I said. "But there's no denying it happened."

"No…I guess not." Willy said. She and Hippo exchanged a glance, which I noticed, and I'm sure Daze did.

"Okay, out with it," I said.

"If Willy is thinking the same thing I am," Hippo said, "We think you are in real danger."

"Why?"

Hippo ticked the reasons off on the fingers of his left hand. "This is a very sophisticated bait and switch. Someone had the pull to get you full clearance at the airport, jobs that at least one of you was totally unqualified for, and identification in false names. They risked the safety of all the passengers on those jets you inspected, and gave you clearance to take off, even though you more or less hijacked the plane by subduing the security personnel. The person who arranged all of it doesn't exist, and you can't even reach the two supposedly aggrieved parties who dragged you into this mess. And you say someone followed you today, and an intruder searched your room?"

"Oh, geez," Daze said, visibly upset.

"What is it, honey?" Willy asked.

"A man followed us here, too. So, we've endangered you two as well. It's one thing for Trip and I to seek pie in the sky. It's another to involve the two of you. Both of you have good jobs. And Hippo just landed the job of his dreams."

I hung my head. Daze was right. We knew the whole thing was crazy, but maybe would pay off. Maybe even be dangerous. But we would never want to hurt our best friends.

Hippo put a stop to our lamentations with a single

upraised, gigantic hand, palm facing us. It was a stop sign, one that loomed almost as large as the real thing. And we stopped. Anyone seeing that would stop.

"We're in this together," Hippo said, and Willy agreed. "We will not let you face this alone. So please, was it the same fellow who followed you before?"

Daze shook her head. "It was a different man." She provided descriptions of both of the men.

"I didn't see the tail this time," I admitted.

"I was a little paranoid after the upheaval in our room, so I paid attention. And there's no doubt. We have another shadow."

The four of us looked at each other for a moment. All of us were considering the best strategy.

"Should we confront him?" I asked. "There's four of us, and one of him. I surveyed our very large friends. Maybe more like six of us. We can find out what's going on."

"He might have friends nearby." Daze said. "With guns."

"I suppose that's possible," Hippo said. "But I think Trip's right. We might not get a better chance to find out what's going on."

So, we created a plan to encircle the guy following us, and confront him head on.

Our shadow was still there when we walked out of the restaurant. We all hugged and pretended to go separate ways. As expected, the man followed us. I could see him through the corner of my eye. We let him follow us for a short distance until we reached a certain spot, at which time Hippo and Willy snuck in behind him. Thus encircled, we confronted him. I could see he wanted no part of Hippo and Willy's imposing figures, and I was thankful they were there. I wasn't so confident of our chances in a physical confrontation ourselves. But the man talked freely. Of course, the guy knew nothing, other than he was to report our movements, and would receive "100 quid." He allowed as how he'd do a lot more to us for 100 quid, but his instructions were explicit. He wan't to hurt us, and all he had was a phone number to call to report and be told where he'd find his money.

"Where did they say they'd leave the money?"

"They didn't say. I was told to report and get instructions at the same time. From what I was told, I expected to pick up an envelope somewhere, but I know nothing more, I swear." He held his palm to his chest to emphasize the sincerity of his statement.

I had a quick thought. "Did you search our room?" I asked it suddenly, and the look of surprise on his face told me he knew nothing about the search. He rapidly responded with a vehement denial.

"Follow and report," he said. "That's it."

"How did you get the instructions in the first place?" Daze asked.

"Um, from a guy on the street."

"What did he look like?"

"Um, I don't remember. He was tall, no, not tall, medium height. Gray sweatshirt. Dark hair, um, maybe, I think so. I don't remember, I swear." Again, the palm to his chest. Very sincere.

"And you believed he would pay you 100 pounds?"

The guy hung his head. "I'd have believed he was the bloody Prince of Wales, for 100 quid. Business has been slow."

"What business? I ventured, followed by an "Oh" when I had the sudden realization. The man was a pickpocket and petty thief.

We all looked at each other and had a group shrug. There was no more information to get from this guy. A tall or medium height man with maybe dark hair had approached him. Obviously, someone who didn't want anyone to recognize him. The description was useless anyway. I supposed we could get his name, but it would be fake. We could bring him to the local constabulary, but accuse him of what? Following us? And we didn't want to take the time to go to the local police. I figured we could follow him to see if he tried to report and pick up his payment, but we had neither the time nor the inclination to do that. So, we let him go, and he just ran off.

Daze and I bid goodbye to our friends, with the agreement to get together the following day. We had one more night paid for at our respective hotels, and Daze and I still hadn't heard from Abby and Jeff. And the network had a few events planned for Hippo and Willy. I was dying to go to the West End to attend a theater production. When would we be back in London to do that? Our friends agreed to go with us. We'd have an early dinner, and be there in time for the 7:30 p.m. performance.

"What should we do now?" I asked as we walked toward the hotel.

"Does it make any sense to call Abby and Jeff now?"

"Probably not. I'm not sure we can reach them at all. It's not like we were able to leave a message, and expect a return call. There was no response at all when we tried before."

"I know. It was like the phone had been disconnected."

"I have a bad feeling about this," I said. "Abby and Jeff incommunicado, men following us, and our room searched."

"I know. But we're richer than we were when we started on this crazy adventure. Maybe we can just enjoy our last day in London, call it quits, and go home."

I had no chance to respond, because at that moment, four burly men surrounded us. Hands covered our mouths, preventing us from calling for help, and I blacked out.

36

When I awoke, I felt groggy, and my eyes had trouble focusing. The outline of a tiny, windowless room gradually appeared, as well as the figure of Daisy in a chair next to mine. Trying to reach over to touch her brought the comprehension that I couldn't move my arm. Someone had secured both my arms to the chair with zip ties. I was immobile. And from what I could tell, Daisy was, too. I tried to speak, but only managed a guttural sound. Daisy was still asleep, or drugged, which I gradually realized these unknown assailants had done to us.

As I tried to bring myself to full consciousness, Daisy stirred. She performed a similar ritual to my own. I watched her look around the small room, then over at me, then attempting to speak and move her arms. She had no more success than me. But my vision and voice were gradually returning, and I could tell her the obvious—we were prisoners, awaiting…we did not know.

We found out soon enough. A short man with sandy hair parted to one side, an oval face bearing round lens glasses and a dark brown sweater came in the room and sat down across the table that sat between us. As I returned to full consciousness, I realized we sat in an interrogation room. But I had no idea who was doing the interrogating. Were we at a police facility? I doubted it. Police don't apprehend suspects by surrounding them and placing chloroform over their faces. Or did they? I assumed the man sitting in front of us would clear it up, but he remained silent. He just sat there for what seemed like minutes, just staring at us. An intimidation technique, I assumed. Well, it was working. I was nervous. Although I had nothing to hide, at least I didn't think so. We'd done a repo job and Imperial paid us for it. We might have done more than that if we'd been successful in finding anything on that jet, but we didn't. And I had no problem admitting that to anyone, including the scary man in front of me.

I guessed he was waiting for us to break the silence, so he'd win the staring contest, but I didn't see the point in continuing the silence, so I blurted out, "Who are you and why have you taken us prisoner?"

Daisy, who was a few minutes behind me in regaining her full consciousness, added her outraged voice.

"You have no right," she said indignantly.

The man, who I had just noticed, had a nasty scar on the left side of his neck, only glared at us.

He finally spoke and pointed to the scar. "You see this?" He stroked the scar.

We both nodded.

"Someone tried to horn in on my…business activities. His knife was ten inches long, and it cut deep. I lost a lot of blood." He paused and cut his eyes away from his scar and back to us.

"But I grabbed his wrist and almost snapped it in two before he could continue his murderous slice. I grabbed the knife and stabbed him eleven times, and spit on his dead body. I will do the same to the two of you if you do not tell me in five seconds where you stashed my product."

His voice never went above a whisper, but it scared me to death, and I was shaking like a leaf in a high wind. I could sense Daisy next to me, shaking as well. And somehow asking this terrifying man what product he meant seemed unwise. We truthfully had no idea. But I couldn't exactly tell him where I put his product, either. So, Daisy and I were going to die, because we'd left our happy, simple life in search of riches. What a crappy way to die.

We said nothing for a long moment, and the man literally began counting the seconds off on the fingers of his left hand.

I blurted out, "Please, give us time to explain."

"Nothing to explain," the man said. "The location. I care nothing about why you stole my product."

Daze spoke up. "No, but you'll kill us, anyway. You might as well hear our story. Waiting a few minutes to kill us costs you nothing."

That was a pretty brazen gambit, and I admired Daze for coming up with it, although I doubted this dangerous criminal would show patience. But he did.

"Okay, I like fiction. Tell me a story. But be quick about it. I get bored easily." He fingered his scar and pulled out a huge knife. "And I have itchy fingers."

So, Daisy and I took turns telling our story, and to my surprise, the man didn't interrupt to stab us. At least not right away. He listened, probably more because it was a totally unbelievable tale that no one would be idiotic enough to tell to avoid being killed. When we finished, he started slowly clapping and fingering his knife. I didn't like the sight of this. It didn't bode well.

"Wonderful tall tale. I thoroughly enjoyed it. And to hear it in two separate voices. A brilliant performance. Now, where did you stash my product? You need more incentive. I will start with the pretty woman. A pilot, you say? You probably need your fingers for that. I will slice them off one by one. He rose and walked toward Daisy.

What could we say more than tell him the truth? And he didn't believe the truth. So, I shouted out "Stop. I'll tell you!"

I did not know even what his "product" was, but I assumed it was drugs. Somehow, I doubted it was a hard drive containing incriminating information, or even a hard drive at all.

But the man stopped. "Where is it? No games."

"We can show you," I said.

"No. You'll tell me right now, or I cut the pretty lady's fingers off."

I had nothing to tell him, and even if I gave a bogus location, he'd kill us anyway. I had no more cards to play. But Daisy did.

"It's still on the plane," she said. "And as the pilot and co-pilot, we can get access to it. But I bet you can't."

The man stared at her. I could tell he was weighing the desire to cause us as much pain as possible against the possibility, however remote, that Daisy was telling the truth. She bet that the thought of losing immense profits would buy time. For what, neither of us knew.

After a long moment, our captor smiled. It was not a kind smile, or even one signifying he believed Daisy could deliver his product. It was more like an evil grin, as if he was going to do something horrible that would give him great pleasure.

I suppose my anxiety created that image in my mind, but this guy made me scared to death that he would start cutting our fingers off, and worse. I shuddered to think of what could be worse than that and came up with too many options.

He broke his smile with a simple statement.

"More lies." The man brandished his knife and

approached Daisy. "I just love my work," he said to no one in particular.

Frantic, I said, "We really know nothing. How can we convince you we're telling the truth?"

"Which is the truth? That you know nothing or that my product in the jet?"

I had to think fast. I had maybe one second to answer his question. And it seemed hopeless. No answer would please him, and likely nothing would keep us alive. This guy was going to kill us either way. Daisy had offered something that might delay that, but he hadn't bought it. At least not yet. It was time for a "Hail Mary."

"Neither," I said. At least that stopped him momentarily.

"A third lie? Okay, I told you I like fiction. Let's hear your tale. And it had better result in giving me back my product."

I mustered everything I had ever learned about acting. This had to be the performance of my life. And it couldn't end like a Shakespearean tragedy.

"My organization wants in." I said it as confidently as I could.

At least that threw him for a moment. "What is your organization? The two of you look nothing like smugglers."

"She's a pilot," I said. "She flies. I'm what you might call a facilitator. I make things happen. And to give you the unvarnished truth you want from us, here it is: I'm afraid of you. But I'm more scared of them. And if you kill or torture us, they will find you and do much worse. But they want in to your organization. And they'll give you your product back. But only under their terms. Neither of us controls them."

I could tell the guy didn't believe one word of what I

said. And it seemed silly to me, too. But it was the best I could come up with to delay…terrible stuff happening to us.

"Tell me who runs this 'organization.'"

I shook my head. "I tell you that, the two of us will be dead the moment we leave here. If we leave here, that is."

"You're hanging by the slenderest thread," the man said.

That statement gave me a scintilla of hope. At least there was a thread.

Unfortunately, the thinnest strands give out easily, and this one snapped right away.

A gigantic man knocked and entered the room, and whispered something in our inquisitor's ear.

The huge guy stayed in the room as the evil grin returned to the smaller man's face.

"I am done here," he said, turning to the big guy.

"Kill them and get rid of the bodies in the usual location."

The man nodded. "Consider it done, boss." He pulled out a handgun and pointed it in my direction, but the little man stopped him.

"Not here."

So, we didn't die at that moment. But once again they chloroformed us, and the last thing I saw was a hand the size of a Christmas ham closing in on my face.

37

I woke up as groggy as before. This time, I was not in a windowless room. They'd placed me in a cramped space where I could barely move. My hands were bound with zip ties, and so were my legs. Not completely conscious, I realized I lay in a fetal position, and the only thing I could see through hazy eyes was a human torso, which I gradually came to recognize as Daisy, similarly prone. I could feel movement and occasional bumps. They had stuffed us in the trunk of a car.

I nudged Daisy's backside, and she stirred.

"We're in a car," Daisy said, without my asking the question. She obviously had awakened before me.

"Heading for our execution."

"We have to get out of here," Daisy said. "But I can't move much, and have little use of my hands or feet."

"I can't move much either. And I don't know what I'd do if I could."

"Pop the trunk, I suppose."

"And roll out of a speeding car with our hands and feet tied? The fall would kill us for sure."

"Which is what will happen if we don't get out of here. But it doesn't matter, because I can't see how we can pop the trunk."

"No. Maybe we can be ready when he opens the trunk and disable him. We'd have the element of surprise."

"The guy is huge," Daisy said. "I've seen buildings smaller than him."

She was right. Not about the buildings, which was just hyperbole, but the chances of two securely bound people with slender builds overcoming a well-muscled human mountain were slim and none. We'd survived the inquisition with all our fingers intact, but we had little chance now.

And doomsday had arrived. The car came to a stop, and shortly after, the trunk opened, with us having no opportunity to mount any defense at all. The man picked us up and unceremoniously dumped us on the ground. He looked down at us and gloated about our imminent fate. Daze and I both said nothing.

"No begging me not to kill you?"

We remained silent. I accepted the futility of our situation, and it seemed Daisy did as well.

"Okay." He brandished a gleaming nickel plated automatic and aimed it squarely at my head.

"Say goodbye," he said.

And fell to the ground, groaning with apparent pain. In my fetal position, I could see him fall and heard his cry of distress, but had no idea what had happened. But I saw the leg of a new person deposit a perfectly placed kick at our attacker's head and saw our attacker pass out. Certainly disabled, and maybe dead. I did not know. But someone saved us. And I soon knew the identity of our rescuers when Hippo and Willy knelt down to set us free.

They had followed us after we parted, concerned for our safety, and had seen where the men had taken us. But they didn't know what to do next, and continued to watch the building, considering how and when to contact the authorities. They'd placed a call, but it seemed no one could come right away. And it seemed no one had believed their story. So, they'd debated storming the building themselves, but worried that might get everyone killed. And then they saw their apparently unconscious friends stuffed into a car, so they hailed a hackney cab and promised the driver a big tip to "follow that car."

"And he did," Willy said with a chuckle.

A short, heavy-set man with a thin mustache and a merry smile stepped forward.

"Just like the American movies," he said, extending his hand. "Willoughby Smithers. They call me Willy just like my new friend," he nodded at our own Willy. "I never had so much excitement driving my hack as I did today."

"Well, a big thank you from all of us," I said. "You saved our lives."

"Happy to oblige," he said. "Next stop New Scotland Yard."

"Yes, sir, thank you. Time to involve the British authorities. And boy, did we have a tale to tell. But we couldn't go it alone anymore. Some terrible people were still out there, with a serious grudge against us.

"What should we do with him?" Hippo asked.

"Is he alive?"

"I think so."

I walked over to him, bend down and picked up his gun with two fingers, careful to not smudge any fingerprints.

"We have no choice. We can't leave him. Maybe the

police will know something about this guy, or can do a ballistics check, or whatever they do with firearms."

"Good thinking," Daisy said. She walked over to the prone man and scoured his pockets, coming away with a wallet and a cell phone, also holding them carefully. "Maybe these, too."

Smithers rummaged around in his cab and produced a small paper bag. "Put everything in here," he said. "I already ate my lunch."

So, we placed all the items in the bag. The five of us together hoisted the unconscious man into the boot, and proceeded to New Scotland Yard.

***

We transported our prisoner successfully to the home of the Metropolitan Police and turned him over to them. But they had a ton of questions for us all. And we had both answers and an unbelievable story to tell. And I mean that as a story no one would believe, not as something amazing. But I guess it was amazing, too.

They didn't buy any of it, but as the police sergeant who spoke to us first put it, "There's no denying you brought in a dangerous criminal." He said this as he left the room in which we all sat so he could find the detective chief inspector. Our story merited a superior officer, and we soon sat across from DCI Arthur Davies. Sergeant Evans sat down and pulled out his notebook, poised to take notes.

After a brief introduction, DCI Davies noted we had a fantastic story to tell, and requested we repeat it. So, I did, with Daisy's occasional input. I could tell DCI Davies didn't believe us any more than Sergeant Evans did. But at least one part of our story resonated with him, and that was that we had delivered to him a dangerous mob enforcer named Oliver Clark, aka The Crusher, for how he dumped people into car crushing machines.

"We've wanted to put him away for a long time, so whatever put you in a position to do that for us, we are much obliged. However…" I waited for the other shoe to drop. That he was going to arrest us for any number of things, including grand theft, kidnapping, fraud, littering. I really didn't know. But our story made no sense to me when I thought about it, so what could it sound like to a seasoned police inspector?

But he surprised me. "However, the rest of your story seems more appropriate to tell to MI5." He looked at us for a moment. "Our internal security service, like your FBI."

"Ah," I said. "Okay, can you tell us where to go?"

"Thames House, but you don't have to go anywhere," he said. "They're sending an officer here. Someone who says he knows you," he added cryptically. And he said no more, even after we asked. So, our imaginations ran wild. Because we knew no one in Britain, much less an MI5 officer.

And when the man arrived, it still flummoxed us who he was.

He was tall, with hair graying at the temples. The man wore a well cut, expensive dark suit probably made in Savile Row, and a starched white shirt. He had steely gray eyes set in an oval face, and he had a wiry frame. He was the picture of fitness. A large gold ring adorned otherwise empty fingers. Even standing a few feet away, the identity of the man baffled me. I glanced over at Daisy, and could see she couldn't figure it out, either. Neither Hippo nor Willy showed any signs of recognition, either.

The man seemed to enjoy our confusion and finally spoke in an unmistakable British accent and a booming voice.

"Pleased to see you in person," he said. "I bet you have a lot of questions for me."

And we surely had questions for none other than Alistair Brooke, who turned out to not be the head of Imperial Reclamation.

"And my name isn't Alistair Brooke, either," he said, and extended his hand. "Michael Graham, MI5."

38

All of us showered him with questions, but he held up his hand, palm facing us. "You told your story to these gentlemen," he said, waving his hand toward DCI Davies and Sergeant Evans. "Please tell it one more time. I know some of it already, but I only have a part of it. Tell your story, and I'll fill in blanks for you, so we all get the full picture."

"That makes sense," Daisy said, and I nodded agreement.

"This is not top secret, but I think we should shrink the number of people in this room," Officer Graham said, and the two Metropolitan Police rose and left the room. He looked at Hippo and Willy and then at us. "Do you want them present?"

"Yes," Daze and I said together.

"Very well, but there's one more person I want to sit in." He pushed a button on an intercom and asked, "Is she here yet?"

After receiving an affirmative reply, he asked to have that person shown in. And a few moments later, there was a knock on the door, following by the entry of a slender woman with dark hair.

"Abby! Or whatever your real name is."

"Let's go with Abby," she said. "Hello Daisy and Tripper." She looked over at Hippo and Willy, and acknowledged them by name as well.

"It was a joint MI5 and FBI operation," said Michael Graham, and Abby nodded.

"What was?" Daze demanded. "We have no idea what is going on. And why we somehow became part of some giant charade."

Daisy was furious, and so was I. They'd manipulated and endangered us, and used us as pawns in some silly game where we were the pieces being moved by unseen players who cared little for our welfare.

Abby sighed deeply. "You weren't supposed to be in any danger. You were supposed to deliver the jet to London, receive payment and have a nice few all-expenses paid vacation days in a truly great city. Some harmless searching for a hard drive that never existed seemed innocuous to us. No one uses portable hard drives to transport sensitive documents. They don't use flash drives, either. It's all encrypted electronic transmissions now. Or maybe a microdot for really paranoid people. They're so small that they're virtually undetectable. They can masquerade as periods in a large book. Anyway, that was just a subterfuge. We did not know who we could trust at the airport, where the heroin was being loaded onto the plane, but we were sure one mechanic was involved, and feeding information to the dangerous people you met."

"Heroin?" Daze asked.

"Two hundred kilos of it, with a street value of about 50 million dollars, and that's just one load."

"I didn't see any heroin when I was servicing the jet," Daze said.

"No, we hoped you might stumble upon it, but they hid

it well.”

“Where was it?”

“A false bottom in the fuselage.”

“I must have looked right at it, and never saw any cracks that would give it away.”

“They sealed and painted it. Tough for a naked eye. Not so hard for an x-ray.”

“Ah.”

“Anyway, we had no reason to think anyone would connect you two with any contraband. We were obviously wrong. People at Jacksonville definitely knew you’d taken the jet, but we sold it hard as a repo. But someone figured you might know something and let the bad guys know. We definitely have a leak in Jacksonville.”

“You have one in Gatwick, too,” I said.

“No doubt. But why do you think so?”

“When our inquisitor demanded we tell him where his product was, he seemed to genuinely not know. We tried every stalling story we could both think of, but he wanted very much to…” Daze shuddered…“cut off my fingers as a way of torturing me to tell him where we hid it. But someone must have told him, because, um, the Crusher whispered something in his ear, and he smiled and told the guy to kill us. Somewhere other than right there. That’s how we ended up leaving. And how our friends over there could rescue us.”

Graham spoke up at that point. “A lucky thing. We watched you closely, first to make sure you hadn’t helped yourselves to the drugs, but after that to make sure you were safe.”

“Then where were you when they abducted us a short distance from the restaurant you arranged? And why didn’t the

Metropolitan Police come immediately when Willy called them?"

Graham sighed. "Because of a monumental cock-up," he said. "Two of them. When you artfully removed our man from following you, our first line of defending you was gone as well."

"Your first line? There was a second?"

"Yes. We. had someone you'd spot, and someone you wouldn't."

"What happened to him or her?"

"He tripped," Graham said ruefully. "Probably on his own feet," he muttered. "And he didn't see you abducted."

I couldn't help it. I chuckled at the thought of someone in the vaunted MI5 tripping on his own feet and allowing a kidnapping.

"I'm glad you find the humor in it," Graham said. "We didn't. And the second cock-up was not advising the Metropolitan Police to prioritize a call from you, although I guess you might excuse us for not expecting a call from Ms. Danvers."

"Anyway, that's the story. It was supposed to be simple. But the best laid plans…"

"The leak in Jacksonville is Alfonso," Daze said suddenly.

"Spot on," Abby said.

"That's why he wanted to help me all the time, and accompany me to Bachenko's plane."

"Yes, ma'am. Right again."

"So Bachenko knew about all this?"

"Yes. He's the one who suggested Daisy. Said she was an ace pilot, and that she had already stolen his Gulfstream once. So, she could do it again. And Tripper here was a perfect fit as well. Who better than an actor to pull off a giant con?"

"Why the elaborate ruse with the fake names and wild promises when you first spoke to us?" Daze demanded.

Abby glanced at Michael, then said simply, "Tradecraft."

Michael was more forthright. "People are more likely to participate in something when they think they're uncovering what they perceive as the truth. Not a nice thing to do, but there you have it."

I interjected a question. "But how could you trust a neophyte like me, even with Daisy's training, to ensure the safety of those jets?"

"We didn't. Not for a second. You met a fellow inspector who had to take a sudden trip back to Missouri?"

"Sure. Connie. I guess he didn't really move to Missouri. So, he was...."

"One of ours, no. He and Skip were just told you were too green to trust, but didn't want you to know, because you were probably some important person's nephew or something like that. So, we arranged for the airport to pay Connie double to pre-inspect all the jets on your list."

"Well, that makes me feel...I guess better to know that I didn't put anyone in danger."

"Good."

"Why did Bachenko even want to be part of this?"

"We approached him, and he was so concerned that one of his pilots or staff was using his jet to transport contraband, he offered to help. He's a very connected man. We might have proceeded differently if he hadn't wanted to stop the smuggling and find out who was a criminal in his own organization."

At Daze's unasked question, Abby said, "And he knew full well you'd never help him personally. He suggested making him out to be a criminal, and it worked."

"I can't stand that guy," Daisy said.

"Exactly. But he did, at our behest, make certain that you can fly anywhere or for anyone you choose without his interference. But we knew you'd do nothing to help Bachenko, so we contrived this fiction in order to get the jet to London without Bachenko's co-pilot or the copilot's crony among the mechanics from knowing. Also, it was better that you two didn't know the details, so you couldn't accidentally give it away. The man you knew as Alfonso is definitely part of the smuggling racket. He can do a lot of things with no one knowing."

"By offering to help you, he wanted to be sure you didn't find the false bottom in the fuselage."

"You know," I said. "We may have something you didn't know." I caught Daisy's eye, and she responded with an almost imperceptive nod. She knew what I was saying.

"What?"

I grinned. "I need an item from my room at the hotel. Can we go there?"

"I'll have someone fetch it for you." He extended his finger to point at the intercom and gazed expectantly at me. "What should we retrieve?"

"My pants," I said, enjoying flummoxing these super-cops.

The two of them seemed unfazed. "Any particular pair of trousers? Perhaps a specific color?"

"They're jeans. Draped over the desk chair."

Graham spoke into the intercom. "A pair of trousers draped over the desk chair. Please bring them here."

In response to a question posed by the person at the other end of the intercom, he responded, "Number 6, Room 16."

So, he knew our room number, and our hotel was number 6. I didn't have time to ask, because he smiled at me and said, "Yes, it's one of ours."

It made sense now. "So, the people who searched our room were…?"

"Our people, too."

"Why did you search…Oh."

"We trusted you, of course, but we wanted to be sure." He smiled. "And of course, you received a really nice dinner for your trouble."

"We did."

39

A short while later, a man knocked and entered the room. He deposited my jeans on the table.

"Your trousers, sir."

I smiled and thanked him, while reaching into the back pocket and retrieving an envelope bearing the hotel's name, and handed it to Mr. Graham. He and Abby looked at me expectantly.

"Be very careful opening it," I said. "It contains what we think is something that masqueraded as a very tiny insect on Daisy's arm."

Abby took the envelope and carefully slit the top and peered inside. She looked at Michael Graham and then at us. "What do you think it really is?"

"I think you suspect the same thing we do. And I bet somewhere in this building is a device for examining it."

Michael nodded. "There is. But it may just be a speck of dust."

"Oh, it probably is," Daisy said. "But worth checking out, right?"

The two law enforcement officers nodded at the same time. Michael pressed the intercom button and requested that someone named Noah come into the room. He turned to us and said, "The Metropolitan Police have an expert right here. Frankly, we've been trying to recruit him for years."

The man arrived in a moment, and they introduced him to all of us. He studied the little dot with a tiny magnifier and said,"Your guess was correct. This is a microdot. You should take it back to Thames House to assess its contents." He eyed us warily. "Perhaps out of sight of civilians. I assume you don't want me to look further?"

"No, thank you, Noah. We'll take it from here. For all we know, we may need to involve Langley and SIS."

"It's the real thing?" I asked, and Michael nodded. "But we don't know what's on it, and I'm afraid it's not something we will be able to share with you, even though you're the ones who brought it to us. You say you just noticed a tiny dot on Ms. Wilson's arm?" He said it casually, but I knew we were being interrogated. But if we were involved, we'd hardly turn it over to them, and Michael Graham knew it. So, I just answered in the affirmative.

"I didn't like the look of it. I thought it might be a tick or some other insect, so we put it in the envelope just to look at it later."

"It must have fallen off something onto your arm," he said to Daisy. "Maybe a book? What books did you look at between Jacksonville and here?"

Daisy thought about it for a moment, and couldn't come up with any books, or even magazines, but she had a sudden thought.

"The flight operations manual. I looked at that during the flight. And it was stowed overhead. When I reached for it, it tumbled down and I caught it midair, but it had opened."

"Could be when the microdot landed on your arm,"

Abby acknowledged, and Michael nodded. "Anyway, we'll see what's on it."

"We won't know anything?" Daisy persisted.

Michael smiled. "Oh, I may give you a clue. You're at least entitled to that. But I have something for you, and the Metropolitan Police have something to tell you. Me first, then I'll call the DCI back in."

He produced four tickets to the hottest, most unavailable show playing in the West End.

"Abby tells me you're fond of the theater. So, enjoy. And let me call in the DCI, who has some good news for you.

The good news was that there was a substantial reward for information leading to the capture of the man known as the Crusher.

"It's 50,000 pounds. Divided among the four of you."

"Not us," Hippo and Willy said at the same time. "Just them. We were just in the right place at the right time."

We argued the point while the three officers looked on. But the DCI had something else to say.

"We hope to wrap up the whole drug smuggling gang," he said. "And when we do, there is a huge reward for information leading to that fortunate occurrence. And the four of you can continue your friendly argument over that."

"In the meantime," he said, "if it's okay with these two, you're free to go, with the Crown's gratitude."

I looked at the clock on the wall. "It's late. We'll all get a good night's sleep and have a great day in London, a fine dinner, and some wonderful theater."

***

The next morning, Daisy received a phone call from Michael Graham, asking us to stop by Thames House at 10:00 a.m.

"He told me we should have our breakfast, and that it was no hurry. But he wouldn't tell me what it was about, saying it wasn't a secure line."

"Very mysterious," I said. "I wonder if they've looked at the microdot."

"I have no doubt," Daisy said. "But he told us they wouldn't tell us what's on it."

"Not exactly," I pointed out. "He said he'd give us an idea."

"That's true," Daze acknowledged.

And I was right. He had something to tell us, and it was both cryptic and brief. He met us in a small conference room in Thames House, and said he had little time, but that because we'd brought the information to him, he thought it only fair to tell us at least something. And he said little and in a quiet voice, but it spoke as loud as Big Ben.

"Two things," Michael said. "MB might not be made of Teflon, and both MI6 and Langley are now involved."

He cut us off in the middle of the proffered questions, saying he had already said way too much, but figured he owed us.

Daze sported an enormous smile, and I knew why. Bachenko was in trouble, and she would shortly be free to fly anywhere she wanted.

"Also," he said. "We've rounded up all your captors, including the "Scar.""

"That's good news," Daisy said. "Thank you."

"The Crown owes you and your friends a thank you. And you will most certainly receive a reward." He paused and smiled an almost impish smile. "As soon as it's approved by the House of Commons and the PM, and initialed by the King in triplicate, and published in the Register of Rewards."

We both stood agape, and Michael laughed. "You won't need all of that. And there's no such thing as a Register of Rewards. Anyway, I have to run. Enjoy the rest of your stay in London."

We thanked him and spent the rest of the day sightseeing and shopping. We dined ourselves, as Hippo and Willy were being wined and dined at an exclusive London restaurant by the network. But we met them after dinner to attend the theater, and we all enjoyed it, although I'm sure I did most of all. I hadn't seen genuine professional theater since I lived in New York, and I missed it terribly. And this was as good or maybe better than Broadway.

***

We flew home in style. Maybe not in a Gulfstream, but someone had arranged for first-class seats home. We sat in the same section and the same flight as Hippo and Willy.

And a few weeks later, I entered from stage-left in our little warehouse theater to assume the role of Feste in the command performance of Twelfth Night.

> A great while ago the world begun,
>
> With hey, ho, the wind and the rain,
>
> But that's all one, our play is done,
>
> And we'll strive to please you every day.

I sang the last lines, and the curtain went down to thunderous applause. My fellow actors took their bows a few at a time, each receiving warm receptions from the audience, and then I came out alone and took my bow to a standing ovation and loud applause, including raucous cheers from my contingent of Hippo, Willy and Daisy. I beckoned to the wings, and Carleton joined me on stage and he took a bow. Then we took a joint bow, after which the entire troupe joined us and we all bowed together.

So, I guess I'm a Shakespearean actor now.

Dear Reader:

Thanks for reading my book!

Online reviews are much appreciated, so it would be great if you took a few moments to write a review on Amazon.com, BarnesandNoble.com, or any other review site. Thanks!

Just click on the link (or type it into your browser), choose which of my books you wish to review, and scroll down to where it provides for a review.

www.amazon.com/author/ericsmall

Eric Small

About the Author

Eric Small is a retired government attorney living in Florida. He is the author of four previous books: *Brazen Gambit; A Tale of Two Freddies*; and *Three Faces of Jennifer*, all set in Middletown, New Jersey. *Out of Sight* is a novel set in the fictional upstate New York town of Standard, New York. *Jet Caper* is set primarily in Florida.